Hidden Treasure

Janet Bennett

Copyright © 2008 Janet Bennett
All rights reserved.

ISBN: 1-4392-0964-2
ISBN-13: 9781439209646

Visit www.booksurge.com to order additional copies..

Preface

Luzetta Hendrich walked her docile, tan and white palfrey into the camp of the Piqui Tribe that lived only a few miles from her Montana home. The chill of the wind whipped around the crescendo of earth surrounding them, biting more forcefully now that she didn't have the trees to protect her from it's sting. The foretelling of snow loomed heavy in the skyline. It would come soon. The pregnant, gray clouds hovering ahead looked more than ready to give up the bounty they held for so long.

Luzetta rarely had contact with the tribal elders in the past. Her father was the one to communicate with them. But today she felt it necessary to confront them about an urgent matter. It pushed her along in earnest to reach her destination, through the cold, over the uncertainty of her reception. In the past the Piqui tribe had proven peaceable toward Luzetta and her father, but her father was not with her any more. He had succumbed to pneumonia last winter and passed away in his sleep.

Luzetta missed her father deeply, but she hoped he was watching over her as she performed the more risky procedures her father trained her to perform. Luzetta's father, the town doctor, was the reason the Piqui was so accepting of their presence so near their camp. When Luzetta and her father moved out West to find a more tolerant, prosperous land she was only five years old. She could still remember the trip and all of it's hardships. They came from the war-torn state of South Carolina in search of the open land, fresh starts, new life teaming everywhere, and the promise of wealth from the hills and streams in the form of precious metals - namely gold. Her father, also seeing the flow of people rushing Westward, knew people were going to need doctors. Most of the travelers were miners, whole families uprooting in the search of riches and freedom. He knew that in all of his wisdom there would be few doctors in comparison to the influx of people hoarding toward the coast.

The further West they traveled, the less Luzetta liked the crudeness of the people she encountered. She sincerely hoped wherever they ended up would be considerably more hospitable.

That such town was Jamestown, Montana. Luzetta's father told her he bought land prospected by their close friend, George Carbaugh. When they arrived to finally see their new hometown, they were both pleasantly surprised. There was a perfect place on a hill for a house and a clearing large enough to farm. There were hot springs of water within walking distance, plenty of game to hunt, and the people in town seemed much more civilized than they encountered in the past. The small town wasn't even on the map, being only 142 in population, it didn't have the tribulations of larger cities. Luzetta and her father frequently took walks to discover new things as they looked for naturally growing herbs and medicinal plants. It wasn't until several months later that they found the Piqui living only five miles away. The Indians had been confined to a reservation of land set out by the U.S. Government. They were a peaceable group with dwindling numbers due to an epidemic sickness that Luzetta later found out was scarlet fever.

Luzetta and her father were returning home through the wooded path not far from their home when a blood curdling scream tore through the hot summer air. Both Luzetta and her father jumped down from the wagon and took off running toward the sound. If it wasn't for the movement of someone running from a still form in the distance, they would have never seen the boy sprawled on the ground. An Indian boy.

Her father rushed to the boy's aid. The two Indian boys must have been hunting in the woods and failed to heed the trap set for an animal. Luzetta never saw such a crude instrument in her young life. She stood and stared at the boy who was clenching his leg, his face contorted in agony. Her father ran back to retrieve his bag from the buggy.

The boy seemed more scared of the white man running toward him than the pain of the trap clamped around his leg. He was prepared to fight when the girl with golden hair came to his side and soothed him with her strange words and her caresses while the man ran back from where he came.

She stroked his hand like she would a favorite kitten. The boy didn't understand a word she said, but knew in his gut that she would not harm him. He had to trust her. When the man approached again with a black bag, the man's intentions were clear. He pried the trap from his leg with two small logs and the boy cried out in pain. Luzetta began to wonder where the other Indian boy went, but didn't give it a second thought as she saw the pain in the boy's eyes and the blood he was losing from his leg. Luzetta took it upon herself to console the boy. She sat next to him and placed his arms around her small waist and laid his head in her lap. The boy held her tightly with all his young strength and squeezed tight, almost taking her breath away while her father worked at the trap.

When the trap finally released it's grip on the young boy's leg, her father began to treat his wounds. "You're a lucky boy" her father said "you'll probably have a limp for the rest of your life, but at least you'll be able to keep your foot."

The boy didn't understand what this man was saying, but he really didn't care. He was fighting just to stay conscious. His leg shot pain through his entire body and he began to shake. With no prompting from the man, the boy watched as the little girl stood and took off her underskirts. They were made of warm cotton and she placed them on his dirt-covered body.

The young Luzetta knew from seeing many of her father's patients in the past that the boy was in shock, but it was in the middle of June and her father was not wearing his coat jacket. The boy lost a lot of blood and both Luzetta and her father exchanged a worried look.

Just as her father was wrapping the boy's leg, they realized they were surrounded by men on horses. Fierce looking Indians on horseback without saddles were standing around them and the ailing boy. The second of the two boys was riding along with one of them, pointing at them and telling them something in his language.

One of the men, the fiercest looking of them all, dismounted and walked over to the trio on the ground. Luzetta and her father could only stare up at the man painted and angry looking. He spoke as if they would understand him clearly. He got no reaction. He pointed to the boy and looked as if he was asking what had transpired. As if sensing the implied question, Luzetta's father raised the trap and his medicine bag. The boy was floating in and out of consciousness and began to moan incoherently. Luzetta stroked his head and shushed him as if she were rocking him to sleep, murmuring words to him that made him settle.

Totally perplexed, the Indian man knelt beside the boy opposite her father. He made brief nods to both of the strangers and scooped up the child gently into his arms. Luzetta imagined he was the boy's father. The man expertly mounted the large horse in one smooth movement without disturbing the boy. Before the band turned back toward home, the Indian man looked down at the little girl, then her father and spoke forceful, unknown words. They both took it as his thank you of sorts.

Before the band was out of sight, the second boy dismounted and ran back to the place where Luzetta and her father were still standing, a little bit dazed. He came close to her, offering a bashful smile. He stood before her and talked to her as if she understood. All Luzetta could do was stare back. Finally he took the necklace he wore around his neck and put it around hers. Luzetta fondled the little flute that dangled from the leather string and smiled at him. The boy smiled back then ran back to the slow-moving band. They traveled through the trees, then across the valley and disappeared as mysteriously as they had appeared.

Chapter One

Luzetta, now twenty-three, still had that little flute. She found no reason to discard it. As time played on, the Indians and the Hendriches worked alongside one another. They kept to themselves for many years, only occasionally rendering each other assistance when needed.

Now it was time to help them again, in the way of a warning. As she approached the reservation, she tried to take in all of the activity going on even on this cold day. Children were playing, a small band of men returned with deer carcasses, women were gathering wood from the forest floor.

After tying her horse with the others, Luzetta marched through the camp, greeted by a sea of solemn faces. She felt her stomach flip in anticipation of her meeting with the tribal elders, if she were allowed.

Not knowing where to go to reach such persons, Luzetta thought it best to stand in the middle of the camp and let them approach her. After all, she was a lone woman encroaching her presence on a patriarchal clan. The last thing she wanted was to offend them and be sent away because of her ignorance. Thoughts of what would happen to these people if she were not allowed to sound the alarm ran through her mind as she waited.

The chill surrounding her seemed to reach clear through to her bones. Her heavy bearskin coat, payment for her services from a local family, served to do little for the chill that ran up her spine and the dread she felt of having to give bad news and the uncertainty of her welcome into the Piqui camp. The wait was agonizing. It felt like an eternity before she spotted someone she recognized.

As soon as he heard she was in the camp he set out to find her. It wasn't hard. He spotted her and walked toward her with the slightest of limps.Still, he kept a straight face, not letting on how glad he was to see her, how he truly felt about her. Moon Star had fallen in love with Luzetta since that fateful day in the woods.

"Moon Star." She greeted him with the same mirrored grim look. Had she come to see him? Had she decided to accept his offer to become one of his wives, be protected by the clan as one of them?

"Golden Hair. Why have you come?" He asked without preamble. This time Luzetta understood those words. She came to learn the language over time from Moon Star and his brother, Running Horse.

"I need to speak with your tribal elders. I need to warn them of a threat to the tribe." Luzetta took Moon Star's acceptance of her request for an audience with the older men of the tribe without further questioning as a sign of respect stemming from past experiences with her father. She didn't see the betrayal of his feelings flash through his eyes.

Moon Star led her to a tent painted with various animals essential to their survival, as they all were, and told her to wait outside. Luzetta waited patiently while Moon Star spoke with the men inside the tent. She couldn't help but notice the curious eyes staring at her the entire time. All she thought to do was offer a small smile.

After Moon Star opened the flap of the teepee allowing Luzetta step inside, Luzetta could hear hushed voices inside the tent.

Luzetta's stomach was doing somersaults. She knew three of the six men accompanying her in the tent. One was Chief Running Bull to whom she never spoke with directly. To his left was Soaring Eagle, Moon Star's father, and Moon Star. The others were introduced to her as Eagle Feather, Red Wolf and the medicine man Bear Hunter.

"The Elders will hear your message that is so important that you risk your life to tell." Moon Star stated, knowing the threat was not from Piqui but from the bitter cold winter looming ahead and she a woman traveling alone. Luzetta paid close attention to herself as she spoke, not wanting to offend her hosts. Luzetta visibly steeled herself and took a deep breath for courage.

"I apologize for my intrusion into your camp," she began "but I felt need to warn you of what is to come." She took another deep breath. Certainly they could sense her nervousness. "Last week I was coming back from town when I noticed Piqui boys playing with two boys. White boys from town." She stated.

"Who were these boys?" Soaring Eagle asked, gently inquiring.

"I don't know, but they were about six or seven years old and one had blue and yellow V shaped markings on his body." Luzetta drew imaginary lines where the markings would be on the boy in question. "The other was tall and had a sling shot they were all playing with." She concluded.

"And what do you need to tell us? Did they do something wrong?" He inquired.

"No, nothing like that. I need to tell you, though, that the white boys they were playing with, along with a rash of other children in town, have come down with chicken pox." Her statement got blank stares and questioning looks. "It is a childhood disease that could be serious to your tribe."

"Tell us more about the 'chicken pox'." The medicine man, Bear Hunter, encouraged.

"Chicken pox is a disease that is noticeable by small blisters that cover the body and cause itching."

"You came to warn us of a disease that will make our children itch?" Soaring Eagle asked with scoffing. Moon Star worried, not doubting Luzetta's statement that this disease would hurt the tribe. Luzetta's brow was furrowed and her hands were rubbing together. The elders laughed prematurely.

"No, I said it was a childhood illness, but anyone can get it. It holds most danger for the very young, the very old, those who are with child or nursing, but adult women and men alike can be hurt by it, too." She informed.

"Go on." He urged.

"For women who are pregnant and exposed to anyone with chicken pox it could cause the baby to be born dead. For the very young and very old they may not be strong enough to fight off the disease and not survive. And men who are of child bearing age could be ..." She tried to think of a way to tell them without confusing them or insulting them. "It could take away their ability to create more children." The tent was deathly quiet for a few seconds before Bear Hunter spoke.

"How do you know that this will happen to the Piqui?" He asked.

"I don't." She interjected. "Once someone is exposed, it could take two weeks before they break out into blisters. It is passed from one person to another during the fever stage until the blisters dry up." The men began talking among themselves.

"How can the Piqui survive this if these children have brought it into the camp?" Moon Star asked, almost desperately. The memory of so many lost during The Fever still fresh in his mind.

"Quarantine." She stated. "Find out first if the boys are sick. If they are then you will have to find all who have been in contact with them. If the boys have not yet shown signs of sickness, more importantly fever, then they will need a tent of their own - or I could take them in my home as I have already had the disease as a child." She didn't know how well received her offer would be. Having a white woman tend to their sick outside of the tribal walls would be quite a novel idea.

The worse that could happen would be for them to reject the information and allow the disease to spread throughout the tribe, causing more deaths. The elders needed time to talk.

Luzetta was ushered safely to the edge of the encampment after leaving the tribal elders to their own council. They agreed to let her know their decision soon. She prayed the entire way into town. After all, there were others who needed her help to get through this crisis in the dead of winter.

There were seven stops in all. Every last one had children ranging from two months old to fourteen years old. Some were afflicted more than others, but each case had it's own worries. Luzetta's last stop was the most worrisome. The Lewis family just recovered from a bout of influenza and they had a two-month-old baby boy. Knowing the family did not yet have adequate time to recover, Luzetta made sure they knew the dangers to watch for, especially where the baby was concerned. Luzetta told the baby's parents to contact her immediately if the boy took fever or started vomiting. Both parents knew this time was critical and prayed the child would fare well so soon after being sick.

Filled with trepidation for the townsfolk and the Piqui, Luzetta headed toward home to await word from the tribal elders. She prayed fiercely that none would come in the way of bad news. Luzetta wondered how long it would take the Piqui to respond to her offer.

Luzetta found out the answer the next morning as she looked out her kitchen window over a steaming cup of coffee. She almost dropped the cup as she saw the group of fifty people or more marching her way.

The tribal elders knew the boys from her description and immediately assessed that almost the entire tribe were all better off camped outside her door. Luzetta mentally fortified herself and dove into the task at hand.

Each one received a thorough examination when their camp was completely set up. The boys exposed to the virus were already showing signs of sickness. They both had a fever and one mother called Young Doe told Luzetta that her boy, the younger of the two, began coughing late last night, sounding like a barking dog. Luzetta knew it was the croup the woman heard. Young Doe looked at Luzetta as if she had seen the ghost of death. She could see the woman had been crying for fear of her sons life.

"Please," the woman reached out for Luzetta with a tearful, strained expression "I can't lose any more children."

"Then we must work together." Luzetta would not allow herself to contemplate the loss of life. She would fight it tooth and nail.

* * *

Luzetta feared more for the babies among the group, hoping they did not come in contact with the boys. It could prove fatal, but she wasn't about to tell the needy faces before her that piece of information. The Piqui were scared to death as it was about what they heard of this terrible disease. Luzetta made sure the boys were separated from the rest of the clan. More would join them, she was sure.

After talking to Young Doe, Luzetta deducted the tribal elders may have told them too much and scared them into the state they were now in, but what was done was done. The Piqui seldom had contact with white men, remaining on their reservation. The thought that the whole tribe could be wiped out by this disease depressed Luzetta, but she didn't breathe a word of her thoughts to anyone lest they go into a panic.

Chapter Two

One week later, Luzetta was tested to how far she could be stretched. The four bedroom house had been converted into a clinic when her father was alive. They had cots and extra blankets, but she never imagined there would be a need as great as there was now.

It wasn't long after arriving that the entire group had been struck with the virus. Men, women and children alike. Luzetta couldn't make the oatmeal packs fast enough.

Despite being covered from head to toe with the hateful, seeping sores, Luzetta was impressed that the Indian children tolerated the inconvenience so well. She could think of some other children who could learn a lesson from them. Come to think about it, some adults too.

The snow began falling three days ago, blanketing the earth as far as the eye could see. Luzetta was almost too busy to take notice, but there were more sick outside in their tepees. She worried about them and checked them often. She couldn't remember when winter was this hard and so long this year. It was mid-March and the warming trends had not yet started. Snow seemed to fall at every available opportunity.

Luzetta knew that the shipment of supplies was to be in soon. Medicines, bandages, instruments and many other things were sorely needed now that her patient load had increased a hundred fold. The supplies she ordered a while back were supposed to be for the entire year. She would be thankful if it lasted one month at this rate. She would have to place another order by telegraph when she was in town. She would have to go soon. The children would need her to be swift. Their mothers would too. It was hitting the Piqui harder than Luzetta anticipated.

Luzetta left the clan in the capable hands of two older women, Spotted Owl and Flying Sparrow, who seemed to resist the disease. They were vigilant in keeping the others comfortable and monitoring them. Luzetta knew that if it were not for them, it would be extremely difficult to keep up the already hectic pace.

Since the Piqui came to her home, three of the remaining unaffected tribesmen were sent to hear a report from Luzetta every morning. Sensing they were afraid of coming close to even her, the men stood at the edge of the forest and would not allow Luzetta closer than 100 feet of them. She had to shout her message to them.

When the elders came that morning, Luzetta stated her need to make a trip to town for needed supplies. They insisted on traveling with her at a distance. Luzetta read between the lines and knew they were pinning the future of their tribe on her and, in order to insure nothing interfered with her coming back, they insisted on the escort. Luzetta didn't mind in the least.

After hitching the horse to the small buggy, as she had done a thousand times before, the men followed her at a good distance. They broke off from her at the edge of town, careful to stay out of sight of the white men in town. They knew how it would look to the white men if they rode into town with a single white woman. It would be as good as signing their death warrant.

"Good morning Reverend Williams." She greeted the young Reverend as he was leaving the post master's office.

"Good morning to you too, Miss Hendrich." He beamed his normal radiant smile at her. "It is nice to see you. It would be nicer to see you on Sundays as well." He was heading for the door, but suddenly turned and walked back toward Luzetta as if he changed his mind and his body reacted to the change instantly.

"As I would like to see you about your stomach." She'd been trying to get him to let her check out his complaints of stomach pain. He always claimed he had prior engagements and would get out to see her when he had a free moment. "Besides, this year's run of chicken pox has kept me hopping."

"Yes, I was meaning to ask you about that. Several of the other families have been hit with it. School has been canceled until the outbreak runs it's course." Reverend Williams was standing beside her as she filled out the slip of paper she needed to give to the telegraph operator. She felt him standing a bit too close for her comfort, but refused to look his way.

"Yes, I know. I went by the Johnson's yesterday. Their two boys are miserable. At least their parents had the pox before."

"Yes, let us be thankful for that" He praised. Luzetta finished the message to be sent and handed the slip of paper to Clevis Owens, the postmaster, with his white starched shirt, black-billed visor and black arm band. She turned her attention to the Reverend, intending to bid him good day and head toward the loaded buggy.

"Well, I have a full day ahead of me." She exclaimed as she tried to move past the Reverend and his pressing presence. He looked down at her and placed a gentle hand at her elbow, keeping her in place. His voice was softer and laced with a strain she hadn't noticed before.

"I really do hope to see you on Sunday, Miss Hendrich." He urged. Luzetta felt uncomfortable with his forwardness. He never acted this way toward her before. She cleared her throat before speaking.

"As it is, Reverend, everyone will have their hands full with the sick. And, if the weather keeps up at this pace, you may find yourself alone come Sunday. I would consider canceling services if I were you." She didn't hold his gaze, but fixed the scarf about her head and tied it securely before trying to pull away from his gentle grasp. "Now if you will excuse me, Reverend."

Fortunately for her, Reverend Williams let go of her without complaint. She said a silent prayer of thankfulness as she walked the short distance to the buggy. She reflected on the sly advances men made toward her in the last year since her father died. She didn't have time to dwell on such matters and dismissed such thoughts as she took the reins and headed home.

Luzetta had been so preoccupied with her pressing time limit that she was unaware of the talk buzzing around town. Two men traveling into town spotted the three Indian men serving as Luzetta's escort. The men jumped to conclusions about why they were loitering so closely to town. Some speculated that they were planning to take advantage of the lack of traffic in town to suit their own needs and rob them. Winter came early this year and settled in for a long stay. The Indians may have run out of supplies and were now looking at their white neighbors to fill their tribe's needs. Since they usually distance themselves from town, their visit could only mean a raid.

The Indian men stayed on the outskirts of town as Luzetta made her way back. It took her longer than she intended. She arrived back home just before dusk. At least it stopped snowing for a short while. Luzetta was too preoccupied to pay any attention to the amazingly beautiful horizon the clear sky afforded as the sun fell.

Two teenage boys approached her cart when she pulled up to the barn. They helped her carry in her purchases and reassured her they would take care of the animal. "Thank you. I appreciate that." She said, distracted as her thoughts ran to the people she left behind. She knew the Indian boys had great respect for the beasts and that it's needs would be met, so she left the horse in their capable hands.

There was no need to put most of the supplies away. They were needed to care for those that stood in front of her, in her house and outside her door. She diligently worked as the night came upon them. Luzetta became increasingly worried about those forced to remain outside. The temperature plummeted to below freezing and Luzetta voiced her concerns over their well being.

"Don't worry, Golden Hair. We have survived many winters much colder." Spotted Owl assured her. "The tepees are warm and dry. You need to rest." She pointed out, noticing the dark circles gradually growing larger directly below her eyes over the last week. "You go to sleep. We will be fine until the sun comes again."

"Okay" she conceded "but you make sure to wake me if someone needs me." The older woman pushed her along as a mother would a reluctant child. Luzetta was gently ushered her into her room, the only room without wall to wall patients. She shrugged out of her dress, leaving the long underwear she wore underneath in place. She didn't have the energy to shed them, but instead fell into a hard slumber as the blankets around her began to warm her blood.

Luzetta slept for only a short time before she was startled awake by the sounds of barking coughs. The sickest of the tribe were inside the house, at her insistence. She quickly pulled her dress back on and bound her hair in a quick knot before emerging from her room. Spotted Owl had fallen asleep and Luzetta didn't have the heart to wake her. She worked as hard as any woman half her age and Luzetta was grateful.

Hearing the croupy cough, Luzetta quickly put more wood in the hearth in the front room then in the cook stove covered with water pots. Even the small wood stove that resided in the back part of the house was put to good use. She refilled as many pots of water as possible. Fortunately there was just enough room for her to heat water for coffee. Soon the house began to fill with the steam coming from the pots.

Concern for the ones remaining outside propelled her toward her coat and the front door. She tiptoed through the crowd of sleeping bodies to reach the door. Dawn was fast approaching and she was thankful for the small amount of light she worked by to keep from having to light a lamp that might wake the sleeping patients.

Reaching the door, she gently turned the knob and opened the door to slip through without detection. She closed the door with equal gentleness to turn around in anticipation of seeing to the needs of those she hoped were no worse for wear despite the plummeting temperatures. Luzetta was brought up short faced by several townsmen.

The men standing in front of her, still mounted on their horses, toted shotguns. They were unsheathed and ready to use if the need arose. All men, townsmen and Piqui alike, kept watching the other's movements with suspicion as Luzetta approached the horsemen.

"Mornin', Miss Hendrich." Said the first man. Luzetta knew him from church. His name was Mr. Minster. He was a farmer that lived on the west side of town, but that was all she knew of him. He was a gruff looking man with a beard down to his mid-chest and dark eyes. They pinned Luzetta where she stood.

"Good morning." Luzetta retorted, closing her coat around her neck to keep the chill at bay. "Is there something I can do for you gentlemen?"

"Yes, Ma'am. You can tell us why all these Injuns are out here." From the look on his face, Luzetta knew he disapproved of the state of affairs he was witnessing. She wondered what he would do if he knew there were just as many, if not more, inside her house. "You all right? Have they taken you over?" Luzetta almost laughed. It had been three weeks since the Piqui arrived at her home and they are just now wondering about her well being?

"Yes, I'm fine, honest. These people are here upon my invitation. They fell sick and I offered my help." She confessed. "And I would appreciate it if you gentlemen would kindly put away your guns. There is no need for them here. These are peaceable Indians. You have no fear of being attacked."

After a few moments Mr. Minter looked over his shoulder and nodded. The others put their shotguns in their sheaths, but they kept one hand on the butt at all times. The action did not go unnoticed by Luzetta.

"Now, is there something you need from me? Any medical emergency?" She asked.

"No, Ma'am. We just saw fit to see that you were safe." Luzetta suppressed her desire to tell the man that he was well from fast off the mark.

"Thank you, but I am in no need of rescuing. You are kind to think of me." For all he knew she could have been dead for the past few weeks and they were just now getting to wonder about her. Certainly they saw her about town, administering to the sick and making her usual rounds that started as soon as the first pock appeared.

With a nod the men began to disperse. "We'll be on our way then." Mr. Minster added. She was glad things had not turned sour. News of the goings on at her house were going to be spreading like wildfire in no time.

After they were out of sight, Luzetta went back to her original plan to check on her crop of patients before her. When she returned to the house, though, she promptly pulled her father's shot gun out of the closet and loaded it. Placing it in her room where the children were not likely to wonder, the gun was securely placed out of reach.

The condition of the Piqui went from bad to worse and the weather followed suit. The croupy cough spread as she knew it would. All Luzetta could do was to keep the pots of water filled to make the inside of the house like a steam bath and apply the mustard and onion poultices to their bodies. Others were vomiting and had high fevers. She mixed herbs and medicines for their mothers to administer. One woman suffered a miscarriage, the tiny life passed without knowing life.

There were others who helped Luzetta with the sick, but she still felt the responsibility of caring for so many and seeing their every need met. The majority of the tribe recovered, but there were still more critical ones that demanded her time and attention.

Luzetta was only able to catch cat naps. She looked and felt bone tired. Her dress and hair stuck to her wet body from the steamy air, and she ignored her own needs in lieu of others.

The women of the tribe recovered and were busy gathering firewood, keeping the fires raging. Prepared meat the men provided, along with the other food stuffs she saw being passed around, were being fed to those who could not feed themselves. Four more bodies were being carried in and lain on the bed rolls. They, too, were full of fever. She wondered how many more nights of sleeplessness, how many more deaths she could endure. Still, she pushed the thought out of her mind and trudged onward.

Falling Water finally succumbed to the strain of caring for others and taken sick. Luzetta knew the woman needed rest and commissioned her to a bed roll. The night came quickly and there didn't seem to be a single star to light the sky. The moon didn't even make an appearance. As she looked out the window, Luzetta thought the night took on her feelings of darkness, despair.

Before she gave into her thoughts, Luzetta made her last round about the camp checking on those who were beginning to recover. The more serious cases were inside the house where she could constantly monitor them. The last few doses of medicine given, poultices rubbed on chests and backs, a few more pieces of wood in each cook stove and fireplace then it was off to bed for a short night. She would have to get up in a couple of hours and start the process all over again. Luzetta fell into the black hole of dreamless sleep just to wake up exhausted.

"Golden Hair." She heard her name calling her out of the abyss of sleep. "Golden Hair." Falling Water was shaking her gently as she spoke to her. "Golden Hair, you must come quickly." Luzetta was surprised to find Falling Water gathering her things at this hour. Something had to have gone seriously wrong for her to get out of her own sickbed to wake her.

Luzetta came instantly awake thinking of the prospects of what the problem might be, peeling her weary body off the warm mattress. Falling Water helped her into a dress before pushing her out of the room. She hadn't even time to pull back her long, curly hair. It was puzzling, though, when she was stuffed into her coat and her black bag pressed into her hand. Falling Water lead her outside and past the camp surrounding her home. Luzetta was lead to the Piqui men on the edge of her land.

What could be wrong? Have the other tribe members suffered the same fate as their fellow clansmen? Luzetta was lifted onto Moon Star's horse before he mounted behind her. It was truly strange to be riding without a saddle. She was grateful she had her father's long underwear hidden under her skirts. Moon Star covered both of them with a thick buffalo hide that helped keep the cold at bay, but the bone-gripping cold bit at her face with sharp teeth. She hid her face inside the warm fur, peeking from time to time to determine her surroundings.

The relentless snow had kept it's vigil for several days now. It came down so hard Luzetta could barely see the lead horse. The horses trudged through slowly but obstinately. Just like their masters.

Fat flakes landed on her hair, the sway of the horse, the quiet darkness of the night all lulled Luzetta to sleep from time to time. Moon Star held her lovingly as she slumped against him. She wished to God she knew where they were taking her.

Moon Star held Luzetta close to him, feeling her strong heart beat through their clothing. His heart swelled with pride as the men and women at the camp told him how hard she was working to keep them all alive. He recalled scanning the landscape and taking in the sight of twenty tepees surrounding the log house.

His people were sick with the white man's disease, dying with it. Looking into the eyes of the sick was tantamount to looking at war-weary soldiers. It was the same look Luzetta carried with her tonight.

He held her tight, letting her rest while she could. Little did she know that they were giving her more than her work to do tonight.

Finally, the horses came to a stop and Luzetta wondered how far they traveled. She had no idea how long she slept, didn't recognize anything around her, could barely make out the trees surrounding them. The snow made it impossible to clearly make any positive identification of landmarks. Moon Star dismounted and took her by the waist, planting her on the ground. He was remarkably strong for his age, she thought. The snow was deep where she stood. Up to her knees.

Red Wolf lead her away from the horses. He was kind enough to let her use his shoulder for balance, part guide as they walked. Bear Hunter followed her into the darkness. They must have walked about ten paces before losing sight of the horses. After five paces more she was convinced the snow flakes were growing thicker.

When Red Wolf stopped, he took Luzetta's hand and pulled her ahead of him and told her to kneel. The realization that she was kneeling next to a man did not come to her until Red Wolf dusted a layer of snow off the naked body. She helped them clear the snow away from him as the sound of rushing adrenaline filled her ears and pushed her tiredness away.

Luzetta could tell the man had not been here for long, but long enough to kill a man. The temperature was at an all-time low, letting animals and people alike become frost bitten and gave them no time at all before freezing to death if proper shelter and warmth was not found.

"What happened?" She asked, her lips moving in slow motion from the cold. She tried to find a pulse in the partially snow-covered man.

Chapter Three

"Other white men attack Scarred By Bear." Spoke Bear Hunter. "His spirit is still alive and strong. You must help him."

"Is he Piqui friend?" She asked, knowing Piqui would not normally go out of their way to help someone such as this man.

"No. He is a white man with white man injuries." Luzetta heard him, but puzzled by his statement, she stared quizzically at him. Bear Hunter guided her hand to the man's injuries. Luzetta felt several bullet holes. As far as she could tell, by feel alone, several bullets passed through his right shoulder, another felt like it could have been a graze, but she couldn't see it. It could have just been a scratch. She couldn't see any others until she had more light and less snow.

"The spirit of the bear runs with this man." Red Wolf stated. He took her hand and spanned out her fingers to draw attention to the markings on the man's chest. "He will survive. You will see." He said with all confidence.

"Did anyone see what had happened?" Luzetta asked as she turned her full attention back to the body before her. "Or who did it?"

"It was Piqui enemy." He stated matter-of-factly. "The men we know from the past. They hunted us, tried to drive us off of our land." He explained. "They brought Scarred by Bear here. They left him for dead on our land to make us look bad, like Piqui hurt him." It took four men to lift the dead weight of the large man. They placed him across a horse brought along specifically for him. Luzetta now understood why the Piqui wanted to see this man to safety. Their survival depended on it. She couldn't blame them.

Luzetta dismounted, preceding the men in hopes of finding a suitable place to put the man. The four Piqui designated to carry the man grunted and strained against his massive weight. The clanswomen cleared a straight path for them to carry the man into the house. They already gathered blankets and brought the fireplace in Luzetta's room to life.

Luzetta knew there was no room to put him except her own. Every nook and cranny had been filled to capacity - except her room. Even if she found a space to put a cot she doubted that it would have held the large man. She didn't even think twice about sacrificing her bed for the wounded, half-dead man. She was pleasantly surprised to see the women prepared the room so well for him.

As Falling Water and Spotted Owl secured Luzetta's room, the men brought the man they began to refer to as Mr. Bear. Luzetta began working on repairing the man's injuries. Bullets were removed, holes closed, stitches placed with expert care. Luzetta worked relentlessly throughout the night. Various Piqui women maintained the fire built at the opposite side of the room and placed warming stones under the man while Luzetta worked. Luzetta was so preoccupied with working as fast as possible that she did not realize more came in to help.

Luzetta was satisfied she did all she could do about the seven bullet wounds. They had concentrated on warming him as fast as possible. They needed to get his body temperature back up to normal quickly before it was too late. While the women piled blankets on him and rubbed his limbs with their hands, as his wounds would allow, Luzetta made a mixture her father invented. After raising his head and forcing his mouth to open, she had poured the mixture in until it was gone. Hopefully the dosage was enough. She took his size and approximate weight into consideration and doubled the normal recipe.

After they did all that could be done, Snow Bird, Falling Water and Luzetta stood at the foot of the bed and stared at the pile of blankets. "Is there anything we've missed, anything else we can do?" She asked the two Indian women.

"When someone has been out in the cold too long, or even fallen into water in winter, it is common to warm their bodies with our own bodies. Use *your* body heat to help warm him." Falling Water pushed her up to the side of the bed. "Here in Piqui land we survive by making heat between two or more." She saw the stricken look on Luzetta's face and laughed. She knew exactly what Luzetta was thinking. "His nakedness is not bad." She said with a smile.

Luzetta realized how ridiculous she was. After all, a man's life was at stake. Who was she to deny him her warmth just because she had never been with a man before? Before she knew it, Falling water helped her out of the dress she was helped into just a few short hours ago. Clad in her father's long underwear, she climbed in between the covers, careful to leave one thin blanket between them.

"No, not beside him. *On* him." Falling Water corrected.

"*On him?*" Luzetta echoed.

"Yes. It will do more good. You will cover more of his body if you are on top of him." She watched as Luzetta awkwardly climbed on the man. It felt strange but oddly comfortable to be atop of the stranger. Falling Water left the room shortly after Luzetta reassured her that everything was under control.

After she was alone, atop a strange man, she began to let her imagination soar and wondered if the man would take a notion to wake up and think he was still under attack, or worse - take advantage of her position. "Please, God." She said out loud. "Please let this be a good man." She decided to better her chances of getting away if anything were to happen. She got back up and tore two strips of an old sheet she was using for bandages. She first tied his right hand to the oak frame, leaving him minimal room to go further than two inches off the bed. Since one side of the bed was almost flush with the wall she had to crawl under the bed to attach his left hand to the frame.

Satisfied she was safe, Luzetta repositioned herself on top of Mr. Bear. She laid her head on his chest and spread her arms and legs to cover his. Had this been under different circumstances Luzetta would have laughed. The lack of coverage she had to offer compared to his needs were more than insufficient. Her fingertips reached his mid-forearms and her toes met his ankle bones. It did not go unnoticed by Luzetta that he was at least twice her width and thickness. Still she maintained her post and kept her vigil. The coolness of his body contrasted the warmth of the covers. The contest made for comfortable sleeping. She dozed off in no time at all.

He was hot and his head hurt was all Trent Longwood knew when he first became aware he was conscious again. Even with his eyes closed he was aware of his surroundings. He could smell the odors that came with hospitals. The smell of bodies, soap and something else stung his nostrils. It could be medicines, he thought to himself. Yes, it smelled like iodine. He could always rely on his senses ... until last night when he failed to sense what was coming.

Trent went looking for trouble and that was exactly what he found. He was actively investigating the theft of gold bouillon that was in transit through this area over a year ago and was approached by a man who supposedly knew information on the topic. Only his quick wit and his reflexes kept him alive. He was out numbered and out gunned, but he filled quite a few of them with lead before something hard from behind him came against his head. It still puzzled him how he could have been taken from behind.

The heat was almost unbearable. He opened his eyes to stare at the wood planks of a foreign ceiling.

Slowly he turned his head to his right and scanned his surroundings. A fire was fully ablaze along with a table stocked with vials, a grinding bowl and doctor's instruments. Instruments he knew were used to retrieve bullets from a person. From *his* person. On his left was a window that illuminated the room fully. He wondered what time it was. The cloud cover outside gave him no indication of the position of the sun.

The pain in his head was more centralized now as he gained clarity. He tried to raise his hand to feel where there undoubtedly would be a huge bump only to be brought up short. He looked down to see his hand tied with a pathetically thin piece of cloth. He also noticed the mass of golden curls covering his chest. How he could have missed having a woman on top of him? And after a night like last night was even more mystifying. He was in really bad shape, details of the previous night surfacing without effort. He raised his head to get a better view of the female covering him. The only thing he could see was the top of her head. He wondered if he should wake her or let her sleep.

He decided to move a little and see what happened. With his left arm flush against the wall he didn't have much leeway. He moved as if in a stretch, moving his legs with instant regret. The pain shot through him like a hot knife. He remembered having to jump out of a two-story window last night. His knees were retaliating along with the bullet wounds he sustained. He was getting too old for this.

As he moved, the woman began to stir. Feeling her soft body move against his was painful on many different levels, but he liked it. She turned her head sleepily and ended up on his wounded arm. The delicious sounds she made reminded Trent of the tabby cat that hung around his place.

The woman's face was still covered by the mass of golden curls. He could see a lock of her hair move with each exhale. With ease, he pulled on his restraint he somehow knew she placed on him. It broke with little resistance. He brought his hand to her hair and paused. Just the touch of her hair reminded him of spun silk. Spun silk colored by the sun, curled by the wind. As he brushed the hair out of her face, he gazed down at her. He was looking at the most perfect, angelic face he ever clapped eyes on. Trent no longer felt the heat from the blankets. His groin took center stage.

He stared down at the sleeping woman, securely on his chest as if she slept there a thousand times before. She had skin that made him think of peaches and cream. Her lips were relaxed and full. He wondered what color her eyes were. Her body was so soft against his. When she moved, he could tell she had a womanly shape to her and it went straight to his head - or rather his groin.

Before he could talk himself out of it, Trent bent his head down, used his shoulder to bring her closer to him and softly kissed the lips that were so inviting. A lightning bolt shot through Trent that had nothing to do with pain. Surprisingly, she didn't wake up. That just encouraged him to continue kissing her. What woman wouldn't want to wake up kissing Trent Longwood?

Luzetta was dreaming she was with her father deep into the hot springs they often ventured to. They were swimming around in water so warm, bubbling around them that Luzetta began to giggle with delight. The water embraced her and held her tight. Her father told her the springs were 'healing waters' and caused many ailing ones relief. She let the warmth of the water hold her, heal her. Completely relaxed, Luzetta leaned back and allowed her legs and body to float carefree in the water. In the background she could hear her father's voice telling her she was his angel, his heaven on earth.

Trent let his control slip as the girl he held in his arms responded favorably to his advances. He wrapped his one loosed arm around her. She began to giggle. Giggle! He leaned in further to access her lips only to be irritated by the mountain of blankets atop them. He gripped the mass and rid them both of the bothersome coverings. The blonde angel had him past his boiling point, relaxed and smiling a contented smile as he looked down at her angelic face.

"You are my angel." He claimed her as his own, for she certainly stole his heart. He brushed back her golden mass of curls and let his fingers dive deep into them. They were no longer hindered by the blankets, hiding her from him. His eyes took their fill at the voluptuous body garbed in men's long underwear instead of the traditional cotton night gown. The underwear allowed him to see the shapeliness he felt before, letting him linger over each curve she had to offer. Of course, he would have preferred the night gown that he could have raised, seen the rest of her, lain next to her skin to skin. The thought made his blood boil.

"My heaven on Earth." He exclaimed. He bent his head down to hers once more, sweetly kissing her, caressing his lips against hers. He didn't even mind the shooting pain through his shoulder and leg, not to mention his head. She took all of that away with each kiss he gave her.

As Luzetta slowly awoke, the tingling sensation her body felt from the bubbles became more real. Somewhere between wakefulness and dreamland, the embrace of the warm water turned into the embrace of a man. Only in a dream, she thought.

Never had she dreamed so vividly. Her body was reacting to a mere fantasy. She let herself become swept away with the feelings. The kiss she was receiving from a faceless man was tender, non obtrusive, gentle. It was exactly the type of kiss she privately dreamed of receiving in reality. The faceless man's kiss was so vivid, so real that Luzetta immersed herself into her dream, kissing the faceless man with her inexperienced mouth.

Trent's control began to slip even more as she began responding with her mouth and body. She let a little mew escape from the back of her throat. Taking his hand from her hip and placing it on her firm, round buttocks pulling her body against his, it was easy to take their kissing to the next level. The tip of his tongue slid across her lips, coaxing her into opening her mouth to him.

Luzetta received the new sensation of the strange kind of kiss with intrigue. She felt the faceless man's tongue slowly enter her mouth then she heard a sound that resembled a growl. Feeling the roughness of an unshaven face and something uncomfortable jabbing into her abdomen, Luzetta realized, to her mortification, she was no longer dreaming.

Luzetta's eyes flew open to meet the faceless man. The man looking down at her was the man she brought in from the snow ... into her bed ... fell asleep on top of him ... and now she was kissing him, something she would not have done had she been in possession of all her faculties.

"Oh my." Was the only thing she could say. She saw the hunger in his eyes as he stared down at her. His dark blonde hair was mussed and his days old beard covered his strong jaw. He was utterly handsome. The knowledge that his palm was spread intimately on her backside mortified her even further and made her face turn bright red with embarrassment. Her embarrassment quickly turned to righteous indignation as she tried to relieve herself from her position, but he had her pinned partially beneath him against the wall. How was she going to get out of this one? She really stepped in it this time. Why had she let Falling Water talk her into laying on him in the first place?

Trent found himself staring down into the bluest eyes he ever saw. They were the color of the clearest, bluest sky. Wide and innocent, then stormy and tumultuous. When she spoke, her voice was light and soft and utterly feminine even when served heated and combative. His heart melted with each bat of her eyes.

"Excuse me." She spoke calmly so as not to make the strange man upset, but firm enough to let him know where he stood with her. After all, she easily saw the predicament she was in for what it was. He was twice her size and could throw her across the room with little effort. She chose to use finesse to avoid possibly offending this man in her bed.

"Would you kindly let me up?" She pushed her palm onto the solid muscle of his chest to emphasize her suggestion. She wondered if the lack of response she got was from him not understanding her. Did he speak another language? Could he be deaf? She needed to communicate her desire to be let up any way she could without upsetting him. After all, he wasn't in any shape to be moving around.

"Please, Sir." She emphatically stated as she pushed at his well-muscled chest with no more strength than a kitten and began to try wriggling free. Her efforts were unheeded and she desperately wanted to get away from whatever it was jabbing her in the abdomen.

Trent knew the angel was trying to get away from the situation as delicately as she knew how. Why didn't she know that her squirming was going to get her into more trouble if she didn't stop? He knew that if he didn't let her up within a matter of seconds she would find out how much trouble he was prepared to give.

"Don't make me use force!" She said with as much vehemence as she could muster, feeling guilty for putting herself in this compromising position in the first place. All she got was a quirk of a smile at the corner of his mouth.

He quickly changed his mind about her inability to protect herself as she filled her lungs to capacity and braced to scream. He removed his hand from it's provocative resting place and rolled his weight off of her onto his back. If waking up in a strange man's embrace wasn't enough, the knowledge that she was nearly naked with a completely naked man sent her over the edge.

Luzetta immediately sat up, ineffectively covering herself with her arms. She was thankful there was a blanket between them. Her face flamed even more. This was the ultimate humiliation. She would never forgive herself for this magnificently huge lapse in judgement. But only half the battle was over. Another loomed before her.

The only way out of the bed was to cross over the man. The small room didn't allot for much. There wasn't enough space to exit over either end of the bed and she was pinned against the wall. She was trapped. The only other option ruminated around in her head as she tried feverishly to think of a way to modestly accomplish the required task.

He was staring at her, listening to her mumble to herself the specifics of her situation. He waited patiently to see what she would do next. It wasn't likely she would ask him to leave the room, or even get out of the bed for that matter. The extent of his wounds would prevent him from standing. "Listen, Mr. Bear" she finally spoke without looking back at him "I don't know if you understand me, but I need your help. Well, cooperation would be more adequate a word for what I need." With a sigh, Luzetta decided to look back at the stranger to gauge his understanding. All she got was the same hungry stare and the corner of his mouth was turned up in a sexy little smile. Oh, why did he have to be so good looking? She turned her eyes away quickly.

"The only way out of this bed is to cross over you. Since you are rather large and I'm ... not decently dressed, I need you to close your eyes as I stand up and walk over you." She was afraid of looking back at him again, but she did anyway. His eyes were still wide open, still full of hunger.

As embarrassing as it may be, she knew she had to get out of this bed. With unsteady bearings and an inadequate amount of room to work with, Luzetta stood and tried to bring her leg over the large man. Her attempt was largely unsuccessful. She landed back on top of him as she had been last night.

She gasped in horror of her predicament. The man lost his smile and a growl escaped him. She tried to scramble off him. This time he lent her his hand to hold onto as she balanced herself. It was then she noticed he was free from the restraint she placed him in last night.

"How did you get free?" She asked when she finally reached the floor, scooping up a blanket for modesty sake. He looked down at his other wrist. It, too, had been tied with the same pathetically thin cloth. It had been just long enough for his arm to rest comfortably at his side. He gave the cloth a tug and it snapped with little effort.

"Oh, my." She said again as she realized her underestimation of the restraint's strength against such a man. Luzetta's face showed exactly what she was thinking. If she only knew how close she was to getting attacked a few seconds ago, she would be running as quickly as she could to get away from him, but her angelic face and her innocent blue eyes cast a spell on him that made his honor stay in check. He wasn't in the business of ravaging innocent virgins that didn't know the effect they had on a man.

Luzetta quickly snatched up another quilt scattered on the floor and wrapped it around her shoulders, wearing it like a cape. She stared back at the man in the bed with large eyes. From the moment she woke up she was aware of the man's intense, watchful gaze. She pulled the quilt tighter around her shoulders and backed toward the door. Once she reached the door, she felt much safer.

Trent had a mixture of relief and loss as the woman slipped out of the room. It was short lived, though. She reentered the room with a look of further mortification on her face. Looking around the room, she located where Falling Water placed her dress and shoes the night before and gathered them up. She could still feel the man watching her.

"Do you mind?" She snapped with more verve than before as the stare of the man became too unnerving to bear. She must have gotten the point across to the silent man because he turned, giving her a full view of his broad, muscular back. Luzetta dressed hurriedly in the semi-private room and pulled her hair back into a neat bun before leaving the man still facing the wall.

"Good morning, Gentlemen." She approached the clan of men gathered in her front room. "Good mornin' to you, Ma'am." Lester Wick greeted her, others just tilting their howdy's. She was still recovering from her embarrassment of encountering the men in a quilt and long underwear. This day was turning out to be full of embarrassments.

"What can I do for you?" She asked as cordially as she could, remembering the last conversation they had.

"We, um . . ." The entire group of four men standing before her would not make eye contact with her.

"May we speak with you ... in private?" He asked nervously. Luzetta knew the men were not comfortable standing in the middle of a house full of Indians that out numbered them ten to one. Even if most were children and sick at that.

"Certainly." She answered begrudgingly. She could have pointed out that they were as private as they were going to get. None of the others spoke English anyway. Lester had inclined his head toward the door leading outside. He helped her with her coat and joined the others outside. Luzetta was hard pressed to smile. "Is this going to take long?" She snapped. "There are some very sick people I need to attend to."

"That's just it, Miss Hendrich. The townsfolk sent us to ask you to come to town with us. A lot of us don't think it's right to let you keep on with these Injuns when there are so many sick in town." Luzetta took offense at Lester's lack of appreciation of life. The other men signaled their agreement when their heads bobbed behind the man. "You are our only doctor and a lot of folks needin' attention won't come out here because they know you have all these Injuns around." He plead. "So we took a vote and we agreed that you should come with us."

"And if I refuse?" She glared back at him. She was furious, but kept a tight lid on her anger. Lester looked as if the thought of her refusal never came to mind. He scratched his jaw and thought for a moment.

Luzetta was furious. The town took a vote to whom she could and could not care for? It was preposterous. Luzetta looked each man in the eye, gauging each one's conviction.

"Why would you refuse?" He asked, bewildered at her stance.

"Because there are more sick people here in my home than in town and these people are much worse off. I have five times the number of sick ones in my house than you have in town. These people need me." She qualified.

"Well, so do the ones in town." He shouted back, unable to keep his frustration in check. "They're just Injuns! Your own kind is suffering and you would rather waste your time on Injuns?"

"The Piqui are people too." She felt like crying. The lid on her temper was slipping and she couldn't control it much longer, but she kept her voice low and even to keep the others from worrying. "They have families to care for, children to rear, breathe and bleed just like you and me. I have not neglected anyone in town or refused treatment of anyone since the Piqui tribe arrived."

"The town counsel voted you to come with us. We've made arrangements for you to stay at Mrs. Stratton's boarding house until everything is under control." He shouted at the woman that had him fit to be tied.

"Under control?" She knew he meant until the Piqui cleared out and on back to where they came from. "Things were never out of control."

"I'll give you just one warning, Miss Hendrich. If you don't come with us, we *will* be back for you." She heard the threat in Lester's voice, but decided to ignore it for now. She didn't have the wherewithal to worry about something as futile as that. She turned toward the house without dismissing the unwelcome guests.

Trent had been on guard since he heard the men's voices outside the bedroom door. It was a coincidence the men chose to assemble under the tree close to his window. Ignoring the chill, Trent opened the sash just enough not to draw attention, but enough to hear what they had to say. He found the conversation very interesting. He learned the woman's name was Miss Hendrich and she was a doctor. That would explain a lot of things. What puzzled him was that they didn't address her with the title. But what was this about Indians in her house?

HIDDEN TREASURE

Trent was aware that, if the band of men knew he was there, they would likely forget the Indians all together. He was sure they had no knowledge of his presence and he wanted to keep it that way.

After the terse words were exchanged, the front door slammed shut. Trent heard voices spoken in a different language just outside his door. Luzetta came through it accompanied by an old Indian woman who immediately began looking him over, measuring him with her hands and eyes. She said something to Miss Hendrich who was mixing something in a bowl with a grind stone. She measured and mixed a liquid into the powder. Turning back toward the bed, she spoke to the Indian woman and they both helped him sit up, propping pillows behind him.

Being fully immersed into her work, fully dressed and chaperoned, Miss Hendrich was more at ease. She turned toward her new patient and began to talk to him even though she didn't expect him to answer her.

"Okay, Mr. Bear. I am going to uncover your leg and apply some medicine and change your bandages." She did as she said. Trent looked at her differently now. He could tell she was stressed and tired. Her voice was different from before. It was almost monotone now as she talked to him absently, telling him what she was doing and why. Trent wondered if the loose-fitting clothes were from a recent weight loss.

"Now, I need you to roll over." She asked, making hand signals mimicking a rolling motion. "This is the last one." She said. "You had seven bullet wounds. Most of the bullets went clean through except one of them that I had to retrieve out of your leg. One day maybe you will be able to tell me how you came to get so many bullet wounds." Not likely, he thought. Luzetta uncovered his right thigh and draped the blanket over one of his more strategic areas. He felt her touch on his skin as she applied the medicine. He wished they were alone as thoughts leapt into his head.

"There." She said with finality. "That should help with any infection." She finished wrapping his leg and covered him up again. "Now, if you will drink this, your pain will subside." She held the shot glass with black liquid in it. He took it and brought it to his nose, trying to decide whether or not to imbibe. "For goodness sakes. It isn't any worse than what you men drink at the saloon." She retorted.

Trent made the quick motion that threw the concoction down his throat and winced, making his face twist into something horrendous. His stomach began to burn and his taste buds screamed.

"God, woman! What was that? It's the most horrible stuff I've ever tasted." He belted out. Luzetta's jaw dropped. It took her a moment before she regained her wits, and her temper.

"Maybe that will teach you." She steamed. She snatched the glass from his hand and fumed over at the table where she began to gather her utensils. "Next time I suggest you speak up and I'll put honey in it like I do for the children." She spat.

"Never again. That stuff is poison!" He accused.

"Only partly." She said smartly.

"What? You gave me poison?" He roared at her.

"Please, Mr. Bear, there are others in this house that are sick just outside your door and they need their rest. Please keep your voice down." She was speaking with her back to him as she gathered her things. "I gave you a mix of herbs. Angelica, black haw, cramp bark, kava kava, rosemary, valerian root, some white willow bark and a pinch of cayenne pepper."

Just before she left, though, she turned to his brooding face and gave him a sappy smile. "You took the cayenne, fresh horseradish and whisky much better last night. I was sure it would have jolted you awake, but it didn't."

After she gathered everything on a tray and headed toward the door, she turned and looked him straight in the eye. "Let's just hope that you don't react to what I just gave you like the last gentleman."

"What happened to him?" He said with narrowed eyes, still wondering if the taste remaining in his mouth was going to make him hurl.

"He died." Out the door she went without expounding on that statement.

"She's just mad." He spoke out loud. "Just yankin' my chain." He reassured himself. He doubted that she could hurt a fly. It wasn't long before he began to feel the effects of the potion she gave him. His pain had subsided, but he was more tired than he ever remembered being. He was out cold in no time.

In and out of feverish lucidity, Trent began to hallucinate. He wasn't sure what was reality and what was fantasy. He laid upon his bed staring at the ceiling, watching it move to and fro. He closed his eyes to stop the motion only to have it reappear when he opened them up again.

Luzetta had a hard time controlling Mr. Bear. He spiked a fever in the middle of the night and had tossed and turned every which way, giving her concern that he might injure himself if he fell out of the bed. Lord knows she wouldn't be able to put him back in. For fear of blood poisoning, Luzetta gave him something to help him fight off the infection. The bullet wounds were easy enough to repair. It was infection that usually killed.

Little time had passed before Mr. Bear falling out of bed was no longer a concern. Keeping him in bed was even worse. The man had the iron will of a bull. At different times it took four or five people to get him to lie back down in the bed. He made it as far as the front door and was trying to escape, chanting something about gold, but they seized him and got him back into bed. It was getting so that everyone was getting used to seeing the naked white man stumble about the house.

Except Luzetta. Each time they had to retrieve him she blushed from the top of her head to the soles of her feet and had to strengthen her constitution. One thing her father never prepared her for was the male sex organs. He told her that no man in his right mind would let her near his 'family jewels' and refused to say anything more about it. She had no idea what to expect then. She does now.

Rising Sun made Mr. Bear a pair of deerskin pants and a shirt. They would have to wait until he was conscious enough to put them on himself. No one was fool enough to attempt dressing him in the state he was in.

Chapter Four

Luzetta hurt all over. She was tired and hungry, but had no real appetite. Two children died in the night along with an old man named Brown Beaver. The house was mournful of the loss, quiet with despair and sadness. Now she stayed by the side of a child only six months old, clinging to life as hard as it was able. Her vigil was strong and determined. Rubbing the child down, forcing him to consume medicine and liquids, praying as hard as she could for the life of this child to be spared.

The one and only thing she could be grateful for was that Mr. Bear had broken his fever and had calmed down. He remained asleep for five whole days. It concerned her considerably, but she continually monitored him.

Luzetta completely forgot about the men that had tried to take her away from the people who needed her most. Luzetta was sitting on a chair beside the exam table where the child lay. Falling Water and the others were getting better, regaining their strength to care for the household needs again and nurse the other fallen clans-members back to health. Luzetta resumed devoting her time to those most in need.

"Golden Hair." Rain Cloud, the woman who lost her baby just yesterday came to her. "Eat this. You need strength." Rain Cloud handed her a strip of deer meat and a cup of broth.

"Thank you." She said. She forced herself to eat it all. Rain Cloud and Song Bird, the sick child's mother, sat together on the floor not ten feet from Luzetta's feet. They chanted softly together to their Spirits and used their legs in place of drums. The same beat was constantly carried on outside her home. The chanting and constant beat worked along with Luzetta's weariness to lull her to sleep. She told herself she would only close her eyes for a moment, rest just until she was needed once more.

When Trent awoke he wasn't alone in his room. An old Indian woman, a different one than the one before, was mopping him with a damp cloth. When he became fully aware of himself, he realized that she was giving him a bath in bed, taking care that his wounds didn't become soiled. She finished with her chore in short order, taking her leave after laying out the clothes she made for him.

First he tried out his arm by slowly swinging it up and over his head. It ached, but didn't hurt any more than a toothache. He uncovered himself and sat up, swinging his legs over the side of the bed. The wrapping around his thigh was tight and neat. He remembered watching Miss Hendrich expertly wrapping it with her light touch.

Trent decided to try and stand. He took a hold of the headboard post and hefted himself up then put pressure little by little on this leg. It hurt like hot coals. He fell back on the bed and let out a little yelp when the pain shot through him. What was he thinking? He had taken three bullets to his right leg. It would be a good while before he could even wobble around.

Luzetta knocked on the door when she heard him struggling. There was no response, but that didn't surprise her. It didn't stop her from entering the room, either.

"I see that you're eager to try your strength." She didn't look at him as she crossed the room to her table. "You should be careful. You could injure yourself again and cause permanent damage." She talked as she mixed, ground, poured. "At least you managed to keep from harming yourself while you were crazy with fever."

"Fever?" He asked quizzically. He didn't remember anything.

"Yes. You had an infection that caused you to have a dangerously high fever. You were crazy with fever for two days." She wasn't about to fill him in on the embarrassing details. She came over to his bedside and instructed him to pull the covers off his leg. Was her cool treatment because of his actions before, or was it from whatever gave her the dark circles under her eyes? Was it his imagination or had they grown larger than before?

Luzetta stopped talking as she began to concentrate on her work at hand. He wanted to keep her talking. He liked to hear her voice.

"What happened?" He asked.

"When bullets hit flesh, they take along with them debris, such as clothing. It causes infection more often than not. I cleaned them out as best I could when you first arrived, but that doesn't mean I couldn't have missed something." She confessed. After unraveling the bandage and examining his leg, she began applying medicine. She was so fully immersed in her work that she didn't notice him memorizing her profile.

Luzetta wrapped his leg and returned to her table only to bring another shot glass of that black poison again.

"Oh, no. Not that stuff again. I think I'll pass." He held up one large palm to refuse.

"It will help your pain." She explained.

"Are you sure that you aren't trying to put me in an early grave with that poison?"

"Positive." Again she offered, again he refused.

"Last time I took that stuff I didn't wake up for two days." He interjected.

"Mr. Bear, the only reason you didn't wake up for seven days was due to the fever from infection." She said rather perturbed. He looked like he was considering it. His leg was throbbing and he was bound and determined to be mobile as soon as possible.

"Okay, but I only want half of it. I don't want to get knocked out again."

"This *is* a half dose. I also gave you only a half dose last time."

"Why?" He seemed put out by the knowledge.

"Because you seemed to be tolerant to your pain that morning . . ." She willed herself not to blush with the memories flooding into her mind. The lip between her teeth was the only thing that gave her thoughts away.

Trent's mind was flooded with memories of that morning as well. Luzetta heard that growl again. Did he have to do that? She stood before him holding the shot glass of medicine. He pinned her with his eyes. Unexpectedly, the man reached out and placed his hands on Luzetta's hips, pulling her close to stand between his legs. Luzetta almost stopped breathing. How could he take such drastic advances toward her?

"Mr. Bear." She protested shakily. Her insides were riotous as his arms encircled her, holding her close to him. He didn't say a word to her as she stood encircled by his muscular arms. He opened his mouth and placed his lips to the rim of the glass. He could feel her heart racing, her breath increase in depth. It made his mind run wild with possibilities.

Luzetta was astonished at the familiarity he was taking with her. When he put his lips to the glass she offered, she poured, watching his mouth as he drank. It did crazy things to her pulse to be this close to a handsome, virile man. What was he trying to do to her?

"Sweet." He commented after swallowing and licking his lips. Miss Hendrich looked absolutely mortified, ready to bolt at any second, but she didn't move or even suggest he let go of her. She looked as if she were going to say something, but stopped herself. He smiled a devilish smile. "Is this the only thing I get, Kitten, or can I get something to eat, too?"

"I can get you something." She wasn't about to ask him what he wanted. Trent let his hands drop and she moved backwards immediately. She turned and remained quiet while she cleaned up after herself. She heard him slip himself back between the covers and adjust his wounded body. She was furious with herself that she let a man become so forward with her. She scolded herself at not telling him to keep his hands off of her. Her upset mind caused her to say the first thing that came to her mind.

"I did want to counsel you on one point, though. Although you may not be worried about it now, your weight should cause you some concern. It will be much harder to lose as you age, and with your size it would be wise to consider your health while you are still young." She didn't wait for any response and closed the door behind her. She only took four steps away from the door before she heard a tremendous roar of laughter. "You would think he would take his health more seriously than that." She said to herself.

Trent had a hard time keeping in the burst of laughter. If she only knew what was causing the blanket to look full. He had a permanent tent whenever she was around. His angel was truly an Angel.

Shortly after consuming the medicine he fell into a comfortable sleep without the throbbing pain of his leg. He woke up to a dark room. He laid there listening to noises that were coming from beyond his door. After an hour or so, he let his curiosity get the best of him.

It took Trent fifteen minutes to get his wounded leg into the pants laid out for him. His shirt went on considerably easier. He couldn't have put boots on if he had any. Prepared for pain, Trent eased himself out of bed. It still hurt, but not as badly as before. He never remembered healing this fast from a gun shot wound before. He hobbled over to the door and listened.

Nothing could have prepared Trent for what he was about to see as he opened the door. There were wall-to-wall Indians coating the floor. As he stood staring out over the people who carpeted the floor he saw the spots that plagued them. Understanding consumed him amidst the coughs, crying babies and parents who consoled them. Only a few were upright, roaming the sea of bodies going from person to person where needed.

Trent used the furniture and walls to help him support his weight as he limped into the front room. When he came to the hallway, he saw two more rooms filled with people struck with the disease. Trent spotted movement toward the back of the house where he saw an Indian woman placing wood in a stove. The surprise of seeing him showed on her face.

Quickly, the woman entered into another room through a closed door. Trent was hoping the woman would lead him to Miss Hendrich. He peered into the room and let out a low groan. There were six cots surrounding what must have been her examination table in the middle of the room. The Indian woman turned the lamp light up.

He spied her, his angel, sitting in a straight back chair resting her head on an outstretched arm. One hand was holding onto the arm of a baby, and her other arm was planted on the baby's small chest. Trent could only imagine it was to keep her aware of the baby's pulse and breathing as she rested.

Taking her by the shoulders, the Indian woman gently squeezed her shoulders and whispered strange words. Slowly, Miss Hendrich's head rose and she looked at the man who filled the doorway, staring at her. He looked bigger standing up, she thought. He also looked meaner with the way the light played upon his strong features, dark eyes and a week's growth of beard

Luzetta stood and walked over to Mr. Bear. "Please" was all she whispered to him and motioned to leave the room. After closing the door, she said nothing as she walked back to his room, giving him the hint that he should follow. Only when they were both inside his room did she speak.

"Mr. Bear, for your health and safety, I feel it is in your best interest to confine you to this room." She stated. "And please sit down before you hurt yourself."

"I will sit down, but I will not be confined." His voice was actually very nice when he wasn't yelling at her.

"And why not?" He took note of the distance she placed between them. "Do you realize that those sick people out there could pass along their disease onto you, making you sick? You may have a false sense of strength right now because of the pain medicine, but please heed my advice." Hands on hips, Luzetta tried to talk some sense into him.

"I've already had the chicken pox." He stated.

"That only covers one area. These people couldn't stand more than they already have. Anything else that comes their way could wipe them out." He knew that to be true. He'd seen white man diseases kill off tribes before they knew what they were dealing with.

"Are you a doctor?" He hoped the change in subject would keep her from hounding him further.

"Yes and No." She said with all honesty, but her chin flew up in the air showing her pride. "I care for the medical needs of this town but I have not been classically trained as most doctors. My father was the town doctor and he trained me from the time I was knee high to a pup." So that explained why the men from town didn't address her with any title other than Miss.

"Is that why the Indians are here?" She looked exasperated by his question.

"Mr. Bear, on any other day I would be more than happy to explain matters, but I have a child that may die tonight. I am going back there and try to prevent that from happening. If you will excuse me." She didn't wait for his approval before reaching for the doorknob.

"Wait." He called out to her. "I just want to ask one question. Why do you keep calling me Mr. Bear?"

Luzetta had been so preoccupied with the Piqui and the strange man's medical problems that she neglected to ask his name. "It was the only name that seemed to suit you."

"Oh?" One eyebrow shot up at the accusation.

"The scars on your chest." She thought to remind him. "And the way you growl at me all the time." She added before slipping out the door.

"Growl?"

Late the next morning, Luzetta's problems compounded. Even though the baby survived the night, the battle was far from over. She worked all night to keep the boy alive and had not stopped to rest. She wouldn't allow another child to die. Not if she could help it. She pulled out some of her father's notes and studied them by lamp light. She tried different things to help the child, but all she could really do was pray. When dawn finally arrived, the baby was still alive. Little relief came with the knowledge. He still was not in the clear.

Luzetta finally took a moment to get some air, removed herself from the despondency that surrounded her. She stepped out onto the front porch without a coat to let the chill in the air wake her. The Piqui were getting their meals ready to serve with efficiency and the constant steam in the house made it hard for Luzetta to keep awake when she was still. She was thankful that only a small group had endured serious complications. It could have been much worse.

Luzetta let her head drop down and roll, stretching her neck muscles. Her body retaliated against the strain of caring for others and the lack of sleep. She stretched her shoulders and her arms as best as she could and stood to stare out into the horizon to turn her thoughts away from being tired.

Over the horizon, though, was a band of men traveling in her direction. Her heart dropped into her stomach as she made out a paddy wagon in tow. Luzetta went straight back into the house in search of her father's gun. She never even pointed it at another living soul, let alone pulled the trigger, but she told herself that it would be for intimidation only. The obstacle she came across, though, was that it was in the same room as Mr. Bear. She hoped not to alert him or cause him any undue stress. He needed his rest and to stay off his wounded leg.

Luzetta crept into the room. Mr. Bear's back was to her and she listened for a moment to his even, heavy breathing before tiptoeing to where the gun was propped up against the wall. As quietly as she could, she picked up the heavy gun and toted it toward the door, placing herself between the man and her gun.

"I sincerely hope you aren't expecting to shoot anything with that." Luzetta nervously jumped at the sound of his voice and spun around. He must have been faking sleep.

"Of course not." She wasn't lying. "I was just thinking of the children. I shouldn't have let it sit out where they could reach it." Her explanation was shaky, but it was the only thing she could think of on short notice. She hoped he bought her story. "I'm taking it out to the barn and placing it high above their heads."

"So it has nothing to do with those men coming this way?" He'd been awake since he heard movement in the house. He would have missed those men like he would have missed a tornado coming.

"No." Luzetta's heart sank. "I don't know of any band of men." Trent watched as the angel's grip on the muzzle of the gun got tighter, wringing it as if she were going to choke it.

"You aren't a very good liar, Kitten." That was the second time he called her kitten, she noticed, with an intimate connotation in his voice. He swung his legs over the side of the bed and she quickly stepped back.

"And you, Mr. Bear, aren't a very good patient. I specifically instructed you to stay in bed." He reached for his pants draped on the end of the bed. She turned her back just in case he felt the need to immodestly expose himself to her. "I should hope that you will take my advice and stay in bed." She said as she slipped out the door.

Not likely. He wanted to see what those men had to say. He wasn't sure if they came for him or for her. After all, who would think they would use a paddy wagon for a kitten like Miss Hendrich?

Luzetta stood on the porch and watched four men walk separately from the other armed men. They obviously thought the Piqui were dangerous enough that they prepared to be forceful if necessary. One of the men, she noticed, was Reverend Williams. The other three were Clarence Jacobs, Bud Jackson and Lester Wick. She assumed they made Reverend Williams come along to try to persuade her into 'Christian service' and abandon her post with the Piqui.

The gun Luzetta held at her side was not giving her the self-confidence she was hoping for. Every man wore a determined, unsmiling look on his face. They were past being sociable since her last refusal. There were no pleasantries, so salutations.

"We come for you, Miss Hendrich." Lester Wick was the one to state the obvious. "Last time we asked you. Now we're telling you. Come into town with us peaceable-like and you can ride your own horse. Refuse and you can ride in this here paddy wagon."

"Who's sick?" She asked him. "Who needs me?" She knew that they wouldn't be able to answer her and it galled her to no end.

"It's for your own good." Was his only excuse. "Put the gun down and come with us." He said cordially enough. He saw the stubborn set of her jaw and the grip on the gun get tighter.

"Come now, Miss Hendrich. Please don't resist." Reverend Williams pleaded. "I give you my word that you will be treated kindly."

"I am not worried about how I will be treated. My concern lies with the ones who truly need me. I saw and treated many townsfolk just days ago. Most parents were well aware of how to handle the situation. The Piqui have never been exposed to this disease, let alone know how to treat it. The children in town were also not as affected. I have seven serious cases in my care now. One of which I was surprised to see survive the night. If I leave now, a six-month-old boy may die." She kept eye contact with Bud Jackson who had a child just that age. "Do you want that blood on your hands?" She said as she turned to the Reverend.

"You can save your breath. We're taking you in. You can send someone for your things later." Lester reached for her. She backed up and pointed the shotgun at his gut. "You're kidding, right?" He looked at her with amusement. "That gun is so old my grandpa would call it ancient. I would be surprised if it even fires."

"Shall we see?" She said with a false sense of bravado in the hopes he would back off. Lester put his hand down and laughed.

"Sure, go ahead." He laughed. Her finger was on the trigger. She knew it was loaded. She couldn't let herself try. She looked away in defeat and allowed Lester to take the gun. He didn't laugh at her. No one did. They knew that she didn't have the heart. He was just lucky that it wasn't someone else pointing the gun at him.

"C'mon, sister. We just want you to tend to your own kind. No sense in gettin' your back up about it. These people can fend for themselves." There was no point in arguing, but she tried anyway. Her words fell on deaf ears.

Luzetta was escorted to the school steps in the paddy wagon as promised. It was a testament to everyone that she came by force, not by will. Several families that stood in the line to be seen were the very ones she'd seen just days ago and concluded that they were well on their way to recovery. Luzetta sensed a conspiracy to make it seem as though the town was really more needy than it actually was.

Regardless of that knowledge Luzetta saw to it that each and every person was treated. It made her angry, though, when she observed that none of the children or adults suffered with any ailment other than itching, yet she hadn't heard so much bellyaching in all her life.

Two armed men stood outside the front and back entrances as if awaiting an ambush. One man even followed her to the privy, evidently expecting her to bolt if she had the chance.

When the last family had been seen, treated and sent home, Luzetta was hoping she could return home.

"Excuse me, but my place is in the opposite direction." She firmly pointed out when the wagon didn't turn in the proper direction.

"Don't worry. We'll get you somewhere safe." Bud Jackson commented, barely keeping the chuckle out of his voice. Luzetta was shocked and dismayed when they pulled in front of the county jailhouse.

"You don't honestly think I am going to stay here?" She gasped.

"Yes. I do." This time he chuckled more openly, and no matter what language she used as she was put into the cell the size of a shoe box, was going to get her out. She was mortified to see the filthy chamber with it's hard bed, scratchy wool blanket and a chamber pot without a lid standing beside the head of the bed. Her heart dropped as she heard the clank the lock made as it slid into place.

"What happened to Reverend William's promise to me that I would be treated kindly?" She cried. All she got were backs turned to her pleas and the door closing her off from any human contact. Luzetta fell back on the hard bed with the scratchy wool blanket and began to cry. The stress she was under was insurmountable in weight. She couldn't take it any more. She cried herself to sleep.

Trent watched the men take Luzetta. He would have killed someone if they hurt his angel, but he knew they needed her. They wouldn't risk her becoming an enemy. He was just glad that he didn't have to reveal himself before he was healed. He knew he was being selfish, but he couldn't stop what had already been set in motion.

One of the men that came for Luzetta had been in the ring of thieves he tried to unveil. If he blew his cover now in the middle of his investigation, he could risk losing it all. He needed to recover the stolen money, not let a female sidetrack his purpose.

Besides, he had a plan. It pained him greatly, both in his leg and for having to leave Luzetta alone like this, but Trent waited until the dead of night and mounted the only horse in the stable and set out for the nearest town in the opposite direction.

Chapter Five

Luzetta was awake by dawn and had been served breakfast. Harriet Johensen, Sheriff John Johensen's wife, was a fine cook. She had a full plate of delicious food. The only problem was that Luzetta couldn't bring herself to eat. She drank some coffee, but she had no appetite for any fare. Another thing she was grateful to Mrs. Johensen for was laying into her husband for treating Luzetta like a common criminal. Luzetta was now allowed to use the water closet instead of that foul chamber pot and Sheriff Johensen didn't lock the cell door while he was in the office.

Luzetta watched as the Sheriff cleaned his plate of food within minutes. He propped his feet up on the desk and popped a tooth pick into his mouth with a loud belch. He didn't even bother to excuse himself afterwards. Luzetta felt sorry for his wife.

"Well, looky what we got here." He said to whomever walked through the door. His feet came down with a loud thump and he grinned like a cat that just swallowed the Canary.

"I caught him tryin' to make off with a horse not his own." A voice from behind the wall stated rather triumphantly.

"Horse thief, aye?" The sheriff swivelled to and fro in his chair, reminding Luzetta of an unruly child. "Do you know the penalty for stealing horses, son?" Luzetta cringed as she imagined the hanging body of a thief. "Who was the fine, upstanding citizen robbed of their horse?" He asked. There was no answer, but the Sheriff looked straight at Luzetta with eyebrows aloft.

"Well, let's just see what she has to say about it. Bring the accused to the victim and get it all hashed out." The Sheriff looked like he had to really work to peel himself off his chair. He waltzed into the room with the gait of a man just appointed judge, juror and executioner. The prisoner and the deputy followed close behind. Her eyes were glued to the prisoner.

He had the deerskin clothes Rising Sun made for him. He also found time to shave. She liked the clean look. His eyes never met hers. He didn't allow himself to look at her for fear of betraying himself. He wanted to appear as guilty as sin.

"Do you know this man, Ma'am?" The Sheriff asked. Luzetta seemed to be in a daze. "Miss Hendrich." He spoke louder to pull her out of the shock she was in. "Do you know this man's name?" She stared back at him.

"No." She said softly. She never in her life felt so bad as she did now about not asking the man his name. She'd been so busy she just called him by the assumed name and treated his wounds. That knowledge made her feel so guilty. When had she lost her bedside manner?

"Looks like you just bought yourself a one way ticket to the gallows." The Sheriff pushed the prisoner into the only other cell available.

"Wait." She called out. "What if I don't want to press charges?" She asked. He looked back at her as if she'd grown another head.

"Why in tarnation would you want to go and do a thing like that for? All's he'd do is go steal somebody else's horse. Or he might just go back to your place and take what he wanted. Look at him. He looks like a mean cuss that would take more than your horse had you been there." Luzetta thought for just a second before she came up with a good argument.

"That would be impossible. I have about fifty Piqui Indians in and around my house. He wouldn't have gotten away with anything." She felt victorious of her debate. The Sheriff looked back at her and huffed.

"What if there wasn't." He countered. "Besides, I can't just let you let a horse thief go free because you don't want to see someone hanged. It is really considered a crime against the community." He explained.

"Is there any other way he could escape hanging? Any other suitable punishment?" Both the Sheriff and the Deputy stared back at her knowing she was someone who would do anything to save a life rather than take one. Both men knew that any other option given to her would be agreed to if it spared his life.

"Not in my book." The Sheriff didn't want to give her any options. She would be better off leaving well enough alone and let them handle this sort of situation.

"There are only two options that the law provides for." Mr. Bear finally spoke when he knew the men were not going to give her the choice. He'd been sitting quietly on his bunk leaning up against the wall with his left leg drawn up to an angle, looking like a true menace to society.

"No there isn't." The Sheriff barked at him. "You just keep your trap shut."

"What are they?" She asked frantically, clinging to hope. When the sherrif returned to his chair and propped his feet up on his desk, she knew he wasn't going to tell her. "You might as well tell me. As soon as you leave us alone you can bet he will." She indicated to the man in the next cell.

"All right." He said begrudgingly. "One is that we could call in a judge, have a long, drawn out trial where a jury will convict him of a crime he was caught red handed at in the first place. All you'll be doing is stalling his death." Luzetta sat and listened to the Sheriff's ideal theory.

"I see." She sat on her cot. "Even if I claim that I do not wish to press charges, they would still convict him and want him ... punished." She couldn't even bring herself to say it. She watched as the Sheriff's head bobbed up and down in response. That was not what she wanted to see. She sat quietly on her cot contemplating the dreadful image.

Sheriff Johensen left her sit quietly. His deputy hadn't realized the sheriff's intention of dropping the matter.

"But he don't have to hang." He offered. The Sheriff shot daggers at the deputy for opening his mouth. Luzetta was ready to listen to anything the deputy had to say.

"What does he have to do?" She urged when the Sheriff's look shut the man's mouth. He figured he might as well let the rest of the cat out of the bag.

"If an upstanding woman of the community wants to make an honest man of him he can escape hanging. And he would have to pay back what he stole." He stated simply. Trent sat on the edge of his cot now with his back to her. His hands gripped the side of the cot. He wanted to give the others the impression he was withholding a negative reply to save his own neck.

"What does that mean, that I have to train him and give him a skill?"

"No, Ma'am. It means marriage." He said point-blankly.

"Marriage." Good thing she was sitting down already. What business did she have getting married to a perfect stranger? She didn't know anything about him. Besides, she was so busy with her practice that she hardly had time for herself, let alone a husband. And children were completely out of the question.

'Wait' she argued with herself 'what am I thinking? A man's life is weighing in the balance and you don't think you have time?' She scolded herself. 'I'll just explain to him that when we get out of this mess he can go his way and I can go mine. He'll be so grateful for me saving his life that he'll have no choice but to honor my request' she thought.

"I'll do it." The soft words pushed past her lips and hung heavy in the jail cell. The Sheriff hung his head and shook it in disbelief that this was really happening. It shouldn't have shocked him that she'd agree to go through with it. He knew her answer before she said it out loud. Later he was going to give his deputy a royal chewing about when to keep his big mouth shut. Trent sat perfectly still as Miss Hendrich contemplated what she just agreed to do. She stared at the same spot on the wall, letting the words rattle around in her head. Luzetta jumped when the sheriff slammed the door as he left.

"Where do you suppose they're going?" She asked softly, hoping that she hadn't just signed her soul over to the Devil.

"Most likely they're fetching the preacher." He'd silently been counting on her to say she would marry him. He watched her debate with herself earlier and knew she was talking herself into it. Little did she know that she just made his job much easier, along with some nice perks on the side. He could play the reformed husband while he investigated the thefts of gold.

"What have I done?" She whispered to herself, not caring that he would hear her.

"You saved my life for the second time." He answered. "Don't worry, Kitten. I'm not a bad man. I'll stay out of the way." He was hoping to take the stricken look off her face. It didn't work. Trent noticed the untouched plate of food on the tray beside her. "You haven't eaten."

"No." She qualified. She felt like crying.

"I'm just venturing a guess, but over the last month, you haven't eaten more than one meal a day, have you?" He didn't wait for an answer. "You're swimming in your clothes and you've lost your color. If you don't eat you'll get sick and you won't be able to take care of a limp ant. It's winter time. You should be putting on pounds not taking them off. Winter is a terrible time to get sick." Luzetta's heart ached even more as her thoughts switched to her father. She knew he was right. She didn't know if his words of concern were genuine until she looked into his eyes. She doubted this man was a criminal.

"I have no appetite. My stomach is too upset." She argued.

"Then I suggest you just eat the grits. It's the only thing on the plate not swimming in grease." She looked up at him as he spoke. "It's better than nothing."

"I suppose you are right." She conceded. As she took bite after bite of cold grits, she thought of his words. Not what he was saying, but how he was saying them. He was articulate and well spoken. She just now noticed that feature about him. Somehow it made him more credible.

After the last bite of grits were gone, the fork hit the plate with a 'clink'. His scrutinizing stare was on her the entire time she ate and was still on her. The temperature of the room began to rise.

"Do you feel any better?" He asked with a voice with smooth and velvety concern.

"Yes, thank you." She didn't want to look at him. And most of all, she didn't want to betray her thoughts to him.

"You're welcome." He lay on his side leaning up on his elbow. The length of his body hung over the edge of the bed. "If we are going to be married, I would like to ask you a few questions." Her heart sank. Married. Was she ready for this?

"All right." She squeaked.

"What is your first name, Kitten?" The question would have been funny if the situation wasn't so sticky.

"Luzetta.." She looked at him without really looking at him. "Luzetta Hendrich is my name."

"Luzetta. That's a very pretty name. Unique." He stood and extended a hand through the bars. "Luzetta Hendrich, I'm pleased to make your acquaintance. Allow me to introduce myself. My name is Trent Longwood."

Luzetta stood and stared at his big, extended hand. She timidly slid her hand in his. Something electric sung through her nerves at the simple touch. Trent pulled her to him through the bars, closing the distance between them.

Trent stepped back and bent his head over her hand, brushing a light kiss on the back. Her eyes followed her hand and she found herself staring into Trent's eyes.

"How old are you, Kitten?" He asked in that smooth voice of his. Trent felt her pulse thrum under his fingers. Her lips were slightly parted, eyes wide.

"Twenty-three." She could barely get the words out. His eyebrows raised in surprise.

"And you have never married? Am I the one that should be running the other way?" He was making a joke, but she didn't laugh.

"Let's just say I've never found myself favorable to the idea." And she still wasn't. If it were up to her, she would remain single regardless of how he was making her feel. She wanted to move away from that line of questioning. "Anything else?" She asked as she pulled her hand back from his.

"How do you know that I'm not a no-account gun slinger that won't ruin you and your good name?" He could have thrown a couple more adjectives in for color, but he knew she wouldn't appreciate them.

"Because" she began to feel a bit warmer under her collar "you leave little clues about yourself." She tried to explain. "Your vocabulary is well rounded and your diction impeccable." She remarked. "While you were hallucinating with fever, you were saying something about gold, so you probably got jumped after a find that brought you to me." A corner of his attractive mouth lifted, encouraging her. "You had a gun at your disposal for the past week without drawing it, so I know you didn't intend to rob or harm me. I'm just assuming that you borrowed my horse to get to somewhere you needed to be. I'll even bet you left a note behind telling me what you did and where I could find you." She listed all the imaginary qualities she could think of.

"Is that your basis for judging me?" He could have been a mass murderer and she wouldn't have known it.

"Yes, and ... you had ample opportunity to ruin me just days ago." Trent saw the pink in her cheeks. It made his heart soften and his groin harden.

"How long have you been on your own?" Luzetta was the only white person he came across was while staying the week at her house, with the exception of the men that came to take her away. No one else came to her aid when she had trouble.

"Over a year. My father died February of last year."

"You mean to tell me that you have been up there all by yourself for the past fourteen months? How did you survive so long?" His voice began to raise and that put Luzetta's back up.

"Do you assume that all women need a man in order to live? Well, not this woman, Mr. Longwood. Long before you got here, I was doing quite well for myself." She held her chin high and her shoulders were back in a regal stance.

"And how you made it this far is beyond me." He was standing, facing her and mimicking her hands-on-hips glare.

"For your information, I always have what I need without fail. Our town may be small, but in these neck of the woods, trade is sometimes the only way some families can pay for things. It just happens that people are particularly generous around here. I have a full pantry, livestock, and plenty of funds to keep me for a good long while."

"That takes care of food and material needs, but who protects you?" The more she talked the closer together his brows became, the thinner his lips became.

"Protects me?" She laughed. "From what?"

"From dangerous men like me." He saw her sober a bit.

"We don't get dangerous men around here." What world did she live in?

"Oh, I guess in your fairytale world you also believe that everyone is law abiding and no one ever does anything wrong." He came to the bars separating them and clenched his hands around them. It was the closest he could get to throttling her. "What do you think this jail is here for?"

"Everyone has a little bad inside. Some more than others." She said as she nailed him with an accusatory glare. "Besides, people call on me when they're in need of medical attention. They wouldn't dare hurt someone who could one day save their life." He wasn't sure if she wasn't applying that to him or people in general. "To our credit, we have never had a bank robbery or a murder like those big towns. We get a few drifters now and again, but with living so close to the Reservation, I don't get many travelers wandering toward my house."

Trent shook his head. "What reservation?"

"The Piqui." Surely he hadn't forgotten the Indians at her house so quickly. "They rarely have contact with those outside their tribe, so most people stay away from them out of ignorance. They're a very peaceable tribe. They live just five miles from my home."

Trent couldn't believe it. Here was a lone woman in the heart of Indian country, high in the Montana mountains and she felt perfectly safe. Go figure!

"You better be glad we're separated by iron bars, Kitten. I have a right mind to take you across my knee. You can't be so naive to think that your profession protects you from all that is evil."

"Why not? Nothing has happened to me so far." Her chin remained tilted up and the look in her eyes told Trent that she was truly convinced of her safety and security.

"Because" he shouted in frustration, raking his hands through his hair "what if some strange travelers saw the smoke coming out of your chimney and decided to see what they could help themselves to. What they would find is a gullible, trusting, beautiful woman with strong drugs, a full larder and pantry and a shotgun that's so old it would probably backfire if it shot at all. They could have you cleaned out and bent over before your pretty little mouth could scream for help."

"That's a big 'if', Mr. Bear."

"Stop calling me that." His frustration mounted as she refused to see reality.

"Then stop growling at me." She shouted back.

"Hey, hey, you two. Pipe down. You are fighting like married folk already." The Sheriff broke in. Both of them sat down and stewed as they were waiting for the deputy to arrive with the Reverend. Luzetta could just hear what he had to say to her about marrying a complete stranger - and horse thief at that.

When Reverend Williams arrived Luzetta got an ear full. He pulled her into the other room and proceeded to give her his opinion about the action she was taking. "Luzetta, I feel that you're letting your kind heart blind your eyes to the reality of how serious this situation can turn out to be. You're risking more than you realize."

"I am not prepared to let anyone be hanged. I tried to explain to the Sheriff that I do not wish to press charges, but he won't comply with my wishes. The only way out of this ugly mess is to marry him."

"Have you ever thought you might be working against God's purpose?" Reverend Williams' suggestion horrified Luzetta.

"Are you suggesting, Reverend Williams, that God purposefully had that man take my horse so he could be hanged? What kind of Divine Wisdom is that? If that is truly how you think, I'll pray for you." She said bitterly.

"As a man of the cloth, I viewed you as someone who would share my conviction to save the life of another, not sit by and watch them be slaughtered because it doesn't make you comfortable to contest the authorities."

"Miss Hendrich, I and others in the congregation have been quite liberal with you and your dearly departed father for quite some time. I'm afraid your actions today may jeopardize your standing in the church." Luzetta's heart sank. Would they go as far as excommunicating her from the congregation because of the stand she took for an innocent man's life? Would they turn her away because of her moral conviction to save this man's life? "This marriage is highly inadvisable and will bring scrutiny from all of those around you. Are you prepared for that?"

"I don't feel I have a choice. My conscience could not bear to let this man to be hanged. The Sheriff said there is no other recourse. What do you expect of me?" Luzetta knew the only way to soften the Reverend was to plead to his calling. "As you know my father instilled in me a great respect for life, just as I've heard you preaching from the pulpit. It isn't something I can just pick up and put down at random. It's with me always, much like your faith in your calling as one of God's servants."

The Reverend's strained look relaxed a fraction and took on a different quality. He was truly afraid for her, but she was not to be swayed. All he could do was perform the ceremony as requested. He stated his objections and now his hands were washed clean of the matter. If she didn't listen to reason, she would be bringing it on herself if things went wrong.

"Fair enough, Luzetta. I understand your frame of mind. I will pray extra hard for you on your endeavor to make a good man out of him."

"Thank you kindly, Reverend Williams. I appreciate your doing just that. Lord in Heaven be with me because I am going to need it."

After the ceremony, Luzetta was escorted to the school house and Trent was put back into his cell. They were purposefully denied their wedding kiss. They said their "I Do's" and the deputy took Luzetta by the arm and escorted her out the front door.

"Okay, Mrs. Longwood, time to get back to work." Trent heard the deputy spout out Luzetta's new name and let it ring through his brain. Back in his cell, he lay in the bed and thought of Luzetta. The way she blushed, the way she held her perfect little mouth, and the color of her sky blue eyes. He noticed they darkened when she got angry, already having been treated to those stormy blues several times already.

Contemplating how fast she was whipped out of the jailhouse, keeping him from kissing her, Trent thought of their first shared kiss. He wanted to kiss her again. Ever since that first morning when he woke to find an angel sleeping on him he wanted to keep kissing her. Honestly, he wanted to do more than that. Who knew when the next chance would come along. They couldn't keep them here forever.

Luzetta was greeted with smirks and glares when she entered the schoolhouse. The usual welcome she felt before was all but gone. News must have traveled like wildfire. It wasn't until the Grove family came in that Luzetta realized the impact of her actions.

Hanshill Grove stormed into the schoolhouse with the strides of a man on a mission. His face was pinched and his hands were fisted at his sides.

"I just want you to know, Miss Hendrich, that the only reason why I am bringing in my boy to you is because he's awfully sick and me and his ma don't think he would last the trip to the next town." Luzetta washed her hands and went out to see the boy laying in the back of their wagon, bundled in quilts and vomiting putrid smelling bile.

As soon as she saw the boy, she knew what was the cause of his troubles. "You're right. He wouldn't have survived the trip." She confirmed. "If it is all right with you, I would like to take him out to my house."

"No way." Mrs. Grove flatly refused. "You got them filthy Injuns at your place. I ain't puttin' my boy in danger."

"There's really no danger, Mrs. Grove. The Piqui are really very peaceful." How many times did she have to say it before someone believed her?

"I don't care about your bein' friends with the likes of them. Like I said, I'm only lettin' you look at my boy because he'll die if someone don't do somethin'. Until we get a real doctor in town, we're stuck with you." Henshill spat.

"Henshill!" His wife whispered harshly. "Why'd you go and tell her that for?"

Henshill lifted his twelve year old son and carried him into the schoolhouse. A table was cleared and Luzetta examined him.

"What will it take to make Jesse right?" He asked.

"I need to operate. I need to take his appendix out before it bursts." Neither of them looked overly fascinated with the idea. "But all of my equipment is at home."

"Make a list. I'll fetch it for you." An armed man named Robert Getes offered.

"No, I would have to get them myself. There are too many things and it would take you longer to find everything. I can't take the chance of something critical left behind or you taking too long." She said in a frustrated rush.

"Let's go then." Within minutes, two armed men supplied her a horse and they were escorting her out to her place.

When they arrived, all but a few Piqui returned home. The men had not allowed Luzetta speak with the remaining few. She wanted desperately to know how the baby was, or if it even survived after she was taken.

Luzetta gathered her things and was back in town within the hour. She began to set up her things and prepare herself. The men moved Jesse onto a larger table where his feet wouldn't hang off the end.

Jesse's parents insisted on being present for the surgery. "We just want to make sure everything is on the up and up." Mrs. Grove sneered with an accusing glare, but she was not able to watch as her son was being cut. She excused herself after the first incision was being made.

"If you see any movement at all, put this over his nose and mouth." Luzetta instructed Mr. Groves, who sat at his son's head.

"You just concentrate on Jesse." He ordered.

Henshill sat in awe as he watched the surgery. After Luzetta removed the swollen member from Jesse, both Mr. Grove and Luzetta were breathing easier. Luzetta was putting the final stitches in the boy's belly when Mr. Grove began to fidget, acting nervously.

"I want to apologize for what I said before. You're a good doctor." He said humbly without meeting her eyes.

"Thank you. I must admit I was impressed when you didn't faint when you saw all that blood." She smiled at him, letting it reach her eyes.

"Aw, that ain't nothin'. I was with Bertha when she gave me each of my boys. If I can handle that, I suppose I can handle most anything."

"You're a mighty fine father, Henshill Groves." That made him feel worse for what he said earlier.

"And from what I seen and heard about you, I 'spect to see Jesse up and running by the end of the week." Luzetta knew Henshill was referring to the fact that whomever she treats, they seem to heal so much faster than ordinary. Much faster.

"You can't believe everything you hear, Mr. Grove." She admonished.

"I don't usually, but I know for sure that you had the touch when I seen Lizzy Eckle. No one in the whole town believed she would have survived after being stung by all them bees. By all rights, she should be dead right now, but you took care of her and she lived."

"I think you underestimate the will a child has to live. They're strong, too. You would be surprised what a child can endure."

"Don't go sellin' yourself short, Miss Hendrich. There are others who think the same way."

"I know and I'm flattered. Thank you." She left it at that. She had also left out that her last name had changed.

Mr. and Mrs. Grove agreed to leave Jesse lay on the table for the night. It wasn't safe to move him so soon after surgery. Luzetta was escorted back to the jail by the same two men who took her home not so long ago. She had blood on her dress and she was exhausted. After making arrangements for Sheriff Johensen to see to it she had a change of clothes and other essentials, she sat across from him and began probing his knowledge about the comment Mrs. Grove made about the new doctor.

"Mr. and Mrs. Grove said something to me today that was rather upsetting." She affixed her eyes on him. "They said that they were expecting another doctor. To replace me."

"Mrs. Longwood" he reminded her of her recent acquisition of a husband "this town, as you know, is growing and there's nothing wrong with getting a second doctor." She knew his answer was hogwash and she wanted him to give her an honest answer.

"The town isn't growing so fast that it can support two doctors. The only way I've survived the last year since Daddy died was the income I've received for my services."

"And your patient load has caused some problems as well." He added to his first answer.

"What problems besides prejudice?"

"The town has other issues as well, but the Injuns took the cake."

"What other issues?" Luzetta was wondering what excuses he would make up.

"Did you know that some townsfolk have traveled into the next town to see a doctor who had actually graduated from Medical school?"

"That's their prerogative." She sailed back at him. "That doesn't change the fact that I've been trained by one of the best doctors around." Luzetta knew she was biased, but she didn't care. "And people have counted on my father and I for years."

"Since your father died the men are uncomfortable with you." She was prepared for that.

"I suppose when a woman needs a doctor we should object when a male doctor comes our way. Why don't we just stock each town with two doctors to make it even. One male and one female." The sheriff shook his head. She took it as him rejecting her solution. "That sounds a lot like discrimination to me. A man can have a choice, but a woman can't?"

"And those who would have absolutely nothing to do with your type of voodoo medicine."

"Voodoo?" She flew out of the chair at the outrageous accusation.

"Those aren't my words." He said, holding his hands up in defense.

"There isn't one bit of witchcraft in any of my practices!" She began to pace. Trent was watching and listening as they talked.

"Then how do you explain the things that happen to your patients?" He countered

"So I am faulted for quick healers? Are you going to abolish good health and clean living next?"

"Let's be honest here. There are people walking around town that should be dead. Because of people like Mrs. Bixly, Tom Hargland, Lizzy Eckle, you have been suspected of something that ain't natural." He pointed his thick finger at her.

"I haven't even been approached by anyone questioning my methods of practicing medicine. Those cases can be easily explained."

"Your explanations won't work. The people of this town have voted to bring in another doctor."

"They voted?" She said breathlessly, sitting as she felt her knees go weak. "When?" Luzetta was totally in the dark about everything.

"Two months ago." She had taken it hard. Her face fell stricken, draining of all color, and she looked like she was about to cry. "It was after Lizzy when people began questioning. They say that you use secret potions."

"No. I use a mix of medicines and herbal remedies." She said breathlessly, still reeling with shock. "No one has ever questioned any of my practices to my face." A spurt of anger ran through her like lightening. She stood and faced the Sheriff. "Let me ask you this. Would the people of this town change their minds about me if the doctor you hired were to examine my patients and practices?"

"I doubt it." He regretted.

"What would it take?" She had desperation written all over her face. Her livelihood depended on it.

"I don't know. But I tell you one thing, it would have to be a miracle to change people's thoughts when they done convinced themselves of something." Luzetta was shaken to the core.

Chapter Six

Sheriff Johensen escorted her back to her cell. She was so preoccupied with her predicament that she hadn't noticed her cell had been changed around. Her bed was now up against the bars. So was Trent's.

Luzetta's face was so full of shock and disbelief. Trent could help but hear the conversation from his cell and knew how devastating something like that had to be to her. She was being cast out of people's lives because of something they didn't understand. She sat on her bunk with her back to him. He could just imagine the look on her face.

Trent waited silently, watching her from behind. He watched as her ribs expanded with each breath. He saw the dress that was probably form fitting before, loose fitting about her waist. He saw the gradual sag of her shoulders as she continued to think about her circumstances.

"Do you want to talk about it?" He couldn't remain silent any longer. He would have paid good money to be able to hold her, comfort her when she was most vulnerable. He was hoping that he could cut out her heading toward a good cry by talking it out. She just shook her head, still reeling in the shock.

Luzetta sighed the saddest sigh Trent had ever heard. She laid down on her bunk, staring at a non-existent spot on the ceiling. In his line of work, sometimes Trent had to wait a person out in order for them to confess. Somehow his nerves couldn't stand the silence now. He didn't know what to say to Luzetta, how to console her. He just knew that she was a good woman and doctor and that she needed his help as much as he needed hers.

"I can see we are off to a running start." He said out loud.

"What?" She said, coming out of her dazed state.

"I said that I can see that we're off to a running start." He had a hard time remembering what he said just moments before when she flashed those hurt blue eyes at him. "If we don't communicate, we will never be able to make this work."

"Make what work?" Her mind still hadn't shifted gears from her conversation with Sheriff Johensen.

"Our marriage." He hadn't taken the offensive. He just wanted to be there for her, even if it was from behind bars.

"Oh." She winced. "Um, can we go back to asking questions?" She wanted her chance to cross-examine him. She propped herself up on one elbow to look him in the eye. He was laying on his back with his hands behind his head.

"I promise to be as honest and forthright as I can." He smiled. He was a good looking man, even when he was yelling at her but, when he smiled, he looked all the more potent.

"How old are you?"

"Twenty-seven."

"That young? I would have thought you older. My goodness, you're only four years older than me." She reeled. "Do you have family?"

"Yes. In South Dakota." He answered her questions without hesitation.

"What brought you this way?"

"I was trying to find a friend. I was told he came out this way. I was hoping to catch up to him before he ran into trouble." He was hoping she didn't probe that response too much.

"Do you think he found it? Trouble, I mean."

"I don't know. I intend to find out, though."

"How did you get in such bad shape when the Piqui found you?"

Trent's eyebrows shot upwards. "The Indians found me and brought me to you?"

Her head nodded. "They are convinced that whoever did that to you put you on their land to blame them. Once Red Wolf saw the markings on your chest, he was sure you would live. He said you had the spirit of the bear." She said. "So, what were you doing with my horse?" She knew if she didn't get the conversation under control, she would be completely off the subject with no clear answers.

"I needed to get to the next town. I was coming right back after I took care of a few things. When those men took you away, I made the decision to hightail it out of there and get help."

"Help to do what?" The suspicious look in her eye made him wonder what she was thinking.

"To find my friend." She didn't buy it. There were too many pieces missing. There was something he was leaving out. It showed in her eyes and he knew he had to fill in those blanks if she were to trust him.

"The same people that shot me were more than likely the ones who may have killed my friend."

"How do you know your friend is dead?"

"Because he would have contacted someone. Anyone. He would have let us know about his progress, where he was going."

"Who is 'us' and what do you mean by 'progress'?" She grilled.

"I am not at liberty to discuss that." He said calmly.

"Figures." She huffed. "No body ever tells me anything."

"I will. Soon." He reassured her. He didn't know how she would take it, though. "Are there any more questions?" He shouldn't have asked, but he couldn't stop himself.

"What do you do for a living?" How was he going to get out of this one?

"I guess you can call me a traveling man." It was the only thing he could think of. "I scout land, I do some tracking and I do odd jobs." Disappointment filled Luzetta's eyes. He was a drifter, a saddle hound as she'd heard it.

Luzetta heard all she needed to hear. She laid back down and looked up at the ceiling in silence.

When the door of the Sheriff's office opened, Luzetta's eyes popped open. She stared at the door, knowing it would open shortly

"Luzetta!" A very pregnant woman filled the doorway. "How awful. Jim told me you were here and I almost fainted. Are you all right?" She asked as the Sheriff unlocked the door.

"Yes, Elise. I'm fine. You should be in bed." She fretted over her friend. "This commotion would upset the baby." She brought her friend to sit on the bed with her and folded her pillow in half before placing it behind her pregnant friend's back.

"I feel fine. I don't have any cramps or anything. I do believe our little bundle of joy will be arriving in the next couple of days, though." Luzetta's eyes lit up with joy as she watched the woman rub her swollen belly. "Thanks to you." Tears filled Elise's eyes, but they didn't drop.

"Don't worry, if the baby comes now it won't be harmed. You'll have a healthy baby before you know it." She beamed at the proud mother.

"And just think, Victoria and I are just about running a race. Jim says that they are taking bets on who will go first. I just hope Victoria has a better time with this one than she did with Jacob." She rattled on. "Her baby seems to grow more each day. She can barely walk."

"I know. I saw her yesterday. She expects to have a ten-pound baby, and I don't doubt her." She said, purposefully not looking over at Trent so as not to draw attention to him.

"How do you expect a ten-pound baby to fit through a reed straw?" Horrified at the thought, Lisa rubbed her belly and admonished it. "You better not be ten pounds." Luzetta laughed at her friend as she scolded the unborn child within her. "I think I would kill Jim if he did that to me."

"Well, let's not think of that. I am sure you will have a normal sized baby. Besides, women have had large babies before."

"Not this one!" She exclaimed. "It's bad enough to deal with the heart burn, muscle cramps, going to the chamber pot every two seconds, cravings, swollen feet ... and that is all before labor starts. If babies weren't such a joy, this wouldn't be all it's cracked up to be."

"I tell you what, you just have Jim come get me when you go into labor and I'll be right out. But for now, I want to get you back home to rest. You need to be off your feet."

"I swear I am sick of that bed. After being in it for the past four months, I think I'll take the notion to run around the house a couple times a day after this one comes along."

"I'm sure you will, but for now, you need to keep your vigil." Luzetta braced herself as Elise held onto her hands and tugged. The two worked together to get the overly burdened woman off the bed.

"Oh, I almost forgot. Here are some clothes for you. I packed a few other things for you just in case you needed them, and you do." She gave Luzetta the carpet bag and a kiss on the cheek. "I'll see you in a few days." She sang out as she left. Luzetta began to rummage through the bag and took out a few items. A hair brush, some hair pins, soap. She left the other things in the bag.

"Sheriff Johensen." She called. "I would like to use the water closet, please." The Sheriff rounded the corner and jangled his keys extra loud.

"I'll give you a few minutes." He claimed.

"I'll need more time than that." Taking the man literally. "I want to wash and change my clothes." She pleaded.

"Look, I have somewhere to be shortly and ..."

"Give her time, Sheriff. She's been in here two days without a washbasin, or any fresh water for that matter. Let her freshen up and we won't give your wife an ear full when she comes here to feed us some of her fine cooking." Trent threatened. "Luzetta has been working nonstop since you threw her in here. The least you could do for her is to let her wash up." Sheriff Johensen gave Trent a leery look, staring him down. Or at least he tried to.

"Actin' like her protector already." He snorted. "Good move. It'll help you later when you get out." He opened Luzetta's chamber with great show, then made a grand sweeping motion to let her know he was obliging her wishes.

"Thank you." She said to the Sheriff as she passed. She stopped before leaving the cell area to look back at the man she barely even knew. How was she going to deal with him?

Luzetta spent the minimum time she could in the water closet just in case the Sheriff changed his mind. There was still her hair to be brushed out, but that could be done outside the cramped closet. She quickly dressed and placed all of her things back into the carpet bag before opening the door.

"Thank you, again. I feel much better." She said to the seated Sheriff as she marched back to her cell.

He wasted no time in locking her back in and leaving the office.

Trent had been standing toward the wall, looking out a window most men wouldn't be able to see out of without standing on the bed. Luzetta sat with her back to him and began pulling the pins from her hair. Pulling the brush through the tangles was painful at first, but the strokes became fluid, relaxing and invigorating. She took pleasure in the feeling of the hard bristles against her head. She wasn't aware she was humming until she felt Trent's hand stroking her hair.

"I don't believe I've ever seen spun gold before, but if I had, I think it would look just like your hair." He said reverently.

"Thank you." She whispered.

Luzetta lay on her bunk again as she stared up at the ceiling. They spent their first night as a married couple in separate beds, in separate cells, in separate worlds.

Trent heard the keys rattling in the Deputy's hand as he walked toward their cells. He became fully awake as the lock was turned, the door opened. The drowsy "What's the matter?" came from Luzetta's mouth by second nature, even before she opened her eyes.

"Grove Boy." He said. Luzetta jumped out of bed, put her coat on, grabbed her bag and made a bee line for the schoolhouse. Trent noticed she hadn't stopped to straighten her hair or smooth out the wrinkles in her dress.

"He's got a really high fever and thrashing around." Mrs. Grove informed Luzetta as she entered into the dimly lit room.

"Has he broken his stitches?" She asked breathlessly.

"Not yet, but if he keeps it up he sure as rainwater will try." The women looked at the boy on the table. He was sweating profusely, but he was not thrashing. He may have been moving around with discomfort, but Luzetta was not about to explain the difference to the anxious mother. Luzetta opened her bag and began putting vials onto the nearby table.

"Wait." Shouted Mrs. Grove. "We don't want any of that Indian voodoo of yours." She spat out accusingly.

"I don't practice nor believe in voodoo medicine, Mrs. Groves." She explained as she went about measuring, mixing, grinding. "These are herbs that have healing properties. When I mix them along with other things, they are very useful to humans and animals. There's nothing secret here."

"It ain't right." She complained. "I don't want my son to be given no brew of yours." Luzetta was trying very hard not to lose her cool.

"Think of it this way, Mrs. Groves, God created these herbs. Don't you think He intended them to be used? If not, why did He give us the knowledge of them in the first place? Many modern medicines are made from herbs." Mrs. Groves still had a pinched face and her arms crossed. "And if I don't give him something to bring his fever down and kill any infection he may die." She waited. Mrs. Groves looked down at her son.

"All right. But I'm gunna be watchin' you. If you do anything strange, you're through." Luzetta finished mixing and ready to give the boy the concoction.

"Will you help me raise his head? He needs to drink all of it." She instructed.

"Let me." The woman took the boy's head in her arm and took the cup from Luzetta. She began coaxing him to open his mouth and swallow, all the while humming a child's nursery song, soothing his brow with her fingers.

Luzetta stayed for the rest of the night hoping against having any further complications. After the sun showed itself and the boy had been resting comfortably with no apparent injuries to his stitches, Luzetta went back to the jailhouse where she slept until midday.

That evening, Trent and Luzetta were treated to a fine spread made by Mrs. Johensen. She made steak that had been simmering all day and was melt-in-your-mouth tender, mashed potatoes with gravy, cooked carrots and fresh baked rolls straight from the oven. Mrs. Johensen handed Luzetta a jar of her famous strawberry preserves and a searing glare for Trent.

"Boy, I sure am going to miss being in jail, Mrs. Johensen." Trent said, turning Mrs. Johensen's lips.

"I did it for Luzetta." She said sharply to him. "She deserves a fine meal. You just got lucky." The condescension was not hidden in her tone.

"I sure did." He was speaking directly to Luzetta. Luzetta looked very nonplused by his statement. "What's wrong?" He asked her when Mrs. Johensen left.

"Nothing is wrong." She said as she pushed her cooked carrots around.

"Why aren't you eating?" He took a bite of his steak and made a sound denoting that it was delicious.

"I lose my appetite when my nerves are frayed." She admitted.

"You should eat anyway. You're losing too much weight and you need your strength." Luzetta looked up at him with surprise on her face. "I can see the way your dress hangs off you just like everyone else can. And maybe there isn't a mirror in the water closet, so I'll tell you that the dark circles under your eyes are getting larger every day." Luzetta was shocked that this man paid so much attention to her, much less showing her this much concern for her health.

Luzetta picked up her fork and forced herself to eat, playing out an imaginary conversation she wanted to have with him since yesterday. At least one person should be able to enjoy their meal. After their meal was finished and the trays were taken away, Trent watched as Luzetta paid extra careful attention to her fingernails, the wrinkles in her skirt, anything to keep from making eye contact or instigating conversation. Finally, Trent could no longer take it.

"Okay, I am going to ask this question once more and this time I want an answer. What is wrong?" He asked

"Nothing is *wrong*." She emphasized.

"Then what's got you looking like you're going to be marched off to the gallows any second?" Getting a woman to stop talking was usually the problem.

"Well, since we talked yesterday I've been thinking." She began, still not looking at him. "We'll be let go soon, I hope, and I think that now we should reach an agreement before there is any misunderstanding."

Trent took a deep breath, waiting for the other shoe to drop. "Go on."

"I don't know how long you plan on staying or if you plan on staying at all, but I don't think you should ... or that we should ..." This was going to be harder than she imagined. "I don't think we should form any sort of attachment so as to avoid any complications later on." There. She got it all out.

"What do you mean?" His brain more than understood what she was trying to say, it was other parts of his body that were looking forward to 'forming attachments' that needed convincing. "I mean that we should take the circumstance we're in and take a businesslike position about it. You can finish whatever you started and I can go on with my life. Complicating matters will not help either of us." Her statement was delivered with as much conviction as her stance on living alone without protection. If only he could tell her he wasn't who he presented himself to be.

"So you just expect me to walk away after all of this is through?"

"Yes."

"And what makes you think I want to do that?"

"Why not? I surely wasn't looking to get married. To anyone. Are you telling me that you were?" No, but it suited his purpose at the moment. He would do anything to catch those thieving scoundrels any way he could. Even if it meant getting hitched to an angel and acting like the family man for the folks in town. He wasn't about to throw her back after he reached his goal, though.

"No, but that doesn't mean I'm about to dishonor a commitment I made." She was flabbergasted at his calmness.

"Honor?" She shot back. "Tell me, what does a gunslinger know about honor?"

"I'm not a gun slinger." He was getting hot under the collar. This woman sure knew how to press his buttons. "And believe me when I say I honor my commitments."

Luzetta sat back onto her bed and covered her face with her hands. "I hoped you would have been less honorable."

"Why?" He quipped. "So you could go play doctor and set yourself up for a fall?"

"No. I don't want to be married. I am not ready yet." She said.

"Ready? You are twenty-three years old. Most girls get married much younger." He pointed out.

"I mean that I am too busy. I have patients to care for, several being expectant mothers, I also have a household to keep up and a garden to plan for. I barely have enough time for myself let alone a husband and children."

"Children?" He sounded shocked, but his eyebrow was cocked and he had a devilish look in his eye. Did she just give him a glimmer of hope of having a family of his own?

"Yes children. That's what comes after you get married. And believe me, I have been delivering babies since I was ten and I don't think I'm ready for that yet. Why are you laughing at me?" She asked, rather put-out at his behavior.

"You" he chuckled "are scared."

"No I'm not. I'm just not ready." Her chin shot up in the air as she tried to convince herself of that.

"Oh, you're ready." He stated confidently.

"And what makes you so sure?" She asked haughtily.

"I'm positive that you're ready because you were this close to it when you woke up on top of me." He held his thumb and forefinger only and inch apart. Trent almost laughed when Luzetta gasped at his statement and turned her reddened face away. He didn't let up. "Don't deny it, Luzetta. You were moving your body like you knew what you wanted. Or maybe it was just your body's way of giving you a clue on what it was made to do."

"Stop it." She said, covering her ears. "I don't want to listen to that kind of talk."

"Face it, Kitten. There is a lot you don't know you need." Trent held his voice calm and steady the entire conversation and it irritated Luzetta.

"I resent you thinking that I can't meet my own needs. There isn't one thing I am in need of." She snarled back. He just stood above her on the opposite side of the bars nodding his objection. "Name one thing!" She demanded.

"Me." He said boldly. "You need me more than you know."

"I don't need anyone. I can handle my own affairs just fine." She boasted.

"I'm not talking about your affairs, Kitten." He smiled.

"Then tell me what you are referring to." She stood, hands balled at her sides. "It's not funny, this game you're playing with me, so stop laughing at me." She glared. "I don't like it when you growl at me like that either." Her voice raised an octave at every argument posed.

"You two fight worse than two polecats in the same bush." Sheriff Johensen walked in with a young man that Trent guessed was about Luzetta's age. He had dust covering his clothes from traveling and a scowl on his face. "Now listen up. This here is Dr. David Schumaker. He'll be replacing you from now on. That being said, you two are free to go."

All Luzetta could do was stand and stare at the man in front of her and remind herself to breathe. Trent didn't know whether to smile or to frown.

"Before you go, Mrs. Longwood, I would like to say that I disapprove of your goings-on out here." Operating on people without any formal training or certification is illegal." He stated with all the righteous indignation he could muster.

"I was trained by the most competent and talented doctor around." Her words fell on deaf ears.

"If I find anything wrong with the way you've treated these people, I will personally press charges without hesitation." He smugly stated.

"You won't find anything wrong." Trent said, knowing that the stunned Luzetta couldn't defend herself to this man. He placed the coat on her shoulders and guided her out the door onto the boardwalk.

"It's dark out. I'll go over to the hotel and secure us a place to stay." He said, already assuming the role as her guard, protector, provider. She wasn't about to let that happen.

"I'll go with you." She spoke up for herself. "To make sure we have separate rooms." Her blue eyes met his with defiant stubbornness.

"Do you think that's such a good idea? What will the townsfolk say when they find out?" He looked down at her, hoping that he could intimidate her into submission. It didn't work.

"I don't give a squat what the town has to say. Not now." She fumed.

"Why does that not surprise me?" He mumbled as he walked away.

They both secured rooms and headed up the stairs after the bellhop. Trent brought up the back watching Luzetta's bottom sway as she climbed the stairs and march down the hall. Maybe she would calm down after a good night's sleep and return home in an environment she was familiar with.

Trent lay awake devising a plan and what his next move would be. He needed this cover in order to penetrate the circle that surrounded the mystery of missing bouillon. He knew that if folks thought this marriage to Luzetta was a hoax, he would be under their scrutinizing glare no matter what he did. He would have to win Luzetta over to get her to make it believable. To win Luzetta, he had to do two things. One was to try to seduce her, letting her believe that he was in this for the reason she thought; to find his friend and to make him worthy of staying alive. The second was farther from doable. If all else failed he would tell her the real reason he came to this Indian infested territory in the first place. The only problem was that she was not a practiced liar. If she was asked, even if she tried to lie, everyone around her would know that it wasn't the truth. If all else failed, he would keep her out of it. For that, he would need help.

Chapter Seven

Luzetta hardly slept that night. She laid awake most of the night wondering about what effect the last few days would have on her life. The most worrisome to her was her livelihood the new doctor was snatching out from beneath her feet. One thing was for sure, she wasn't about to hand over the entire town. More specifically Elise and Victoria. She was going to continue to support them as long as they agreed. Elise and Victoria were her two closest friends and she was not about to allow some green boy to see them through the roughest part of their pregnancies.

But how was she going to survive without income? Her father had put some money back for them, but he lived by the same method Luzetta did, letting people pay them by material things or provisions. Most were perishable items, but she had chickens and a cow for milk. Her garden was large enough to feed two people plus the dozen or so visitors they would have over during the year, but Trent was much bigger than her father. Trent would have to pull his share if he was going to stick around. She was sure he would eat three times as much as she did, easily.

By dawn, she came to some definite plans. She mapped out how she was going to handle this marriage thing and when he chose to leave there would be no difference, as if he'd never been there at all.

They met in the breakfast room and said next to nothing to each other. She drank a glass of milk and ate one poached egg with dry toast. He, on the other hand, had three eggs, a side of ham, grits, griddle cakes and coffee. She watched as he used extremely good table manners devouring the food on his plate.

"Is something the matter?" He asked when he was through with his meal. She shook her head.

"Nothing." She said quietly.

"It's evident that something's on your mind." He stared at her with those brown eyes that seemed to see right through her every time.

"Yes, but I don't wish to discuss it in public." Her blue eyes flashed.

"All right." He said as he wiped his mouth on the napkin. "I spoke to the Innkeeper and she agreed to give us credit for the stay and the meal." He said quietly.

"Thank you." She said as they stepped out of the hotel and onto the street.

"What for?" He wasn't even looking at her, but watching all that was around them.

"For arranging the stay and breakfast." She said softly. His dark eyes looked down at her and studied her face.

"My pleasure." He said slowly, thinking of ways to convince her they were a couple, not just two separate people caught in the same situation.

Since they had no transportation besides Luzetta's old nag, Trent asked the livery boy to give them a ride out to Luzetta's place.

"I'm sorry, Sir. I'm the only one here and I can't just drop everything. I can let you rent a wagon if you promise to bring it back later on today." He said as he mucked out one of the empty stalls.

"I'd be much obliged." He tipped his hat to the small, gapped tooth kid.

"Hey, ain't you the one who married Miss Luzetta?" He asked.

"Yep." He replied. He followed the boy to the wagon in question.

"This one should suit you fine." He qualified. "I'm glad Miss Hendrich found herself someone to be with out there. I think she's the only woman I know who would live out there alone and not be bothered by it." The young sprout said. "Name's Henry Stout." He held out his hand.

"Trent Longwood." His had grasped the youngster's hand.

"Nice to know ye." Henry began hooking up the rig to the horse. "I'd like to give you some advise, if you'd be willin' to take it from someone like me." He said as he worked.

"I'm a good listener. Can't say as I'm too good at following advise, though." He wondered what the kid could tell him that he didn't already know.

"I'd be mighty careful around here. I been hearin' folks talkin' and If'n my ideas are right, I 'spect some folks aren't too keen on your new bride no more. We had a bunch of Quakers squattin' here for some time now. They started sayin' that people like Luzetta got hung for what she be doin'. They think she's some kind of witch or whatever. After people got wind that she took up with them Injuns they think she don't care 'bout no white folk no more.

Now I don't know what's what here, but I'd be figurin' they got it in 'em to make Luzetta an outcast." Trent weighed the serious words from this observant livery hand.

"Do you think they would hurt her?" The boy thought about it for a second at most.

"No, they wouldn't do anything like that, but if certain people had their way it would be hard for her to do any business in town." His forthrightness held favor with Trent.

"Yes, I know. They already have a new doctor in town." He qualified.

"Well, there you go." He said, reinforcing what he just predicted. "I sure hate to see a good woman put out like that."

Trent thanked him and headed toward the front of the hotel where he left Luzetta. He watched as each person that passed her by turn up their noses. She raised her hand and waved to someone, only to have the gesture ignored. Everyone was snubbing her. He felt sorry for her as the disappointment crossed her face.

The ride home was a silent one. He didn't know what to say to her and she didn't feel much like talking. Her hands were gloved and placed neatly on her lap. Her gaze fell blankly on the horizon.

Trent and Luzetta could see the remaining single teepee in front of the house and smoke of the fire beside it. An older woman, Wind In Hair, was sitting by herself at the fire, warming herself. Trent got down from the wagon and lifted Luzetta down. She was light as a feather and his hands fit perfectly around her small waist.

Trent didn't let her go when her feet were on solid ground. It forced her to look up at him. When Trent didn't make any move to let her go, she panicked thinking he might make a move to kiss her.

"I'm so glad to be home. I need a hot bath." Despite her rambling, Luzetta still held onto his arms for support.

"I'm going to kiss you now." Trent warned.

Luzetta's insides turned shaky. She was afraid of this. "What about just being friends?"

"I'm a married man, but I've been denied my kiss. I want it." Trent moved her closer to him.

Panic shot through Luzetta. Her eyes instinctively to his mouth. "I don't think that is the best way to handle things." She tried to push away from him as he pulled her forward. He put his arms around her, cradling her head with one large hand, taking all control from her. She braced for the worst.

Trent's mouth was soft, his lips warm. This wasn't as bad as she thought it would be. She relaxed against him, letting him tilt her head to the left. He played with her lips, sucking them ever so slightly. After that she couldn't have told you who was kissing who.

Trent felt her soften toward him, giving him all the more reason to deepen the kiss. He toyed with her mouth, lavishing on her full, kissable lips.

"Let's go inside." Trent's voice was pure sultry gravel. The meaning was unmistakable.

"No." She shook her head to confirm her statement.

"We're married now."

"I know. I just can't."

Frustration built up inside Trent. "Can't or won't."

"Both. For the same reason."

"What reason?"

Before Luzetta could respond, an Indian woman called out to Luzetta in her language.

Luzetta broke away from Trent went directly to the Indian woman.

"Hello, Wind In Hair. How are you feeling?" Luzetta sat down beside the woman and caressed her face, feeling for fever. Wind In Hair took her hand gently away.

"I feel good." She looked into Luzetta's face. *"I am more worried about you. Are you sick?"* She asked.

"No, just tired." She admitted.

"You were taken away so swiftly by the white men. Why?" The concern for Luzetta had shown itself in Wind In Hair's eyes.

"The white men wanted me to take care of their young." It was no surprise to Wind In Hair to hear that the selfish white men took something else away from the Piqui. Wind In Hair looked over at the man standing on the porch, leaning against the post with his arms crossing his wide chest.

"Scarred By Bear was taken too. Was it because he took your horse?" She speculated.

"Yes. He has been let go, though. I didn't let them hurt him." At that Wind In Hair looked into Luzetta's eyes, studying them.

"He stays?" She asked

"Yes. For a while." Disappointment crept into Luzetta's face and eyes.

"*Good. You and Scarred by Bear have good spirit. Work together.*" She said

"*What do you mean?*"

"*The male bear is strong, fierce, protects and is a good hunter. Golden Hair needs good protector.*" Luzetta's eyebrows shot up at her explanation. Wind in Hair chuckled. "*I see more than you want to see.*" Wind In Hair said as she watched Luzetta's facial expressions change while she looked over at Trent. Wind In Hair and Luzetta stood and walked to the house as Wind In Hair recounted what happened after she left. Luzetta was relieved to know that the baby survived and was thriving.

Wind In Hair and Luzetta reached the house and Trent interrupted their conversation to introduce himself. Even though the language barrier was there, he still held out his hand to the Indian woman.

"Would you care to translate?" He asked Luzetta. She nodded and he began. "I'm Trent Longwood. I recognize you as one of the women who helped me when I was ill." He took the woman's firm handshake as a sign that she didn't think of him as a threat.

"I am Wind In Hair." She smiled at him.

"Well, I thank you kindly for your help." His eyes were honest and true. She knew only few white men, but this one was the only one she liked.

"Luzetta was help to all. She is the one who should be thanked." They both looked at Luzetta, who was modestly smiling back at them. She wanted to change the subject.

"Why don't we go inside and I'll make some coffee?" She was leading the way to the door when Trent snatched her up, carrying her across the threshold before she could object.

Surprisingly the place was tidied and put back the way it had been originally as if the Piqui hadn't been sprawled across her living room floor from wall to wall.

"This is wonderful." Trent put her down and she went from one room to the next.

"*Thanks to you, there are no more sick. Piqui can take care of themselves now. Winter is over and we have time to build ourselves up again.*" Wind In Hair spoke as she removed the blanket that was wrapped around her shoulders. Amazingly Luzetta watched as the woman went straight to the kitchen and removed a loaf pan and a covered bowl with dough inside. The cook stove had been lit, along with the back stove for warmth. Wind in Hair had kept up vigil for her return.

"*Wind In Hair, why did you not return with the tribe? You are well and there is no more sick to care for.*" Luzetta inquired.

"*Chief Running Bull wished for me to stay.*" She volunteered.

"Since I know you are home and safe, I'll get that wagon back to the livery." Trent stated as he headed for the door. He felt like an intruder when they spoke Indian like that. He didn't want to ask Luzetta to translate every single thing they said, but it irritated him to not know what they were talking about. For all he knew they could be trading recipes, but it still bothered him.

At supper that night, Luzetta figured it was high time she told Trent of her way of handling him. Wind In Hair left to go back to her teepee, refusing to eat what she helped prepare. They were alone and silent through most of the meal.

"It might be a good time to talk about sleeping arrangements since we are so close to nightfall." She peered over her coffee cup at him across the table. He was polishing off his third plate of beef stew and dumplings. He stopped chewing for a second when she brought up the subject of tonight. He was thinking of that very subject himself.

"What did you have in mind?" He had a silly smirk on his face as he spoke.

"Since the bed in the front bedroom is the only one you can fit in ..." she didn't like the wolfish grin that crossed his lips "you can take that room and I'll take the single bed in the back." The wolfish grin disappeared and a small growl escaped his throat. "You can growl all you want. We both know that we didn't get married for the right reasons. Let's just carry on as if we are just friends and there will be no hard feelings when you leave." She said.

"Who said I was leaving?" He asked

"Not leaving?" Trent heard the crack in her voice.

"I was planning on sticking around for a while, now that I have a wife." Her cup hit the table with a clank.

"A while? Mr. Longwood, I would appreciate it if you wouldn't play head-games with me."

"I'm not playing any games, Mrs. Longwood. And since we're married, it would suit better for you to call me Trent." He watched her closely, analyzing her thoughts from the play across her face.

Luzetta knew by his face that he wasn't joking around. Was he seriously thinking about staying? What a mess she had gotten herself into! Luzetta excused herself from the table and took her plate to the wash bowl. Trent brought his up as she began pouring hot water into the bowl. He placed his plate down and put his hands on her shoulders. Luzetta instantly tensed.

"Listen, you're beat and you didn't get much sleep since before the jail. You go on to bed. I'll take care of the dishes." He offered.

Luzetta was completely shocked by this man. Never once had her father washed the dishes for her. His concern for her touched her heart. It didn't take long, after the shock wore off, before Luzetta took his advise and accepted his help.

"All right, but I want to check your stitches first." She toweled off her hands and walked toward her room.

"You can check them in the morning." He argued. "I wouldn't want you poking around while you can't keep your eyelids open." Luzetta accepted his plea and went to fetch her nightdress. She quickly changed out of her clothes as if he were to waltz in on her. That thought had crossed her mind.

Luzetta could hear the clanking of the dishes as Trent washed them. She already covered the stew so they could have it for lunch tomorrow. As she let her hair down and brushed it, Luzetta began to think about what Trent said earlier. What if he were to stick around? She heard of men taking a wife they'd never even met before. They would promise themselves to a woman far away, have her brought out to them and marry her. It was no different than her marrying this complete stranger.

Luzetta made up her mind that she was much too tired to think logically and went to bed. She was asleep within minutes.

The next morning, Luzetta woke up rested. She also felt very relaxed until she remembered exactly why she was sleeping in the back bedroom. One thing she was certain of was that someone was up and about in the house. It had been a long time since she had awaken to a warm house. The thought made her think of her father. She missed him dearly.

Quickly dressing then pulling her hair up, Luzetta checked her reflection in the mirror that sat above the wash basin. She decided then that she was going to get the longest tub bath she ever had tonight. She was tired of the short sink baths that she had to take for the sake of time and convenience.

Wind in Hair was in the kitchen stoking the fire, causing the cook stove to flame up. "*Good Morning*". Luzetta greeted her with a smile. Wind in Hair didn't smile back. Actually, she looked rather miffed.

"*Scarred by Bear has already eaten and gone.*" She pronounced. Luzetta looked over and saw the used plate and cup by the wash bowl.

"*Did he say when he will return?*" She pulled on her apron and tied it behind her back with deft motions of practiced hands.

"*No*". Wind in Hair was gruff this morning. Luzetta hated not knowing what was amiss.

"*Wind In Hair, did Scarred by Bear do something to upset you?*" She thought to ask. Wind In hair looked back at her with an unsmiling face.

"*No.*" This was going to be a fishing expedition.

"*Are you unhappy here? Did you want to return to your tribe?*" Maybe she was homesick.

"*No.*" Again was her response. Luzetta was becoming exasperated.

"Then what could be wrong? You are not happy. What can I do to make you happy again?" Always the 'fixer', Luzetta offered anything in her power to eradicate Wind In Hair's sadness.

"Scarred by Bear and I spoke this morning." Luzetta was brought up short. *"I speak English. I don't like to, but I do. I understand it when it is spoken, though. He told me that you and him were married."* Uh-oh. Luzetta's face looked disappointed.

"Yes, the Sheriff was going to hang Scarred by Bear. I couldn't let that happen."

"I know. Scarred by Bear told me." She still had a frown on her face.

"You don't approve?" She wouldn't be the first.

"That is not my place. It was your decision." Wind In Hair huffed.

"Then why do you look angry?" Wind in Hair took a moment to reply.

"You are not honoring your husband." She blurted out, not knowing how to say it any gentler. Luzetta's brows came together in an expression of confusion. Wind in Hair knew it was an honest look, for Luzetta had never had a mother or any female to raise her. *"You sleep in separate rooms. You are supposed to mate with your husband in order to strengthen your union and your*

family." She felt the need to explain. To Luzetta's embarrassment, Wind In Hair had brought up the one subject that she least wanted to discuss.

"*I see.*" She raised her chin. "*Scarred by Bear will be leaving soon. Call me selfish, but raising a child on my own does not suit me.*" She said, having felt as if the excuse was plausible. "*I have no one to rely on, no relative to support me and a child. I feel it is the responsible thing to do.*"

Wind in Hair had accepted Luzetta's reason for not consummating her relationship with her husband, but Luzetta still felt the cold shoulder she was given.

Later that day, Trent trotted back just before noon. He had shot a deer and hung it at a reasonable distance from the house. Luzetta knew instantly when Trent had arrived. The pounding of his huge boots on the wooden floor announced his presence. Luzetta had been busying herself with her father's files in the small room at the back of the house that served as his office. The dust and the cobwebs had not dulled the feelings of sorrow she felt as she remembered her father spending hours in this very room writing of his patient's health and progress and whatever gossip that was handed down at the visit. He would also read any and all things regarding new or improved medical practice, even if he didn't subscribe to such changes.

She missed those walks in the woods when he taught her about the bark of the willow tree and how it can be processed into a pain killer, how the hot springs helped those with ailing joints and arthritis be comfortable, at least for a time.

Despite the dust, Luzetta dove into the piles of happenstance filing her father had used. She was determined to find out any methods she could to have her cake and eat it too.

"Luzetta." Trent called out in the hallway.

"Back here." She called back. Trent made his way back to the room, finding Luzetta in a faded blue dress, a dirty apron and watery eyes. He figured it was from the dust. She still looked like an angel.

"We have visitors." He announced. He watched as she tried to straighten herself.

"Visitors, you say. Fine time to show up. I'm in no shape to entertain. I must look dreadful." Luzetta stated, trying to skirt past him as she felt his eyes baring down on her.

"Nope. You look perfect." Trent's complement made Luzetta aware of herself and of him. Why did he have to be so good looking? And the way he looked at her just made her want to turn tail and run. Clearing her throat, Luzetta passed Trent and walked through the door.

Chief Running Bull and several others stood at the steps of the porch. Among them was Wind in Hair. "Good afternoon." She greeted the crowd of Piqui.

"Golden Hair, it is good to see you unharmed by the white man." He spoke perfect English, as she knew her father had taught him. "The Piqui tribe would like to thank you for saving us much misery. Your father's legacy continues." Just the mentioning of her father made Luzetta sad again. "Much like your father, you show Piqui good faith and honesty. In Piqui tribe, such acts of selflessness merits reward. Wind in Hair will stay here, be a companion and helper."

"Thank you. You are very generous." Luzetta knew that declining this gift would be insulting them and they knew Luzetta would not mistreat Wind in Hair like other white men, turning her into a slave to abuse and order about.

"You and your father have been very kind to us over many years. It is the least We can do." He paused as if to collect a reply, but when Luzetta tried to speak Chief Running Bull began talking again. "Wind in Hair says you and Scarred by Bear are wed." It was more of a statement, less of a question. Luzetta stood silent. "I had feared you would weather another winter without protection."

Why did everyone feel as if she needed protected? She'd never been in need of protection before. From man or beast. She just bet Trent was smiling behind her.

"Thank you. We will come to see another winter because of you." Soaring Eagle commented. With that they mounted their bare backed horses and left Trent, Luzetta and Wind In Hair standing on the porch.

Luzetta didn't know what to say. She'd never been given a person before. She felt awkward to say the least. Wind In Hair was probably feeling just as awkward. Luzetta looked at Wind In Hair and then to Trent, who shrugged his shoulders, showing her that he had no idea of what to do either.

"Lunch is ready." She said to the others, walking past them in a reconciled fashion.

Lunch was filled with awkward silence for the fist five minutes of heaping ladles of beef stew into bowls and setting the table up for the meal. Luzetta pulled out a pan of biscuits and placed them in the oven. She busied herself with anything to keep the awkwardness at bay. Finally she sat down with Trent and Wind In Hair.

"I would like to get to know you better, Wind In Hair." Trent spoke softly. "Why don't we talk a bit."

Wind in Hair just nodded. "Can you tell me a little about yourself?"

"I Chief Running Bull's wife." She held up three fingers. "Others young ..." She patted her belly and made an arching motion that gave the clue she meant pregnant.

"The Piqui" Luzetta clarified "believe that polygamy is the best way to ensure the tribe's success and survival." She said matter-of-factly. "Wind In Hair was the wife of Mountain Wolf, Running Bull's brother, who died some time ago."

"To provide for you?" Trent asked Wind In Hair.

"Yes. Make family strong." Wind in Hair again resorted to hand motions to convey her thoughts. She pointed to herself and made an arching motion at her belly, then held up two fingers. "I not young. No babies to Running Bull. I come to help." Then Wind In Hair pointed at the two sitting at the table. Luzetta thought it was awful to be shuffled around and then pushed out when her usefulness ended.

"Well, now you are welcome to join our family and help Luzetta and me strengthen our tribe." Trent's comment amazed Luzetta. Her eyes flashed up to his and her face began to turn pink.

Luzetta couldn't believe Trent just said they were a family and wanted to 'become more'. She felt a choking lump at her throat. She quickly finished her meal and got up and away from Trent's stare. She filled the wash bowl so her back was turned to the others. Trent continued his conversation without her.

"How long have the Piqui been here?" He asked, innocently as if he hadn't unsettled Luzetta's world.

"Since before settlers. This our home." Wind in Hair didn't hide any resentment in her voice for the white men who tried to push the Piqui off their land. "We not let white man take our land. White men use tricks. Piqui not trust." She spoke with a pointed finger at Trent.

"I can understand why." Trent heard how some tribes were tricked out of huge chunks of land by the whites. They would get the Indians drunk then have negotiations, ending with a treaty saying they would stay on a small portion of land that wasn't fit to piss on and they would take what they were given. "But not all white men are bad."

"Yes, Piqui trust some." She watched Luzetta busy herself. "Golden Hair trust. Father trust before die." Trent noticed something was missing.

"What about her mother?" Luzetta's movements slowed and she turned back to look at him.

"My mother died when I was born." She admitted. At least she was talking to him.

"And your father never remarried?" Luzetta turned just in time to miss the look between Wind in Hair and Trent.

"No. It has been just the two of us since I can remember." She talked as she resumed her chore of cleaning off the table. "I was only five when we moved out here. The Piqui were the first civil bunch we came across in a long time. The town folk were all up in arms about the Quakers moving in and condemning every single thing they did. Needless to say, they weren't too keen on anyone outside their clan. To a certain degree, it's like they formed their own community and they only allow in certain ones."

"Sounds rather persnickety." He wasn't going to comment any further on her insight, knowing she was pretty close to hitting the nail on the head. Only a few were trusted to keep secrets.

"Yes, I know. They'll only do business with you if you pass inspection, but don't you dare try to ask them any questions or inquire about their personal lives." Luzetta returned to the table and reclaimed her seat. "It was easier making friends with the Piqui, and we didn't even speak their language."

"Do you know why they are like that?" Trent asked, forming ideas as she talked.

"Just prejudice, I guess. They are easy to get all riled up, too." She had been a victim of their getting all riled up just days ago. She should know better than anyone.

"I noticed." Trent stared at Luzetta over his coffee mug, noticing how easy it was to talk to her, listen to her, watch her as she sat across the table and met him with those sky blue eyes. "Why do you stay?"

"Where would I go? Besides, Papa's grave is here, just out back. I'll probably die here too."

"Does the town get many visitors?" He pried.

"I don't keep up with the goings on in town too much. We get some cattle ranchers through here and some friends of my father's come around often enough. I wouldn't call them strangers, though. Most of them I've known all my life." Luzetta began to get a little irritated by his bold stare. "Let me get the pie." She pulled a pie off the pantry shelf and set it on the table. "I hope you like rhubarb." She said, apologetically.

"Wow, isn't this a treat. I hadn't had rhubarb pie in ages." Luzetta sliced each a piece and poured more coffee. At least she wasn't concentrating on Trent's gaze any more. "You can really cook. I haven't tasted pie like this since I was in Texas." Trent gobbled up three large pieces. Luzetta placed a fourth on his plate.

"What are you trying to do, feed me to death?" He said laughingly.

"No, I'm just trying to keep up with your appetite. I'm accustomed to feeding hungry men now and again, but you now have successfully eaten more than anyone I know." She said shaking her head and tisking her tongue.

"Well, save that last piece for supper. I can't eat another bite. At this rate, I am not going to be able to fit through the door." He stood and rubbed his belly, thinking back when Luzetta counseled him on his 'weight' issue. "Although, I am not complaining." He assured. "I'm going to be gone for a day or two. I have to get some clothes and supplies. If you wish, make up a list and I'll get them for you while I'm there." He finished his coffee with a flourish.

"I have a few things I need. Are you sure you won't mind?" She asked as her blue eyes met his across the table.

"Yes, I'm sure. I'll be purchasing some things I'll need anyway. It's no bother." He assured her. He watched as Luzetta took out paper and a pencil from her desk drawer. She made her list in short order then consulted with Wind In Hair as to her needs before giving it to Trent.

Trent read over the list. 3 yards of durable cloth of good color, several spools of thread, sugar, raisins and a shotgun with ammunition. He knew exactly why she requested the last two items. One thing is for sure, he was more likely to see Luzetta climb to the roof naked and cluck like a chicken before he would see her shoot anything. Luzetta handed him some money, enough to cover her purchases.

"What is this for? I have plenty of money." He qualified.

"Maybe, but I would feel better if you just take it and buy what I asked for. There is nothing wrong with a woman paying her own way." She stated with her chin aloft. Trent let out a sigh of resignation. He knew he had to pick his battles and this one wasn't worth fighting. Yet. Trent bent forward and placed a soft kiss on Luzetta's lips. Luzetta mustered a genteel smile as he walked out of the door without saying good-bye or telling her where he was going. Of course, she hadn't said good-bye to him or asked his business. She wanted to keep their relationship to a minimum so her heart would not break when time came for him to leave. Those kisses were going to have to stop if she was to keep her heart out of it.

Supper was uneventful with Trent gone. Making conversation with Wind In Hair was increasingly easier as she took up more and more English. Wind In Hair made her declaration to learn the language since Trent didn't have the time to learn Piqui. Luzetta thought that was a lovely idea.

Later on that night, Luzetta asked Wind in Hair to help her wash her hair. She placed the tub in the middle of her room and began filling it with water. Wind in Hair brought in two towels for Luzetta. After completely washing and rinsing her hair, Wind in Hair left Luzetta alone to bathe herself.

It felt good to sink into the hot water and let the bubbles surround her, absorb all her tension and frustrations away. She didn't hurry herself. It had been too long since she'd been able to soak in the tub. She would do this every day if she could. The heat of the water worked wonders on her tense muscles, making her relax. Her body had been so tense lately she barely noticed until now.

She was tired and worn today. She would turn in early and try to catch up on the sleep she missed over the past month. Wind In Hair came back after a while and brought a clean night gown to her. Luzetta had begun to prune, so when Wind In Hair brought up the towel, signifying that it was time to get out, Luzetta stood up. It was then she had realized another reason she felt tired and worn. The bright red streaking her legs was unmistakable.

"I'll go get the menstrual clothes." Wind in Hair hurried out the door after wrapping Luzetta with a towel.

Chapter Eight

The next week flew by like Trent had never been there. He was gone before she awoke and she heard him come in well after she had gone to bed for several days in a row. She wondered what mischief he had been up to, but wasn't bold enough to ask him. That would require caring and she didn't want to care.

Luzetta resumed her self-appointed duty to search through her father's notes for the mysteries it may hold. Certainly he must know of some way to prevent a woman from conceiving. It didn't look like Trent was going to be leaving anytime soon and she had a feeling she wouldn't be able to hold him off forever. The search was a long one, mostly because Luzetta got so caught up with her father's writings. With each medical visit written, he chose to explain the goings on of the town, the political climate and any gossip, true or not, in his comical way.

Wind In Hair was pleasantly settling herself in and taking lessons from Luzetta on how to speak better English. She was a fast learner and had taken off like a child eager to learn. One afternoon, during Wind In Hair's lesson, Trent strode in the kitchen and announced he had to go to the next town to do some business. He looked rough and dead-tired.

"I want to check your leg before you go." She stated.

"It's fine. You can check it when I get back. I'll need to get going right away. I might be gone a day or two." He said as he strode out of the house as fast as he came in. He mounted his horse that looked just as rough and tired as his owner. "I'll be back as soon as I can." He said as he trotted off. He must have found his friend with the way he was riding out. She hoped it didn't mean trouble.

The next morning, while looking for herbs and vegetation in the woods, she began to daydream, wondering about with her head in the clouds. She drifted to the hot springs she visited so many times before with her father. She wasn't thinking of him now. She was trying to think of a way to convince Trent to move on or get a divorce. She didn't want to be married to anyone. Couldn't be married to anyone. Her fate was sealed. Her father told her of the curse that fell upon the women in her mother's bloodline. Her mother and her grandmother both died at childbirth. Her father didn't go into details,

Luzetta knew it pained him to talk about her death, so sudden and all. She was sure to follow in their footsteps if she were to be with child. She didn't want to die. She would rather live the worst life imaginable than die at such a young age. There were so many things that she could do, learn, explore.

Luzetta took her shoes and stockings off and sat by the pool. Her feet dangled in and she was lost to her own thoughts and desires. She was so wrapped up in her own misery that she didn't hear the man approaching her from behind.

"Luzetta?" He said, not but ten feet away from where she was sitting. Startled, she turned to see who was behind her, only to break out into a smile at the visitor she hadn't seen in almost six months.

"George!" She escalated. She swung her legs around and held her hands up for him to help her up. She gave him a kiss on the cheek and a hug on the neck and smiled up at his face that had been browned by too many days in the sun. "How nice. I didn't know you were coming this way." The hat that had been perched on top of his head came off, showing a full head of salt and pepper hair. He'd been his father's closest friend back East. The only times he and his boys came by were when the cattle they ranched were taken to California or when they had been visiting other family members through the years.

"Actually I had been in town for quite a while, but when I came to visit you were being invaded by the Piqui." He admitted.

"Yes, they had an outbreak of the chicken pox. They're quite all right, now." Lacing her arm through his, she pulled him further toward the pool. "Come and take your shoes off. We have a lot to catch up on." She encouraged. "How is Joe?"

"He's fine. His ribs healed quite nicely, but his leg gives him fits every time a storm front is moving through." Joe had been riding back with his father on one of the cattle runs last Fall when they were caught in a mud slide and Joe's horse had rolled over him. "But not too many people can say that a horse landed on them and lived to tell about it."

"I'm sure. He's very lucky." She said, sticking her feet back into the warm water.

"He was lucky to have you to help him. I don't think there are too many doctors who wouldn't have cut his leg off for the break he had." George shook his head in memory of the scene. "But enough about us. I heard some talk in town about you gettin' hitched." He came to the point rather fast, as always. Luzetta rolled her eyes at his statement.

"It's true, but hopefully not for long."

"My goodness, the honeymoon isn't over yet and you already want to get rid of him?" He chuckled, sliding his boots off and sticking his feet into the water.

"It isn't like that and you know it. You know about my family history. I can't take the chance of not surviving childbirth." She said, knowing George had been there when her mother died.

"Yes, I know." He hung his head solemnly. "So who's the lucky soon-to-be ex-husband?" Luzetta let out a little grunt.

"Someone I'd saved from a hanging." George looked at her with a raised eyebrow. "He borrowed my horse. They thought he was steeling it."

"Luzetta, they don't hang men for 'borrowing' things." He scolded. "Where were you when he 'borrowed' it?" He asked.

"In jail." George began coughing.

"My Lord, Luzetta. I promised your Papa that I would look after you when he passed. Am I going to have to watch you like a hawk?"

"No, it's nothing like that. The townsfolk took nasty to the fact that I was helping the Piqui and they made me abandon them to look after the people in town who hardly needed my help." She huffed. "Besides, I'm a pretty good judge of character and Trent is a good man, even if he is a saddle tramp."

"What do you mean by saddle tramp?" George never heard her use that term before.

"He goes from place to place doing this and that." She made flitting motions with her hands. "His current interest is in finding some friend of his."

"What does he do for a living?" He asked.

"He said he takes in odd jobs." She confessed. It sounded to George that he needed to investigate this new man of Luzetta's for himself. She was like a niece to him and he wouldn't want to see anything bad happen to her.

"Sounds interesting." He said, nonchalantly.

"Yeah, if you like that sort of thing. I just wonder how long he is going to stick around." She thought out loud.

"I see that you are putting in a bigger garden this year." Luzetta welcomed the change of subject.

"I needed to if I want to feed us through next winter." She let her head fall back and let the sun warm her face.

"I thought you said he wasn't going to stick around?" He retorted.

"I was talking about Wind In Hair. Chief Running Bull gave her to me as a companion and helper for taking care of the Piqui. I'm sure we'll get along just fine. Even if the crops are a bust, I'm sure the Piqui will help us along."

"You are always the optimist. Everything will always be right in the end. Truly, I wish things were always like that." He lamented.

"One thing isn't right, though, George." The sadness in her voice was blatant. "They got a new doctor. They told me they didn't want me any more." She looked at him with hurt in her eyes. He wrapped one arm around her. "I never saw it coming."

"Did they tell you why?"

"Sheriff Johensen said that it was because I didn't go to medical school, I wasn't male and that everyone is convinced, by the Quakers no doubt, that I practice some kind of witchcraft." Luzetta let her head fall onto George's shoulder, his arm came around her, comforting her. "They wouldn't even let me explain or give me a chance to defend myself." She felt tears come to her eyes, but refused to let them surface.

"Maybe there's a reason for it all." Luzetta's head popped up and looked at him as if he was the spawn of the Devil himself. "Look, there is usually a reason for everything. Maybe if you try hard enough you can try to reason with this new doctor and share in the work load."

"That is impossible. He believes whatever they told him. He told me he's going to investigate my practices and bring me up on charges if he finds anything wrong."

"Hogwash. There isn't a thing wrong. I bet you had a more thorough training than he did, by a better doctor than any of those professors at his college."

"Thank you." She emphasized. "That's what I told Sheriff Johensen, sort of. He just said that the people made their decision and that is that."

"Well, then they brought it on themselves. You just watch, they'll come running back to you once they realize what a great doctor you are. Certification or not." Luzetta smiled up at him.

"Thanks, George." She nudged him with her shoulder. "You always knew how to make me feel better."

Luzetta and George sat for a half an hour catching up on old times and times passed. They sat with their feet dangling in the water and staring up at the clouds, just enjoying the day until George announced that he had to get back to camp.

"Tell the boys I said hello. Y'all be careful, now." She ordered.

"We will." He said before placing a kiss on her forehead. "You take care and keep up the fight. I'll come by in a week or so and see how things are going. Me and the boys are going to stick around for a little while, so you'll be seeing us."

"Glad to hear it. Good-bye." After George left, Luzetta put her shoes and stockings back on and headed back to the house. It wasn't until the next night when Trent had come back.

Luzetta had been at the end of the porch throwing out the dirty dish water when she noticed him riding in. He was wearing new clothes and riding a new horse, with hers in tow. Trent looked more tired, even at a distance, than he did when he left. She could tell from the sag of his shoulders that he was pulling himself up by his bootstraps to get himself back home where he could rest. Luzetta wondered what had gotten him into such a state.

Trent saw Luzetta standing on the end of the porch as soon as she came out toting the wash pan. It was nearly seven o'clock and it had been almost three days since he last slept. He wasn't so far gone, though, that he couldn't think with a little clarity. He had been ridden hard and put away wet, as the saying went.

The time was getting close when he needed to let Luzetta in on his little secret and he was needing to know what kind of ground he stood on. He needed to know if he could trust her.

Trent wanted to trust Luzetta, but he wasn't sure how to find out without coming right out and asking her, making her ask him questions that he couldn't answer. He had to be sure whatever he told her was going to be kept in check. His life depended on it.

As Trent dismounted, he knew the one way to test her. One way she would probably not like. He needed to get into her head and see what he would find. Of course, when she found out that he'd been deceiving her all along, using her for his own gain this whole time, she would be furious. That was a chance he had to take. What if she were to talk to the wrong person in town and let vital information out that broke all he had worked to build?

"You're limping." She hadn't taken her eyes off him since spotting him on the horizon.

"I'm fine." He crossed the yard to the front porch, temporarily tying the horse to the post. He climbed the steps to stop at the next to the last one. Luzetta followed the length of the porch and met him at the steps, standing in front of him. Her head was tilted ever so slightly and her amazing blue eyes were inquisitive. This was it. Time to test the waters.

Trent stood, looking like he would be knocked over by a stiff wind, and he smiled at her. Not just any smile. He smiled slowly, starting with the corners of his mouth that stretched to finally bare his white teeth and reach his eyes. It was a 'glad to be home' smile. Luzetta found herself smiling back at him. Trent took her chin and tilted it to face him and pressed a soft kiss on her closed lips.

"It's nice to be back." He grumbled, noticing the shock of energy he felt when he kissed her. Luzetta was shocked to her socks by the way she felt when Trent smiled at her. Her heart did a little loop-de-loop and a lump formed in her throat. It felt natural for him to kiss her. He was gentle and tender, allowing her the option of pulling away. She didn't.

Remembering the kiss they shared not so long ago, Luzetta let him manipulate her mouth, coaxing her into deepening their kiss. His arm came around her and pulled her in. Her arms found their way around his neck of their own accord. A small growl came from him as he pulled her tighter against him. She was so soft and willing. He wanted to carry her into the house and make love to her so bad it hurt. When he broke the kiss and looked down at her closed eyes and angelic face he was almost lost.

"Make love with me, Luzetta." He pleaded as he nuzzled her neck. She was reeling in the sensations he was giving to her and her body was reacting in ways she never felt before.

"What?" She was so lost in the feelings that she didn't hear him correctly.

"Make love with me." He said louder, desire dripping from every word as he found her mouth again.

Suddenly, Luzetta came to her senses and pushed away from Trent. She hated the way he made her forget her own name so easily. "I can't" She said as she hugged herself, feeling the lack of warmth she felt just seconds ago.

"It isn't for the lack of wanting to." He accused, breathing hard from the excitement he built himself up to.

"I know." She admitted, covering her face with her hands and sitting on the porch swing to keep her legs under her. Her admission shocked Trent, enough to render him speechless. He hadn't expected her to admit it.

"Why not?" Was the next logical question. He came to sit beside Luzetta, careful to give her the space she needed.

"Because I don't want to die." She cried. Trent uncovered her face and made her look at him, seeing that she was serious about her statement.

"Luzetta" he had to make sure he said this with a straight face "in all of human history, no one has ever died from making love."

"That isn't what I mean. I can't have children." She sobbed.

"Have you ever tried?" He needed to lighten the mood, but it failed.

"No." She shot out. "And I'll never have the chance."

"I don't mean to point this out too bluntly, but I'm giving you the chance right now." He confirmed.

"You don't understand. My mother and grandmother both died while they gave birth. My father said that it was a rare defect that probably passed on to me. I don't want to run the risk of dying if I can help it." Trent began to get a clearer picture of why she didn't want him to stick around. Her father placed the fear in her, a very real fear. Trent felt like a pile of cow manure just then. He hadn't understood, or even asked before, why she was so adamant about not 'complicating matters'. He gathered Luzetta up in his arms and kissed the top of her head.

"I had used this last week to go through my father's notes and see if he had any knowledge of how to keep a woman from conceiving, but I haven't found anything yet." Trent was surprised and pleased to know that she was trying to find a way around her predicament. She probably hadn't had to worry about it before now. He wondered if her father even had the belief of a woman controlling the conception of children.

"I wish I could help. I don't know anything about that." He admitted. "Maybe I can help you look through his files."

"I doubt it. He had the handwriting of a five year old. It's even hard for me to read. That is why it is taking so long. Besides all of the rigamarole he put in to spice it up."

"Rigamarole?" He asked.

"Gossip. Politics. Whatever." She added. Trent hummed his understanding. Luzetta stayed in Trent's embrace for some time before it began getting dark.

"Let me get the horses settled in and I'll be inside in a little bit." He said, shuffling her off into the house. Trent knew she was worth trusting, but had a hard time letting her in on his deception. He would do it first thing tomorrow, he promised himself. He needed to have a clear head before he got into it with her. Right now he was dead tired and in need of some rest.

When Trent came back into the house, Luzetta was waiting for him in his bedroom. She had her tray of utensils and medicines on the table next to the bed. She instructed him to get ready for bed and she would be in to examine his leg when he was finished. She left the room with him standing in the middle of it thinking that it would be nicer if she stayed.

"I'm ready." He called. She opened the door to see Trent draped with the bed sheet with his leg uncovered. Whatever he had been doing had caused little disruption to his stitches and she went to work removing them. He had healed nicely. When she was through examining all of the wounds, Luzetta handed Trent a shot glass of the pain medicine she gave him before.

"This time I'm going to welcome this. I hurt all over." He exclaimed.

"It will help you sleep, too. The less pain you feel, the more restful your sleep will be." She was speaking to herself, because as soon as Trent's head hit the pillow, he was asleep. Luzetta cleared her supplies from the room and let him sleep. Maybe she would have the courage to ask him what he had been doing for more than a week.

The next morning Luzetta hadn't the heart to wake up Trent. She let him sleep the morning through. Wind In Hair set out to make the most of the morning chores and kept busy most of the time. The windows were washed, rugs beat, the house was swept and dusted. Luzetta was just itching to get outside on such a bright, warm day, so she and Wind In Hair set out to find what they could do. Luzetta set her sights on weeding her garden she planted just last week and Wind In Hair said she wanted to visit her family.

"That is a wonderful idea. Tell everyone I said hello and I send my love." She saw Wind In Hair off, insisting she ride the palfrey. Luzetta waved to her from the horizon then set back to work on the weeds.

Humming a little tune, Luzetta was content working with the soil that would yield the winter's portions of vegetables. She planted corn, green beans, carrots, cabbage, green peppers, white and green onions, potatoes, and the list went on and on. She was proud of her efforts. Last spring was her first garden planted without her father's help. She managed to plow the plot straighter this time and she knew exactly what she wanted to plant.

With the chickens that were the best layers she had ever seen and a generous milking cow, Luzetta had hopes of not being in need of much over this next year. She even planned to pick as many wild berries as she could find to can and save for pies and deserts. She found herself smiling at her accomplishments, humming a cheerful tune the whole way.

Sam Sheets had been circling the place for the last hour. He took out his spy glass and looked in every possible angle at the surroundings and the place itself. The folks in town told him where to find the runt know as Trent Longwood, but there was no sign of him at the moment.

Two days ago Trent's brother, Clint, received Trent's telegram. It wasn't exactly what he would call conclusive. It read: "Hit Jackpot. Stop. Need Backup. Stop. Got Married. Stop." Trent's family knew the gravity of his mission and was ultimately confused on whether he needed help with the findings from his investigation or needed help with his new wife. Sam knew Trent was as sharp as a tack and thought it was just an announcement, but his mother took it upon herself to read the telegram differently. So, Trent's mother, Harriet, and four of his brothers Clint, Trayton, Isaac and Aaron and Aaron's wife April, along with their two sons, were all on their way here just a few hours back. That gave Sam the opportunity to investigate Trent's surroundings before bringing the family in. The simple directions left for them at the livery stable would lead them right here.

So where was Trent? Sam rode in from the south, facing the house. Sam couldn't help but notice the shapely rump pointed right at him. The woman had been working in the garden for at least thirty minutes, after seeing some Indian woman off. Maybe she would have some answers for him. Sam rode in quietly and dismounted his horse, fastening him to the porch railing. He walked over to stand beside the woman, finding it odd that she didn't even seem to hear him approach. Now he was standing beside her, listening to her hum and watching her weed the garden that had not yet produced anything but little sprigs of green here and there. He squatted down on his haunches and tried to peer underneath the sun hat she was wearing.

"Hello." He said, startling Luzetta.

"Oh." She jumped. "Hello." She said back, laughing a little. "You'll have to excuse me." She said apologetically, dusting her hands off then wiping them on her apron. "I wasn't expecting anyone and

I wanted to get out here while the sun was warm." She explained without prompting. The man that approached her was wearing black from head to toe and covered with traveling dust. He was tall and reed thin, evident even under the duster he wore. The hat on his head remained as he extended his hand to help her up. She accepted with a smile and a "thank you."

"Yes, the sun is warm today." He acknowledged, furrowing his brow at this beautiful woman. "My, aren't you just a slice of peach pie." He remarked as she looked up at him with dreamy blue eyes and inviting smile he'd only seen on children that were not yet aware of danger. It disturbed Sam to his core.

"Well, can I offer you something to drink? I have iced tea in the house if you care to join me." She invited. Sam's jaw almost dropped. She didn't ask his name, his business here, nothing. She invited a complete strange man into her home with no qualms about her safety. Sam was now doubting whether or not Trent's telegram was read correctly by his mother.

"Actually, I would love to, but I have some business with your husband." He stated.

"Oh, well, he's sleeping right now. He should be awake soon if you want to wait. Or if it is urgent, I could wake him." She didn't seem the least bit worried about her husband sleeping in the middle of the day. Sam was shocked for the second time within minutes of each other and he had the feeling it wouldn't get any better.

"I have a hard time believing that Trent would be sleeping midday, Ma'am." He followed Luzetta up to the front porch steps, then stopped.

"It's only because I gave him something to help him sleep last night. He must have been more wore out than I anticipated." She said, opening the front door and making a sweeping motion for him to enter her home unaware of the derogatory statement that came from her mouth. "Like I said, I would be happy to wake him for you."

"No, that won't be necessary. I think I'll take a glass of that iced tea, though." Sam knew he would be able to glean a lot of information from this woman, so he decided to let Trent sleep and see what he could find out.

"Have you been traveling a long way, Mr..." She asked, letting him know that she wanted to know his name in her own way.

"Sam. Sam Sheets. I came from South Dakota." He said, taking off his hat as he entered the house.

"Trent said that was were his family comes from. Are you part of his family?" She asked with baby trust in her eyes and words.

"No, but close enough. I started out as Trent's oldest brother's friend and it grew into a family friend as the years wore on." He said, taking the glass of tea she promised.

"Please, have a seat." She offered him any chair in the living room. Just as he moved through the living room, though, she heard the distinct sounds of a hungry stomach. "Let me get you something to eat. You must be starving after traveling all that way." She began busying herself in the kitchen.

"Thanks, Ma'am. I would hate to be a bother." What bothered him was that this woman was treating him like she'd known him for years.

"No bother. Just let me make you a sandwich. Do you like pickles?" She asked as she worked.

"Sure do. I would like it better if I knew the cook's name." Luzetta put her hands of her face and stared at him, shocked.

"Oh, where are my manners? I'm Luzetta Hendr ... Longwood." She corrected. "Sorry, I'm still getting used to the name change."

"How long have you and Trent been married?" He moved to the table and pulled out a chair to sit on, watching as she sliced three hunks of ham and placed them between six slices of bread. She decorated the plate with a good sized pickle on the side and set out a small round of cheese and mustard.

"Three weeks." She said, sitting across from him. "Would you like anything else?" She offered.

"No, no. This is more than I expected. You must be used to feeding Trent." He stated as he looked down on the heaping plate of food.

"I've been known to serve some big eaters in my time. Besides, you look like you could use a good, hearty meal." She said before she could stop herself. "I'm sorry."

"Nothing to be sorry for. You're right. I guess my bones do need a little padding." He admitted. Luzetta smiled at him as he bit into the first sandwich.

"How did you meet Trent?" He asked between mouthfuls. Sam could hardly keep from choking as Luzetta told him about the condition Trent was found in, ending the story when she had said she would marry him to keep him from hanging. Sam quite chewing all together and stared at her, brows furrowed. He cleared his throat and made himself swallow. He didn't like this one bit.

"Did he tell you to be expecting company?" He asked.

"No. He said that he was looking for some friend of his, though, and he had been gone for the better part of two weeks doing God knows what. I just figured he must have found him." Sam was getting angrier by the second. He was ready to go into Trent's bedroom and pound his face in for leading this lovely lady along, and then praising him for finding her before she walked herself into some no-good scoundrel's path. Right now, Sam felt like Trent was no better.

Sam and Luzetta talked until he finished his lunch and coffee. He was gleaning much more information about her than she probably knew she was doling out. Sam knew Luzetta was genuine and feared nothing and seemed to have no reason to. She had been called to the aid of so many others that it came naturally to her. Giving, he supposed, was her nature, along with her unassuming personality and easy manor.

"I think I hear Trent. I bet he is going to be happy to see you." She said, with a cheery grin.

"No he isn't." Sam said to himself.

Chapter Nine

Trent came strolling down the hallway, stretching his arms above his head as much as he could without hitting the ceiling. As he rounded the corner into the kitchen, he saw Luzetta and his old friend Sam Sheets sitting as comfortable as he may, giving him a look that told him he'd done something wrong.

"Good morning, Runt." Sam stood and shook Trent's hand. Hard.

"Good to see you too. How did you find the place?" Trent ran a hand through his hair, wondering why Sam was upset with him.

"Little fellow named Henry Stout pointed the way. Say, do you think you and me could step outside for a minute." He let go of Trent's hand and gave him a look that told Trent he'd better follow if he knew what was good for him.

"Sure." He said, passing Luzetta without a word. The men got a good distance away from the house before speaking. "Do you mind telling me what this is about?" Trent asked as he kept stride with his friend. "Not until I get you behind the barn so I can realign your jaw." Sam said, not breaking stride.

"What?" He wasn't sure why Sam was so angry at him. "I don't understand."

"Then you really do need a beating." He rounded on Trent. "I should knock your teeth down your throat for what you've been doing to that woman." He pointed to the house. "I've been here for at least an hour and almost got her whole life story already, not to mention that she didn't even take alarm when I rode in. She didn't even know I was there until I was right beside her. If I was a snake I would'a bit her." Sam felt like belting Trent, but knew that it wouldn't change Luzetta. "That woman has no place out here. How she survived this long without her father is beyond me. If she knew this place was crawling with men like George Carbaugh and his boys, Russ Turner, Linus Fort, just to name a few, she wouldn't be that trusting."

Trent ran his fingers through his hair and didn't object to Sam's rantings. There wasn't anything he couldn't say that Trent didn't already know.

"And what is this about her not knowing the truth about you?" Sam poked a stiff finger in Trent's chest. "You got no right playin' games with her head. If she finds out that you been swindlin' her like you have, I hope you know how to duck and cover." Sam ranted, breaking down in his usual form of speech to his way of talking when he was extremely mad, and Trent knew that was a very rare occurrence.

"I was going to tell her today." He stated, confident that his friend would believe him.

"Well, you'd better do it quick because your Ma is coming." He watched Trent's face turn white over the announcement.

"Why is she coming here?" He asked in a strained voice.

"Because of your telegram. 'Hit Jackpot. Need backup. Got married.' How was she supposed to take it? For all she knows, you hitched yourself to some sidewinder and needed marital advice and moral support." He spat. "Even little April could chew Luzetta up and spit her out, for God sake. And she probably will." Sam paced the length of the barn and came back again. "Now how are you going to handle this?" He asked with finality.

"I plan on doing just as I set out to. I'll go in there right now and tell her." He said, turning to head for the house, only to be caught short by the sight of the wagon that held his mother and sister-in-law. Trent's four brothers were riding along side coming his way. Trent muttered something under his breath and knew his time had run out. He just hoped Luzetta hadn't learned how to load and shoot the shotgun he just purchased for her.

The covered wagon pulling into the yard sported Trent's mother, sister-in-law and his two nephews. His mother, Harriet, was a sturdy woman, almost as tall as any of her sons. She had to be sturdy to handle all of them. She had ten children. Six boys, four girls. Trent's brothers flanked all sides as the wagon pulled in. They began to make whooping sounds as they caught sight of their youngest brother. Ma pulled the wagon to a stop.

"Well, where is she?" She hollered out without saying as much as a hello to the son she hadn't seen for more than two months. "I want to meet the woman who tied you on." She wasn't kept waiting for long because when Luzetta heard all of the whooping and goings on outside, she went to investigate.

Luzetta stood stunned as she looked out and saw six men, four looking almost exactly like Trent, just older. Everyone was standing before her, looking at her as if she were some marvel never seen before by human eyes. Luzetta was speechless. The four men she hadn't met dismounted and took off their hats to her, placing them over their hearts.

"Afternoon." The first one said. "My, Trent has picked the prettiest of the bunch, Ma." He yelled back. He took her hand and guided her down the steps. "Come on out and meet the family." He said. Luzetta almost had the wind knocked out of her. Luzetta let an accusing look fly toward Trent. This surely was an underhanded move of Trent. He would have her meet his family and she would get emotionally attached. Was her plan to get out of this marriage to him impossible? It was looking like it. Luzetta looked out at the crowd of strange faces and smiled. "Hello." She said to the crowd. Trent came to stand beside her.

"Let me make the introductions." He said, gently placing a hand at her elbow. "This is Clint, Tray, Isaac, Aaron." He pointed to each one. "This is Ma and April, Aaron's wife. Their children are Aaron junior, 6, and Walter, 4." He couldn't read the look on Luzetta's face, but it looked like she was scared to death from his standpoint.

"Come over here and let me get a good look at you." The tall woman said, jumping down from the wagon. She was broad shouldered as any man Luzetta had ever seen. "Why, you ain't no bigger than a minute. How old are you, child?" The blond woman of indiscriminate years asked.

"Twenty three." She allowed.

"Well, isn't that just keen. I was thinking Trent wouldn't be able to find anyone out here in the woods and all, but here he found himself a fine piece." She boasted over her new daughter-in-law. "Ain't that right, April." The dark haired woman still sitting in the wagon seat was holding a sleeping four year old. She didn't seem to take to Luzetta very friendly.

"Sure enough." She said, peering at Luzetta as if trying to figure her out, not trusting her until she got to know her better. Luzetta stretched her arms up to take the child so April could get down from the wagon. As the child transferred from the comfortable arms of his mother to a stranger's the child awoke.

Walter was, at first, wide eyed and ready to cry when he found he was with a stranger, but he decided not to as he looked at Luzetta. He stared at her for a moment, taking in her light features, blond hair clouding about her head and the sun directly above her, creating a halo effect. Taking her face into his tiny hands, the child placed a gingerly kiss on her lips. "Are you an angel?" He asked.

"No." She whispered back. "But you are." She smiled. She instantly like the child. April took the child back after getting down from the wagon, seeming to be perturbed by something. Trent seemed to be perturbed about something, too.

"You all must be hungry from your travels. Why don't we settle in to the kitchen and get some food into your bellies." She offered.

"Sounds good to me." Clint raised his voice first, then the other's followed suit. Ma took Luzetta by the shoulders and walked into the house with her, effectively cutting Trent off from stealing her away for a minute or two. Ma made Luzetta aware that no special treatment was in order and there wasn't anything that they all couldn't pitch in and get done.

"If you don't mind, pull on that side of the table and I'll set in the leaves." She asked Ma. "This table can fit twelve people at it, so I don't think there will be a problem seating everyone." She said, trying to adjust to the sudden influx of guests.

"My this is nice." Ma said. "I'll help you with lunch." She announced. Luzetta accepted her offer and they went to work on preparing the lunch while the men stood out in the yard talking and April settled the children in the parlor, still sleepy from their naps.

"You have lovely children. At first I thought they took after their father, but when I got close I saw more of your features in their eyes and mouth." Luzetta commented. April smiled. "Thank you. Not many people look past the blonde hair and size." She stated. "And they're always referred to as 'Aaron's boys' like I had nothing to do with it." She reluctantly admitted.

"I must say, Luzetta, that we were all very surprised when we received Trent's telegram that he was married." Ma said, busy with needing the bread dough. "Trent hasn't ever set his cap for any girl back home, and to have him take a wife so suddenly was rather shocking."

"That's because he had no choice in the matter, seeing that his other choice was hanging from a noose in the town square." Luzetta said without missing a beat. Ma and April looked at each other inquisitively.

"What kind of trouble was he in to need a hanging?" She asked, toweling her hands off to pay more attention to Luzetta.

"He borrowed my horse. Sheriff Johensen wouldn't let me drop the charges, so it was marry him or see him hang and I couldn't let that happen." She clarified.

"Where was his horse?" Brows furrowed, Ma came to sit by Luzetta at the table who was peeling potatoes.

"He didn't come with one." Luzetta realized his mother might not take the news of the condition

Trent had arrived in very easily. She didn't want to be the one to shock this woman with how close Trent was to death. She averted Ma's eyes and paid attention to the potato she was peeling.

"How did you two meet?" Ma was too close to her, pressing her for information she didn't want to give. Luzetta stilled her hands and took a deep breath before looking the woman in the eye.

"Please, Mrs. Longwood."

"Ma." She barked in the motherly commanding way she perfected over the years.

"Ma, I don't want to tell you what Trent should, by all rights. All I can tell you was that I was the town doctor." She hinted.

"And that is all you can tell me?" She asked, squinting one eye at her, pressuring her to expound on her admission.

"Yes, Ma'am." She cleared her throat to loosen the knot. "Unless you expect me to lie and I am terrible at it." Ma cracked with a loud boom of laughter.

"I am sure you are." She laughed. "Don't look so stricken. It's a good quality, being a bad liar. It's the good ones you have to watch." She said. "Now, from what I gather, Trent didn't tell you what his line of work was, did he?"

"Yes. He said he took odd jobs while he was looking for a friend who may have fallen into trouble." She said, wondering if Ma would enlighten her further. "Is that true?" Harriet could tell Luzetta was becoming less sure of what she knew about Trent.

"As a wise woman said 'I don't want to tell you what Trent should, by all rights'." Ma left it at that. "Why don't we let him have his confession time come lunchtime. The old one-two at a table full of people he can't lie to ought to do the trick." A malicious grin coated Ma's face.

"Teach him a lesson, too." Added April. "A husband should talk to his wife."

"Amen." Ma seconded the motion.

"I have a feeling I'm not going to like this." Luzetta said to herself.

Chapter Ten

"So, Trent." Aaron began. "Start talking." Everyone gathered round.

"When I said I hit the jackpot, I meant it. I was able to get into close circles with the men we've been looking for. George Carbaugh and his sons, Russ Turner, Linus Fort, Manny Wainright and Mack Crinshaw." Whistles sounded all around. Sam took off his hat and began hitting it against his leg, knocking all of the dust off. "The only one missing from our little party is John Beck."

"And I take it you know where they're hiding." Sam assumed. Trent nodded, looking at an imaginary spot on the ground. "Any chances they know what's going down?"

"Not likely. Closer to none than slim. We have to work fast, though. I think they are beginning to get restless. I saw some of them talking privately several nights ago." Trent urged.

"How do you figure this is going down?" Isaac asked, knowing the odds of six against nine, maybe more, were not the worst he's been in, but these guys have gone without getting caught for over twenty years. They must be doing something to escape unscathed.

"I don't quite have that figured out yet. All I know is that they seem to meet pretty regular at George's place. I figure we ambush them." He suggested.

"Men like that don't wait around with their pants around their ankles, Trent." Sam argued. "They're going to be ready for anything. Ambushing them is like attacking a house full of rattlers." Sam countered.

"I know. That means we are going to need every single angle covered. I'll take all of you out there tonight and we can take a look around. After that we'll come back here and make a plan of action." It sounded good enough to work.

Come lunch time, the men were called in and corralled into the kitchen around the large table flanked with two long benches brought in from outside and two high-backed chairs on both ends. Ma took the head seat, as Luzetta thought she was accustomed to doing. Next to her on the left was Sam, Trent, April and Aaron Jr. everyone just called Junior. Aaron Sr. headed the other end of the table. Walter sat on his other side followed by Clint. Isaac and Tray flanked Luzetta. She was deliberately seated across from Trent. Despite Luzetta boasting the table could seat twelve, the sheer size of the men took up more room than she anticipated.

The table was full of chatter and laughter. Walter was sitting two seats down from Luzetta, but she could feel him peeking around his uncle at every chance. Luzetta noticed and started a little peek-a-boo game with him that he enjoyed immensely. Trent watched the interaction go on between Luzetta and Walter, wondering if they would ever be able to have children of their own.

"With nine other siblings" Isaac said "we had a line of hand-me-downs that went a mile long." He cracked. "Did I mention that I have two older sisters?" Everyone laughed at the connotation he made about being made to wear girls clothes.

"If I didn't have any manors" Luzetta broke in "I would reach right over Tray's plate and shake your hand. The most children I've seen around here is six. You sure are a brave woman." Luzetta lamented.

"Nothing brave about it. I had to have someone to work the fields when I got old." Ma jeered. "I only got one farmer, though. Kyle is back home keeping the home fires burning. He has a wife and four of his own children and Isaac's wife is expecting in summer. She didn't feel like traveling."

"I don't blame her." April broke in. "It looks like Isaac put twins in her. She's as huge as a water buffalo." She snickered. Luzetta's eyes met Trent's.

"Do twins run in the family?" She asked.

"Kyle and Aaron are twins, I also have twin girls, Faith and Hope, who are back home." Ma confirmed. Luzetta began paying attention to her plate in deep thought. "Makes me wonder what will become of you two." She broke in, hoping the new couple will give her more grandbabies soon.

"We'll do just fine." He said to his mother, but he was looking at Luzetta. Ma knew what was going on. It was that way with new couples.

"So tell us how you two met, Trent." April couldn't wait any more. Trent cleared his throat before starting. Luzetta felt like a heel for playing this little game with Trent.

"I woke up with Luzetta on top of me." Trent joked, but wanted to retract it as soon as he heard the gasp across from the table and seeing the flaming face and round, surprised eyes. No one else seemed to be bothered by the statement. "She took me in after I was jumped by some hooligans." Trent revealed, trying to glaze over the event.

"You've been jumped before, Runt." Sam used the nick name most when he was peeved at something Trent had done. "Never needed a Doc before." Sam didn't know about the plan to out Trent, but he was helping it along.

"Yeah, I know. This time I was shot pretty bad." He admitted.

"How bad?" Ma's fork hit her plate with a clink and stopped eating to stare at Trent.

"A few times." He didn't want to tell his mother the whole story, fearing she would faint on the spot. "Nothing major." Luzetta rolled her eyes.

"Luzetta, is that true?" Knowing that Luzetta was not a liar, Trent knew the truth would be coming out. About everything. Tonight. Luzetta looked at Trent then his mother.

"Might as well. Trent's too chicken." Sam elbowed Trent in the ribs.

"Okay, I'll tell you." He finally spat out. "Luzetta didn't know the whole story anyway." He put his fork down and addressed his mother. "I was meeting an informant that had some information about the train robbery. When I met him, he and some of his friends jumped me. They beat me up pretty good, shot me a couple of times and left me for dead." He stated matter-of-factly. Ma raised an eyebrow to Luzetta.

"Seven times." She paused. "Naked." She added. "In Indian country." She said, almost inaudibly. "In the middle of a blizzard. He was almost frozen to death." She couldn't make herself take a bite to avoid eye contact. "That's why I was on top of him. I was warming him up." Ma looked over at Trent, so were his brothers.

"Is this true, Trent?" She asked. Trent bobbed his head. Ma's face had gone pale for just a moment before regaining her color and composure. "You should have called for help sooner." She chastised.

"No sense in beating a dead dog. What's done is done. We're here now. Them suckers will get what's coming to them." Clint said with resignation.

"Wait a minute. You told me you were looking for some friend of yours, not some train robbers." Luzetta said. Again, all eyes flew to Trent.

"I was doing both." He said, leaving it at that.

"There should be no secrets in a family, Trent, least of all in a new marriage. She has a right to know." Ma dictated. The whole family was behind Luzetta now. There was no getting out of it. If he didn't tell her, she would hear from someone else and that would be even worse. The trick was finding the words to tell her. Those sky blue eyes were staring at him, waiting for an answer to the question she had asked two weeks ago.

"I'm sorry." He began. "I meant to tell you sooner." He hated to hear what was coming, but it had to be done. "I'm a United States Marshall. So are they." He said, indicating the other men sitting around the table. It didn't take her a split second for the information to register. He saw the sky blue eyes turn dark and stormy instantly. He had used her. He lied to her. When she told him she didn't want a husband, he pushed the subject. He could have gotten himself out of trouble with the law. Instead he used her for his own purposes. He just lost major trust points with her at that very second. But all she did was sit there and look at him. She didn't yell, pitch a fit, didn't even blink.

Everyone at the table was waiting for the explosion that should have erupted by now. They watched as Luzetta sat primly in her seat, holding her thoughts to herself, giving Trent a look that would turn most men to stone. She didn't break the stare she was giving Trent for a full minute, but then she returned to the ham and mashed potatoes on her plate. Absolutely every one, except the children who were unaware of the conversation, admired Luzetta's ability to control her temper. The news she was just given would have set off any other woman. Luzetta's respectability shot skyward with all, including Trent. She was truly a strong woman.

Slowly everyone started eating again, making small talk and filling Luzetta in on the family as the meal progressed.

"Since Isaac and I are finished" Clint suggested "We'll go on and check into the hotel and get everything squared away."

"Nonsense." Luzetta broke in. "You'll stay here with us." She demanded.

"Do you have enough room?" Aaron asked.

"If I can fit fifty Indians in this house, ten won't be a bother." Everyone stopped what they were doing and looked at Luzetta. Trent just shook his head and smiled.

"You had fifty Indians in here? What for?" Isaac asked, dumbfounded at the logic of having fifty filthy Indians in the small house.

"It started with two Indian boys playing with two white boys who happened to break out with chicken pox soon after." She explained. "The majority of the tribe broke out and didn't have a clue how to deal with it. I took them in and helped them out." Everyone was staring at Luzetta still, amazed at the talk they were hearing. Everyone was bewildered by this new family member, intrigued by her way of thinking.

"Where did you find these Indians?" Clint asked.

"They live five miles North of here. They were here before we moved here." She explained.

"We?" Clint asked

"My father and I. He died the Fall before last." She just then realized that she had eight pairs of furrowed brows staring at her and little room to move.

"She'd been up here fourteen months by herself." Trent confirmed, sounding almost proud.

"Well, don't that beat all. I didn't know there were any women that tough. Not many women are as brave as you are, Luzetta." Ma commended.

"What do you mean? I had plenty of food and my practice to make a living." She questioned.

"Yeah, but that only takes care of food and things, but who was here to protect you?" Ma asked the exact same question Trent asked three weeks ago. It still didn't occur to her that she needed any protection, except from her husband.

"Almost everybody knows that these hills are crawling with thieves and robbers and the like. Real low lifes like to hide where there are a lot of spots to hide. I suppose that's why Trent followed them here." Isaac confirmed.

"How come I never heard about any of this?" Luzetta asked.

"Beats me." Isaac just shook his head. "Maybe you're too far into the forest to see the trees. These men don't want to draw too much attention to their hiding spots." Luzetta instantly thought of George and his boys. She hoped that they would be all right.

Trent noticed that she was starting to believe there was indeed a need for him right now. He saw the questioning and fear in her eyes. Was she really deep in criminal lands?

"I see." She said, standing to take her plate to the sink, only to have it whisked out of her hands by April.

"I'll do the dishes. It's the least I could do for putting us up. Or should I say putting up with us?" She jibbed.

"It will be nice to have company again. It's been a long time since I had someone out here." She said absently.

"Here, Kitten. Let's go for a walk." Trent took her hand and guided her out the door. They walked a half a mile before he got Luzetta to speak what was on her mind.

"I'm just trying to let everything sink in." She said, gathering her arms over her mid-section. She stopped at a place where a fallen tree served as a place to sit. "There must be a good reason you deliberately deceived me. Otherwise you would have listened to me about not wanting to get married in the first place." She was making Trent feel like a heel, but he deserved it.

"Yes, I did use you. I needed to keep my cover. I didn't want the wrong people to find out that I was a Marshall. Things would have gone bad for me if they found out." Trent tried to place his arm around her, but she pulled away from him.

"I still don't want to be married, Trent. It was a pretty rotten thing for you to bringing your family here to meet me."

"I didn't intend for them to come. I just sent word that I needed my brothers to come help round up the people responsible for the majority of the crimes around here." He tried to explain.

"Sam told me what the telegram said. I didn't get the message that you weren't wanting everyone to come out here and celebrate with you." She accused. Trent stood up to look at her, hoping to talk some sense into her.

"I understand you are upset, but this marriage is what you needed." He rubbed her arms in mock warming motions.

"Explain to me how this is what I needed. I don't want it, Trent." She took a deep breath and stepped back from him. "I'm sorry I led you on, thinking that this will last, but it won't." Trent was looking down at her with curious eyes. She spoke confidently, willing herself not to be swayed. "In light of your deeds, I think it's appropriate for us to refrain from any physical contact." Her eyes were a pale shade of smoky blue as she talked. "I'll play the part as a wife until your family is gone and you're finished with your investigation. Afterward, I'll travel with you to another town away from here and we can obtain a divorce."

"A divorce?" He spat.

"Or an annulment. Whichever will suit me fine." She stood perfectly still as Trent walked a couple paces away and then back again.

"Listen, Luzetta. I have had it up to here with you trying to shove me out the door." He held up his hand to his forehead. "Whether you like it or not we are married. I certainly didn't plan on it working out the way it had, but it did." He raked his fingers through his hair. "You and I both stood in front of the preacher and said 'I do' and I plan on making good on that promise."

Luzetta's knees began to shake, but Trent never saw them, thankfully. How was she going to get rid of him? Why did he have to be so stubborn about this?

"And how do you plan on doing that when you are off chasing bad-guys?" She hadn't moved, expression hadn't changed. Trent looked at her and decided to bluff.

"Who says I have to go anywhere?" He spoke softly, but the effect was seismic.

Supper was full of cheerful talk and spirits. Wind In Hair had not returned home yet and everyone was having a good time, except Luzetta. Ma noticed the tension between Trent and Luzetta. She figured Luzetta was still raw from finding out she'd been used and Ma didn't blame her. Trent would have a hard row to hoe to win her trust back.

As the night drew in, Luzetta made sure everyone had somewhere to sleep. She soon realized that she didn't have anywhere to sleep but Trent's bed. Luzetta made a mental note to bring in a rocking chair from the living room when everyone retired.

Gathering around the fire place, the men began to devise their plan of attack. They spoke in hushed voices as the women were about the house getting things ready, put away, tucking in the children.

"Luzetta, are you still up?" April asked as she stepped out of the shadows of the hallway.

"Yes. I want to make sure Wind In Hair gets here safely." The made up excuse sounded plausible. "I'm pretty sure she would appreciate me telling her there are extra people in the house."

"Do you think she will be long?" April asked.

"I hope not." She said, yawning behind her hand. Just then Wind In Hair stepped quietly through the door and came over to Luzetta. "Wind In Hair, I would like you to meet April, my sister-in-law." Both April and Luzetta looked at each other as it spilled out of Luzetta's mouth. Luzetta felt a strange feeling in the deep part of her heart as she spoke the words. Was she too far into this relationship with Trent's family to carry through with her plans? She had a feeling they already had a firm grip on her heart.

"Nice to meet you, April." Wind In Hair smiled, winking at Luzetta.

"How is everyone? Doing well, I hope." Luzetta asked before she would have to explain Wind In Hair's behavior.

"Yes, all send love. Ask me to send gifts." She stated. "Two Feathers will bring in morning."

Sure enough, Two Feathers was there at the crack of dawn toting along buffalo meat and hides. The meat was already prepared and the hides were of fine quality. The entire family came out of the house to inspect the parcel behind the boy's horse.

"This is mighty fine." Clint whistled.

"I guess you weren't kidding when you said your doctoring kept you comfortable up here." Aaron said before sampling a piece of jerky. "My, this is the best I ever tasted."

"And look at these hides." Isaac held one up. "You could completely cover ten small children from just one." Everyone was pleased with the gifts from the Piqui.

Luzetta invited the boy in and fed him breakfast while gathering some things for him to take back. She made a package of salt, sugar and some preserves she kept in the pantry. When she approached him, handing him the parcel, the boy stepped back and held his hands in refusal. Even though everyone but Wind In Hair was ignorant of their foreign speech, they weren't blind. The body language he was giving was screaming "this was not a trade".

"Please, take and give to the elders to thank them." Luzetta pleaded.

"Running Bull said you would try to do this. He gave you this gift. Take it and be happy. He knows two women on their own need help, even if one is as stubborn as a mountain goat." Two Feathers said. Wind In Hair hid a chuckle behind her hand. "But I will tell him you accepted me kindly and fed me in your own house." Luzetta knew the tribe would see that single gesture as far more significant than any return gift would have. "And I will tell them you are very grateful to have received our gift." After Two Feathers left, everything went back to normal. Animals were being tended, children were being taught, chores were being done. But it still took all of Trent's might to not think of Luzetta and her determination to be rid of him. He had to do something. He didn't want her to think she could just demand a divorce of him and expect him to walk away. Lie or no lie.

Trent set out to make things right with Luzetta. He decided to start off with a shooting lesson. He gathered up the gun and ammunition and hoped his plan worked. He was hoping to scare Luzetta's independence right out of her.

"Put the butt of the gun at your shoulder" he said, nestling her body in with his, whispering into her left ear as he held her close "that is, unless you have something else to put it up against."

"Why?" She asked, feeling the heat of his body against hers.

"Because the gun will knock you off your feet if you aren't careful." He put her hands into position on the gun. "Now, look through both sights at the same time." He instructed. "Do you see the target?" God, she smelled good.

"Yes." She said, more aware of him than the task at hand.

"Okay, when you're ready, pull the trigger." Luzetta wasn't ready. She could barely breath, let alone concentrate on a target between two sights with a gun as heavy as a small child. Trent was shoulder to shoulder to her, bracing her for the shot. His mouth was at her ear, whispering words of encouragement.

Luzetta pulled the trigger and got the shock of her life. If Trent hadn't been right there, she would have dropped the gun. With a terrified scream, Luzetta let go of the gun and spun around into Trent's body, burying her face into his chest. She felt defiled, like she had just worked one of Satan's own tools.

"It's all right." Trent propped the gun on the post and gathered Luzetta into him. "It's always a shock the first time." He soothed. "Does your shoulder hurt?" He asked, rubbing the offended part with long, soothing fingers.

"No." She sniffed. Trent kept rubbing it anyway.

"Do you feel like trying again?" He asked after a few minutes.

"No." She said adamantly. Trent smiled at his success.

"Maybe tomorrow." Luzetta didn't say anything to that. "You did good." He commended, knowing she hadn't even come close to the target.

"I want to go back." She stated coldly.

"All right." Trent let Luzetta slip out of his arms. "Luzetta." He caught her just as she was turning around. She turned her face to him and he lost his train of thought, so he kissed her. His kiss was searching, wanting her to open up to him. His arms were strong but gentle, trapping her in the most lovely embrace. At first she had to remind herself to breath, but when she did, she took in his scent, his feel. She liked kissing him. She told herself she was just playing a role as his wife, and this was just a perk. She was leading herself onto a dangerous path.

Trent broke the kiss. He looked down at her half closed eyes, half drugged. Letting out a sigh of resignation, he let her arms go and picked the gun up, heading for the house. Luzetta took a moment before returning to the house to compose herself.

During the next two days, Ma, April, Luzetta and the children were left to fill their time while the men were off hunting other men. Luzetta became increasingly fond of Ma and April, telling them about her father, whom she hadn't talked about openly for over a year.

"He was a brilliant man. He loved medicine and nature. We would go on walks and he would teach me about every single tree or flower we came across. There are hot springs not far from here that we would go swimming in even in the winter." She was lost to her memories as April mended a rip in the seat of Junior's pants that got caught on a renegade nail in the barn.

"He sounds like a good man. He lived a full life and raised a fine daughter along the way." Ma complimented.

'Thank you, Ma. I miss him so much it hurts. Sometimes I can't even look at his grave without drawing up a tear." She admitted, almost shocking herself.

"That happens when you lose a loved one suddenly like that. I lost my husband when Joy, my youngest daughter, was just three years old. He, and Sam's brother, was killed while guarding a transit car full of government money. I don't think I'll ever get over the shock of having them jerked away from me like that. And with ten children to raise at that."

"How you did it still amazes me, Ma." April broke in after cutting the thread with her teeth.

"Is that why most of your boys are lawmen?" Luzetta asked. Ma nodded. Luzetta saw the pain in her eyes as Ma thought of the past.

"They are still chasing the men who are responsible. It was twenty two years ago and them slimy cusses still haven't been caught. They have good motivation though. With my boys after them, they know what's coming to them when my boys catch up to them." She said.

"And what about Trent's friend he was looking for?"

"Jake Forester. He was tracking them when he disappeared. We think he met up with bad terms. We would have heard something, anything from him if he was still alive." The somber turn of the conversation made Luzetta begin to worry about Trent and the others.

Chapter Eleven

Wind In Hair came in from drawing water, looking rushed. "Golden Hair! Rider coming. He ride fast." Luzetta jumped up and peered in the direction Wind In Hair pointed.

"Oh good. It's Jim Crump. His wife must be having her baby." She rushed and gathered everything she needed and met Jim at the door.

"Luzetta. You gotta come quick. He ain't doin' nothin'." Jim said, out of breath.

"Who isn't doing anything?" She asked.

"The new Doc. He's just sitting there watching her scream. It's been almost two whole days. Hurry." He urged. April and Ma decided to travel with Luzetta. Leaving Wind In Hair with the boys, the three women climbed into the buggy meant for two and rode like the wind to Luzetta's closest friend's aid.

When they arrived, Luzetta heard Elise's scream of pain from outside. "Oh, Elise." She Prayed. She marched into the house, determined to take over. As she was told, Luzetta found the new Doctor Schumaker peering into the open legs of Elise Crump. He hadn't even taken his overcoat off.

"What's going on here?" Luzetta demanded with anger she never felt before. Dr. Schumaker quickly pulled his gaze over to the furious lady standing at the door.

"You just march yourself right out of here. You're no doctor." He shouted, pointing back at the door whence she came.

"And neither are you, from the looks of it. Jim tells me she has been in labor for two days. How long has she been screaming in pain, Doctor?" She accused as she washed and readied herself. Ma and April came in behind Luzetta, but they were ignored by the doctor so full of himself.

"Not long. She's doing just fine. Her progression is normal." He spat.

"Liar." Jim said, caustically. "She's been screaming at the top of her lungs since yesterday. She's begged him to do something. She said the baby was stuck. She can feel it. But all he did was look at her like she was some sideshow freak."

"Let me take a look at her." Luzetta started toward her friend who was so exhausted that her eyes were lackluster and her hair was drenched with sweat along with the sheets she was laying on.

"You won't touch her." Dr. Schumaker pushed Luzetta back. It was then that Jim Crump had reached the end of his rope and punched the doctor out cold. April and Ma watched as the young man take a sucker punch to jaw, laying him sprawled out over the bedroom floor.

It was worse than Luzetta had hoped for. "Elise, your baby needs to be turned. He's breech and face up, altogether wrong. I'm going to have you get on your hands and knees." She explained, pointing out the other women that were going to help Elise with the positioning. "Elise, this is going to hurt, but it is the only way to save you and the baby." Luzetta turned the baby in record time, reducing the pain that Elise had been in. "Okay, one more push. That's it. Pushpushpushpush." She cheered. "Here's the head. Now slow down." She instructed. "Here come the shoulders. It's out." She said with tears in her eyes at the glorious little boy she held in her hands. "It's a boy." She said. Jim looked like he was about to faint, but whooped his joy instead.

Elise was completely exhausted, falling to sleep as soon as the baby was out. Luzetta pulled the placenta out and stitched her back up with deft hands while the baby was held by his father. Elise woke up when Luzetta and Ma were repositioning her while changing the sheets. She smiled up at Luzetta and asked for her son.

"Here he is." Jim held the precious boy beside his mother. Ma saw a distinct yearning in Luzetta's eyes as she watched the mother and baby together. After helping Elise begin to nurse, the first stirring of the Doctor was the main focus.

"What happened?" He asked as he stood up, noticing that Mr. Crump was across the room.

"Luzetta just saved my wife and child, you no good saw bones." He spat. "Don't think you're going to get very far in this town treating your patient's like that."

Luzetta stood and began gathering up her supplies. "Good-bye, Elise. I'll be back to check up on you in a couple of days. Jim, you make sure she stays in bed until I see her again. You can get out of bed to only use the chamber pot or to sit in a chair. That's it. Jim, when she feels good enough to get out of bed I want you right there at her side at all times."

"Yes, Ma'am." He said, thankful of her talents.

Luzetta had her bag in hand and ready to leave, but instead of heading out the door, she stood directly in front of Dr. Schumaker. "If you want to learn how to deliver babies, I'll be glad to teach you all that I know. Otherwise, I would leave it up to midwives or myself."

"And what makes you think I'll do that? This was a special case."

"Yes, it was. But you have to take the bull by the horns, Dr. Schumaker. You did nothing." Her eyes nailed a steeling look at him. "I've delivered babies since I was ten and I have never lost a mother or child to the birthing process. You almost lost both in one fell swoop. I suggest you get some additional training before you go into another birthing situation or you might find yourself losing patients." She said before turning on her heal and walking out the door.

The ride home was quiet, with Luzetta sandwiched between April and Ma. "Thank you for coming with me. I don't think Elise could have been able to position herself if she had to and her husband would have fainted in the process."

"You're welcome." Ma said soberly.

"You're welcome to deliver any of my future babies any time you please." April commented laughingly. "You've really been delivering babies since you were ten?"

"Yup." Luzetta confirmed, rather proud of herself today.

"What a way to grow up. I don't think I would have the stomach to do that. Having them is one thing. Delivering them is something completely different, especially at ten." April was still reeling from the experience.

"Well, I'm proud of you." Ma said, patting Luzetta's leg. Luzetta was struck with a feeling she hadn't expected. It was the feeling of being a part of something bigger. Part of a family. It caressed her heart, comforting it's tender spots.

These last few days made it harder for Luzetta to envision leaving Trent. How was she going to let down this perfect family? Even though she wasn't going to be there to tell them, she could just see the disappointment in their eyes, especially Ma's and April's.

Later that night, Trent came into the kitchen to where Luzetta was wiping the counter, removing the crumbs from the pies she just cut. Trent saw the book she had been reading and knew it was one of her father's journals. It encouraged him to know she was still searching to find an answer to her problem. He stood behind her and rubbed her tired muscles.

"Your shoulders are in knots." Trent's masculine voice soothed and relaxed Luzetta and she closed her eyes as she felt the heat from his hands and the massaging motion from his fingers seep into her aching body. He had an irresistible urge to kiss her outstretched neck. She slapped him away.

"I know." She conceded.

"Still wound up from Dr. Schumaker?" He asked.

"Not really. I'm probably stiff from sleeping in the rocking chair for the last three nights." She said, not realizing who was around her to hear her, which was Aaron, April, Ma and Sam in the Living room not far away. Their eyes flew to Trent with questioning looks. As soon as Trent stopped massaging, she looked and saw her error and instantly regretted it. Certainly she would get an earful if they knew the truth about their relationship. Trent stormed out, more than likely from his pride being bruised than embarrassment. Luzetta didn't have any doubt that she just put the thorn in his side a little deeper. Aaron and Sam followed him.

Ma and April came over to the kitchen table. Luzetta had the sinking feeling she was about to spill her guts.

"Come sit, Luzetta." Ma patted the seat beside her. Luzetta obeyed. "Now, Luzetta. You aren't still making Trent pay for the mistake of keeping secrets from you, are you?" She asked.

"You have to learn how to forgive him or your marriage will fall apart." April placed her hands on Luzetta's, drawing her eyes to meet hers.

"It isn't that." She really didn't want to go into this. Not right now.

"Than what is it?" April urged. She saw the battle waging inside Luzetta's head.

"You'll find out soon enough." Luzetta resigned herself to breaking the news herself. "After you leave, I fully intend to divorce Trent."

"Divorce?" Both women reeled.

"Now, just wait. I didn't want this marriage in the first place. Trent and I haven't even consummated our marriage yet."

"Why, in God's name, not?" April asked, puzzled. "Don't you like him?"

"Well, yes." Luzetta pinked.

"Don't you find him attractive?" April drew further. Luzetta's cheeks pinked even more.

"Yes." She admitted.

"Then what's the problem?" Ma blurted out.

"It is more complicated than that." She played with her fingers nervously.

"Then explain it to us." Ma demanded. Both women were staring at her, eager to hear the reason why she was dumping the man she married almost a month ago. Luzetta reluctantly told them her story of how she had been cursed with the family line of women who didn't survive child birth and her argument to not remain married to Trent in fear of becoming pregnant.

"Did your father tell you what that problem was?" Ma asked.

"No. He didn't talk too much about my mother. It was too painful for him." She remembered. "But I am going through his journals" she held up the book she'd been reading "to see if he had any methods of contraception." She admitted. Ma and April sat and thought for a minute.

"Have you found anything yet?" April asked with more interest than Ma desired.

"No. I haven't." She began to look defeated in her struggle.

"Maybe you are going about it wrong." Ma interjected. "Maybe, instead of looking for contraception, you should be looking for what exactly happened to your mother. You said that you were well versed in child birthing because of what your mother and grandmother went through, maybe he wrote something that would give you a clue as to what caused it."

"I don't understand." She said.

"Your father was the one who delivered you, right?" Ma asked.

"I suppose so." Luzetta thought.

"Then he should have it written down somewhere what exactly went wrong." She suggested. "That way you could find out if it was preventable." Ma was particularly proud of her idea. "And we could help you." She volunteered.

"Only if you can read his writing." She handed the open book to Ma.

"My goodness. It looks like Walter got in here and started scribbling."

"No, that's just the way he wrote."

"Was the earth quaking at the time?"

"He was rather old. I guess his hand was a little bit unsteady."

"How old was he?"

"He was sixty five when he died." Ma and April had their mouths open at Luzetta's statement.

"Maybe it wasn't the problem of the delivery, but the age of the woman." April suggested.

"I don't know how old she was, though." She regrettably admitted. "Many men marry women much younger than they are."

"Well, we'll just set out to find the answers to our questions." Ma encouraged.

Luzetta didn't see Trent that night or the next day. They had ridden out saying they were to return by the next day at the latest. All three women fretted with all the men gone off to do what they knew was dangerous work. Luzetta couldn't concentrate on reading that morning and told the others she needed to go for a walk.

"Do you want me to go with you?" Wind In Hair asked. "We can pick more herbs." She suggested. Luzetta just shook her head.

"I won't go far." She assured them. "I just need some air." Luzetta stated then set out for the small stream behind the house.

"I think she's more attached to Trent than she thinks." April said to Ma after Luzetta left.

"I think you're right." She seconded.

Luzetta meant to walk to the stream and back, just enough to stretch her legs, but ended up lingering longer than she intended. She sat along the bank and poked at the water with a stick she picked up along the way. She was pleasantly surprised to see her old friend, George, galloping toward her.

"George, how is everything?" She asked, placing a small kiss on his cheek when he dismounted.

"It sure is good to see your smiling face, Luzetta. Especially after staring at the boys for so long." Luzetta laughed and they walked a bit along the stream.

"Did you come to tell me you are riding out?" She asked.

"Yes, I did. We'll be leaving soon and I didn't want to leave without seeing how you were getting along with everything." He gestured toward the house. "Looks like you have a packed house again."

"It's not that bad. I've had worse." She didn't have to remind him of the Indians he witnessed.

"I hope you don't mind me poking into your business, but how are you and your new husband coming along?" He inquired.

"Fine, I guess. His family is here." She admitted. "They are all pretty nice." She reinstated her poking the stream.

"So you don't need me to whisk you away somewhere?" He joked.

"No. I can handle everything." She assured him. "Speaking of family, how are the boys? Did Linus and Russ come with you again?"

"Yup. They're real sorry they couldn't come out, but we have other business to attend to before heading out. Manny and Mack are with us too."

"Really, oh I wish you could stay a little while longer. I miss Mack's campfire stories." She smiled. "Tell them I said hello and that I expect to see them the next time they are here." She scolded. "It's been over a year and that is too long. I'm likely to forget what they look like." She cajoled.

"Not likely. Those are some of the *ugliest* men I know. When you see them, you aren't likely to forget." They laughed.

"I suppose you are right. Anyway, tell them I send my love. Be careful out there." She cautioned. George kissed her on the forehead, as he always did, and mounted with the ease of someone born in the saddle.

"I will." He saluted her good-bye and slowly meandered off into the horizon.

When Luzetta walked back to the house, Trent and the others were riding back in. Luzetta's stomach gave a little lurch and her heart skipped a beat. She knew she had feelings for Trent and his family.

He had everything she didn't. Sure, she had a loving father to raise her, but she missed out on brothers and sisters. Even a mother. Ma told her that Trent's father was killed when Trent was just five years old. At least they had that in common, not growing up with one of their parents.

"Find anything yet?" She asked as she entered the kitchen, finding two squint-eyed women at the table.

"No." April grumbled. Ma rubbed her eyes from the strain.

"I think I'll take a break. The boys are back anyway." Ma excused herself to fetch some water.

"Well, I didn't expect you to get this far." She said, noticing April halfway through the book Luzetta had given to her.

"It's not so hard after you get used to it." April flipped another page. Trent and Isaac waltzed in as Luzetta was putting a pan on the stove to heat. Noticing the book April was reading, Trent went over to Luzetta and spun her around, letting her land in his arms.

"My, it's good to see you." He said, smiling down at her with a devilish grin.

"Than why are you growling at me?" She asked, rather perturbed at the conflict of his actions. Was he trying to confuse her, holding her and growling his disapproval?

"I'm not growling, Luzetta." He couldn't understand this obsession she had with him growling at her. Trent closed in softly on her mouth for a gentle kiss.

"Trent!" She pushed at his chest. "Not in front of everybody." She pleaded, looking at April, who was pretending to read, but wearing a smile from ear to ear.

"Don't worry. She's done this before." He chortled, nuzzling her neck.

"But... Trent." She was losing her battle. "Please." With a face as red as an apple, Luzetta tried to pry Trent off of her.

"Okay, Kitten." He said, noticing how embarrassed she must feel at the public display of affection she was getting. He reluctantly let her go, giving a wink to April as he left the kitchen.

"Oh, my." She said, covering her face with mortification.

"Luzetta." April said slowly. "Can I give you a little personal information about Trent?"

"I guess." She said, sitting across from April. "If it will help."

"That little 'growl' you thought you heard" she informed "is a sound he makes when he is sexually aroused." April watched as Luzetta's jaw dropped, her face turning red again.

"No." She argued. "It can't be. He does it all the time!" She qualified. April just smiled and wiggled her eyebrows once or twice, leaving Luzetta to make a conclusion for herself.

"Aaron makes the same noise." April admitted. Luzetta stood and turned her attention to the meat she was going to brown. Could this really be? Could Trent desire her that much? Luzetta wondered if Trent felt love for her or just physical attraction.

Later that night, after pie and coffee, everyone once again congregated in the living room, talking about anything that came to their minds. Walter and Junior began to fuss and were whisked off to bed by April and Ma. Luzetta was sitting, gathering up the small blocks the boys were playing with when Trent reached down to her and pulled her to sit across his lap. Luzetta's face went instantly red and her spine stiff as a fire poker.

"Relax." Trent whispered into her ear. "Lay back on me." He guided her back to lean against his chest. It took a while for her to get used to the feeling of sitting on a man's lap. He took a stray lock of hair and threading it through his fingers. Luzetta's pleading eyes fell on Wind In Hair, only to be disregarded. She felt she had no allies in her vigil of remaining uninvolved.

Ma and April returned from putting the boys down. Luzetta almost jumped off Trent's lap when they entered the room, but he kept her pinned tight. Both women smiled at the new couple getting close, knowing that Luzetta was still not intimate with Trent. Luzetta's eyes flew to April's as she heard the growl come from Trent. It took April a mighty large dose of control not to laugh.

"Here." Trent pressed her head to his shoulder. Luzetta decided to make the most of this precarious position she was in and moved to a more comfortable angle. "Better?" Trent asked, stroking Luzetta's back and arms.

"Yes." She conceded. She hated to admit how comfortable Trent felt. She was at eye level with his throat and could see the strong pulse beating beneath the skin. "Ma tells me that your father was killed when you were just five." What ever made her say that was beyond her.

"Um-hum." He said, not missing a beat. "He was a guard working for the government and they were transporting money for the US Treasury Department.

Everyone on the train died that day. Sam's older brother was one of the guards, too." He told her.

"Then how do you know who did it?" She asked.

"By knowing who was in the area at the time and how the people were killed." Trent kept stroking Luzetta, relaxing her body as she sat on his lap. She thought about what he said. "Especially the way they were killed." He continued. "My father and Sam's brother were killed by a man named John Beck. They call him Butcher Beck, by trade. He has a pretty gruesome technique in killing his victims." He knew he was scaring Luzetta, which had been his intention.

"Yup" Sam commented "he knew just where to cause the most pain and the longest death." Luzetta hadn't even been aware Sam was paying any attention to their conversation.

"It's harder to nail the others who just like to shoot first and ask questions later, like George Carbaugh." Trent felt Luzetta stiffen instantly. She pushed herself up to look him straight in the eye.

"Trent Longwood, you take that back." She said with anger in her voice.

"Take what back?" Trent was momentarily puzzled by Luzetta's outburst.

"About what you said about George Carbaugh." She huffed. "He couldn't have done that." Trent's face turned white as she spoke.

"How do you know him?" Sam asked, an ominous tone coating his words.

"He was my father's best friend. He's like an uncle to me. Papa and me came out here after George scouted the land and told my father about all of the wonderful advantages to be had as a doctor out here." Luzetta tried to pry Trent's hands apart in order to stand, but Trent wouldn't let her. The other five men and two women were advancing on her as if to examine her under a magnifying glass.

"Luzetta." Ma said in a soft, but reprimanding tone. "Them Carbaughs are as bad as they come."

"No." She cried, tears streaming down her face. "I don't believe you." Luzetta began to breath harder in effort to keep her emotions under control as she stared back at unbelieving, accusing eyes. "All my life I have had George and his boys sit at the very table you sat at and not one hair on our heads were harmed. My father wouldn't be associating with criminals if they are who you say they are."

"Well, I'll be a monkey's uncle." Isaac said. "Them boys are as mean as two rattlers with their tails tied together." He said, wondering how a woman as beautiful as Luzetta escaped the Carbaugh boys' foul play they were notorious for.

Aaron, with his heart in his eyes came to kneel beside Luzetta, taking her hands in his. His hands were rough and his voice was smooth as honey. "Believe me, Luzetta. We're not trying to spread false stories about anyone. We're in the business of finding the worst of the worst and bringing them to justice. Now, them Carbaughs wouldn't be on our list if they weren't needing to be brought in." He said. Luzetta searched his features.

"Kitten." Trent addressed her. "We aren't saying this to hurt you. We didn't even know you knew them." Trent gathered Luzetta up in his arms as she covered her face in her shame. Slowly the realization of it all hit her and she looked about the room at the only family she will ever have for the rest of her life.

"If the Carbaughs are known criminals, then what about Russ Turner?" She asked, looking at Sam, nodding his head. "Linus Fort?" Clint nodded. "Mack Crinshaw?" Isaac nodded. "Manny Wainright?" She looked at Trayton. He was reluctant to give the confirmation.

"They call him 'The Mangler'." He said softly, not wanting to break her heart as he knew it would. Luzetta's body bore the weight of all the information she was given. Trent felt her slump with defeat as she knew what she was told was the truth. Tears came with no sound.

Luzetta turned into Trent's chest and protective arms and let him soothe her. He rocked for a long time, letting her deal with everything. Everyone remained quiet and in deep thought over the nights revelation.

"You said you've been looking for some train robbers." Luzetta finally spoke. "What was on the train?" She asked.

"Gold. Bars, mostly." Trent qualified softly.

"And your friend. When did you hear from him last?" She asked, trying to fill in the blanks that were vacant.

"Last September. Jake said he was making headway and would be close to getting a location on their hiding place."

Luzetta finally sat up and removed Trent's arms from her, stood and walked into another room. Everyone was looking at each other, wondering what to expect from her. Luzetta walked back into the room. She was carrying a small, brown leather drawstring bag in her hands, holding it in cupped hands. She looked at it with haunted eyes as if she were offering up a soul for the price of what she held.

"Here." She said, handing the bag to Trent. "Tomorrow, or whenever you have time, I will take you to the place where your friend is most likely buried." Trent stood in shock as he looked into the bag. Everyone stood to look at the contents of the bag. It was a crudely cut block of gold, distinctly shaped like an end of a bar that the US Mint used. Trent gathered her up, held her closely.

"Carbaugh?" Sam asked, holding the chunk of gold loosely in his hand.

"Yes." She sniffed. Luzetta had been putting away the shipment of medical supplies she had recently received when Clarence Jacobs came to her place riding like a bat out of hell. She had heard from townsfolk that a hermitic man in the backwoods had been swept away along with his cow and small crop by landslides. The spring rains had brought mudslides that were dangerous and lethal.

Mr. Jacobs said there was a man near his home that was wounded. He said he discovered him while hunting, and of course she accompanied him back to the site.

When she arrived, there were seven men, six surrounded the seventh that lay on the ground. Luzetta dismounted and approached the crowd, realizing it was Joe Carbaugh who was wounded.

"What happened?" Luzetta asked as she tore Joe's pants further up his leg to assess the damage to see the bone of his lower leg protruding out of the skin. He was in considerable pain and Luzetta hated knowing she didn't have anything with her to dull it. It was Randy who came to the rescue and handed Joe a bottle of whiskey. Joe guzzled it like a man dying of thirst.

"His horse" George volunteered "fell on top of him as they were coming down the mountain, here." He pointed to the crest just above him, but Luzetta didn't look. "The ground was too soft and the horse lost it's footing. Can you help him?" George asked with concern lacing his voice. Luzetta looked over the moaning patient, assessing him for any further damage he may have sustained from a horse landing on him.

"I think so. We will have to fashion a leg splint and find a way to get him back to the house." They all worked quickly to accommodate Luzetta's demands.

Mr. Jacobs pulled his flatbed wagon within a few feet away from where Joe was positioned on the still wet ground. Luzetta stood back as the men worked to get Joe on the wagon as carefully as possible. That was when she noticed the unmarked graves and the shovel leaning against the tree. Luzetta asked George about the graves.

"You see them fallen trees over yonder?" He asked, pointing to the trees in question.

"Yes."

"When we came down, so did those trees. It was something awful. Mr. Jacobs told us there was a mudslide just before we came through. I guess them trees wasn't rooted too strongly. It landed on two of them before we could shout out." George's remorseful face convinced Luzetta to believe his story.

"It didn't occur to me to question his story." Luzetta said, feeling the pain of loss.

"Of course not. You didn't expect them to be hardened criminals." Trent consoled, swaying with her ever so slowly. Suddenly she looked up at him.

"Trent he said he was leaving soon." She warned.

"Carbaugh? You talked to him?" He asked, shocked again.

"Yes. Twice. The last time was this morning. He said that he and the boys would be leaving soon and he wanted to say good-bye." Instantly the room became charged with restless agitation. "Good. We planned on moving in on them tonight anyway." Trent smiled down at her, tracing her face with his finger. He placed butterfly kisses on her forehead, nose, then mouth. This time she wasn't embarrassed by the affection. As far as she was concerned, She and Trent were alone in the room. "I may be gone all night." He whispered. "Will you miss me?"

"Yes." She said with no hesitation. Her blue eyes burned into his. "I'm scared, Trent." She admitted.

"I know. That makes ten of us. Everything will be fine." He smiled. "I promise." Placing another, deeper kiss on her lips, Trent felt Luzetta shutter. He didn't want to leave her just now. He wanted to hold her, protect her and whisper beautiful things into her ear.

"Let's Go." Aaron called out to everyone. Luzetta, Ma and April stood, arms around each other, watching the men mount their horses after arming themselves. Luzetta had never seen so many guns in one place in her life. She sent up a silent prayer for them all to be kept safe in their quest for justice.

Chapter Twelve

None of the women could sleep that night. They sat silently before the fire letting their imaginations take hold of them. Luzetta became so agitated with her thoughts that she knew she needed a distraction. She took a lamp into her father's study and began rummaging around.

"What are you doing?" Wind In Hair asked, standing outside the room watching Luzetta pilfer through her father's desk.

"Just looking." She said without looking up.

"Anything in particular?" Ma pried. Luzetta looked up at her with red eyes. She didn't know if it was tears beginning to form or strain from the lack of proper lighting and all the dust.

"I need to know why my father kept company with the likes of those men. He brought them into our home, probably knowing what they did." She ruffled through files and drawers, slamming them shut without regard to how noisy it was. "I want to know why." She vented. Luzetta looked and looked all night to find anything personal her father could have written. The journals he kept were of patients and local gossip from the town, nothing of his own activities or dealings.

April and Ma stood at the doorway watching a very determined woman ransack the stacks of papers, books and files. "Can we help?" April asked with a concerned voice.

"No. There isn't enough room in here for more than one ..." She stopped. There, in the corner, under a stack of books, was a pocket sized book, pressed into the footstool long ago forgotten. The book was at least three inches thick, bound with leather.

Luzetta picked up the book and slowly cracked it open. The pages, full of her father's scribbling, were yellowed with age. Holding it as if it held the answers to life, Luzetta carried it and the lamp out to the living room. April and Ma knew that Luzetta would be lost with reading all night with the size of the book, and they weren't about to go to sleep with the men out on the job, such as they were. So all four women settled back into their chairs as time ticked on. Wind in Hair was the only one active. She kept the fire going and tended to the needs of the other women, always offering them food and drink. After a while Ma told her to sit down before she drove her crazy.

Luzetta sat Indian style on the floor beside the fire wrapped in a blanket. She squinted and read slowly for the first two pages. At first she didn't understand what she was reading. Listed were a bunch of dates, locations and money amounts. Luzetta never heard of these places and wondered how anyone could have come into that large of sums of money, except by way of robbery. Before giving up, Luzetta looked up at Ma and April and thought about all she had learned tonight. A lump formed in her throat and she read on. She hoped her suspicion was wrong.

April nodded off first, then Ma soon followed. Luzetta wondered how many nights they had sat up, sleeping in rocking chairs waiting for their men to come home from a raid. Luzetta placed a blanket on both of them and returned to her reading. Wind In Hair had been leaning against the wall unmoving for the past hour. Luzetta was pretty certain she was asleep as well.

Luzetta was not aware of the crickets singing their tune outside, or the crackling of the fire just a few feet away. Immersed in the words her father wrote, Luzetta ignored her sleep deprived brain and her aching eyes to investigate further, knowing there was something to uncover.

After pages and pages of places she had never heard of and jargon she was unfamiliar with, Luzetta was starting to wonder if she had wasted her time.

Then about midway through the book, her father's writing style changed. He began describing his surroundings, albeit blandly, but she felt it was a refreshing change. It wasn't long before she found what she was looking for.

"Chicago, 1864. Met up with George and the boys for a little R & R. George said his contact said the Eastbound Suffolk and Western would be full of loot. Even though it was heavily guarded, the route was full of opportunities to be taken." Luzetta began to pull at her collar, finding it hard to breath. "We had a fool-proof plan. We took the train easily. Manny got hurt, though. He got burned on the face while fighting with the conductor. Why he didn't just shoot him is beyond me. I took care of some guards with Russ and Mack." Luzetta knew what 'care' they were taking with those people. It made her want to vomit. "Linus and George took care of the passengers that were in a fancy car in the back. They were fine looking folk, with their silk gowns and tall hats. I saw them beg before George and Linus gunned them down. Their money couldn't protect them now. The funny thing was, though, that when we went to loot the passenger car, there was something there we didn't expect. In a small carpetbag was a child. A little girl about a year old." Luzetta feared for the child, even twenty some odd years later. "She had a full head of curly blond hair and the bluest eyes you ever saw." Luzetta couldn't believe her eyes.

She pulled on her collar, needing to get more air. It wasn't coming. The next few sentences gripped her lungs. "I picked her up and looked at her knowing that I couldn't harm this child. She looked like a little angel. She didn't even cry as I held her. George said he knew in my face that I would keep her. I couldn't do anything else but hold her and call her 'Luzetta'." Luzetta lost it. She couldn't breath. Luzetta thought her heart would leap out of her chest and her lungs were being squeezed by her shock.

April woke up to see Luzetta hyperventilating, pulling at her collar. "Luzetta." She called to her without response. Ma and Wind In Hair woke up when April called out. Luzetta flung the book across the room as hard as she could, making it land with a thump. Luzetta was close to hysterics. Ma took Luzetta's arms firmly.

"Luzetta. What is it, Child?" She demanded. Luzetta couldn't think, she couldn't speak. She lost her mind with grief and heartache over the man she'd known as her father.

"No." She said with a guttural voice. "No." She chanted again and again. She shrugged out of Ma's grip and went back to her father's study. She flung papers, files and books everywhere, screaming at the top of her voice. "Liar. Scoundrel. Thief." She cried. Looking as if she had gone mad, Ma called out to April to call for help.

Ma tried to hold onto Luzetta as best she could, to try and calm her, but Luzetta was filled with the strength borne of fear, shock and rage. Renting her collar off her shirt, Luzetta heaved in gulps of breath. She felt like she was drowning. Both Ma and Wind In Hair heard the three gun shots go off in quick succession.

"Luzetta." Ma demanded, close to tears herself. "What's wrong. Tell me, please." Luzetta was scaring her half to death, but Luzetta was lost in her own madness. Suddenly, Luzetta pushed past the women and took off from the house through the back door. She ran as fast as she could to the tree standing proudly over her father's grave. With as much strength as she could muster, she tore off a branch and kneeled down to the ground, stabbing it with all her might again and again and again.

"What's going on?" Trent and Aaron rode in.

"It's Luzetta. She's gone mad." April exclaimed in fright. Trent jumped off his horse and ran through the house, stopping at the room littered to the hilt with papers and such. He heard the ranting and screams from the back of the house.

Trent opened the back door to see his mother and Wind In Hair standing over Luzetta who was stabbing the ground with all of her might, flinging chunks of dirt at the stone grave marker in front of her. She screamed, kicking the headstone, spewing words that were sacrilege coming from her innocent mouth. Her stark outrage and vulgar words spoke volumes to those gathered to witness it. Several moments passed before Trent shook off his shock and dismay and took matters into his own hands.

She didn't hear Trent call to her. She didn't feel the bands of steel wrap around her. She was being dragged away from the grave and all she did was kick and scream. After Trent got her into the house and pulled her in to sit in his lap, Luzetta stopped kicking and screaming, but she was crying uncontrollably, pushing her face into Trent's Chest.

"It must be something pretty bad, if she got that upset." Ma stated worriedly. April searched around and found the book that Luzetta had been reading. "Where are the others?"

"At the jail baby-sitting." He confirmed. "We got them all." He said into Luzetta's hair. He didn't feel much like celebrating the good luck they had tonight.

"Ma." April gestured to Ma to follow her into another room. They left Luzetta in Trent's capable hands to search the book. "I think this is what Luzetta found." April read aloud as Ma listened.

"Oh my God." Ma's knees went weak. She sat down with a plop. "Do you think?" She asked April, knowing they thought the same thing.

"I'm guessing, but there is one way to find out for sure." April followed Ma and sat down, needing relief from the weight of the situation. "We need to ask Luzetta if there are any pictures of her father."

"Maybe later." She said, still white and reeling from the passage written.

Trent took Luzetta to their room and shut the door. She'd stopped crying, but the shock was putting her in a catatonic state. Trent stood her up beside the bed. As he began unbuttoning Luzetta's dress, he watched to see if she would react, come back to reality. She only had a blank stare in her sad, sweet eyes. Trent took off her dress, leaving her under things on, and slid the night gown on her. It was just like dressing one of his nephews or nieces. He gathered up her sleeve and pulled her hand through. Luzetta let it fall to her side.

"Come on Luzetta. Let's lay down for a while. Everything will look better to you in the morning." Trent swung her legs up and placed her on the far side of the bed. Luzetta had been quiet, except for the occasional hiccup. He lay beside her wondering what could have put her in such a state. When Trent was positive she was asleep, he crept out of the room in search of an answer.

Trent walked into the living room and looked at the four sitting at the kitchen table. By the looks on their faces, he wasn't sure he wanted to go into the kitchen. He decided to, against better judgment, for Luzetta's sake. He searched his mother's face, only seeing a combination of pain, grief and confusion. She could barely look him in the eye.

In the middle of the table between them all was a little brown, leather-bound book that kept everyone's attention. Trent sat silently, waiting for someone to speak.

"We found out" Aaron said solemnly to his hands, not wanting to look at Trent "that Luzetta found her father's diary." He continued slowly. "He wrote it before Luzetta came along. Trent" he took a deep breath in sorrow "I think that her father was John Beck." Aaron let the information sink in before looking at Trent.

"Are you sure?" He asked, breathlessly.

"Yeah. He gives dates and places and money amounts at first, then he goes into detail. He described things he had done to people. To our father, to Sam's brother, to Luzetta's parents." There was no denying the book belonged to Butcher Beck. What amazed everyone was that the man could have raised a daughter who was as gentle and kind as Luzetta.

"Sitting here" Ma began "I began to wonder if she wasn't his saving grace." She said with tears in her eyes. "He said he knew instantly when he picked her up that he was a changed man." She choked out, not believing a man as ruthless as Butcher Beck could have ever been anything but evil.

"But it doesn't make sense." Trent argued. "He hadn't changed, because he kept on with the robberies and killings, just not as much." He interjected. "I think he wanted a family and knew he wasn't going to get it the old-fashioned way."

"I think it's destiny." April said, fingering the book as if to make sure it was real. "She wasn't meant to be killed with the others that day. She must have had a purpose for living, to be taken by him." She sniffed. "Maybe it was a way to redeem himself. Luzetta said he was the town doctor and had taught her many things." She rambled on. "Or" she thought "maybe it was that she was to find this book and see to it that those men got what they deserved."

"No. I don't believe that. I've never been a believer in destiny. You make out of life what you can." Trent shook his head in rejection to the idea.

"But we'll be needing that book for evidence." He reached out and took the book, flipping through the pages. He came to the part Luzetta found and read it. Trent's heart broke for her. To find that the man you loved and adored and idolized had been a murderer and a thief was hard enough. It was something more unnerving to find out that he killed your parents in cold blood and took you for his own. It would be, in Trent's mind, just as shocking as watching the murder take place.

Trent hoped that Luzetta would let him help her through this. For now he wasn't going to leave her side while she needed him. It would take the hand of God himself to take him away from her right now. Trent excused himself and returned to their bedroom. Luzetta was still in the position he left her in. Although he wasn't sure she was asleep, he was hoping she was. Sleep would be her only reprieve right now and he would be there when she woke up.

Trent undressed and slipped between the covers as quietly as he could. He wrapped his arms around her and held her tight all night long, listening to her soft, even breathing.

The next morning, Trent woke up with Luzetta still in his arms. She hadn't even stirred. He looked to see if she was still asleep. Her eyes were wide open, staring at the wall in silence. Trent kissed Luzetta's shoulder and tried to think of something to say. He knew her feelings would still be raw.

"I need to get out of here." She whispered to Trent.

"Okay. I'll get up." He mistakenly thought.

"No. I mean I need to get away from this house, away from this town." She clarified. Trent understood her feelings.

"Okay." He agreed. "I'll take you home." Home. He was dying to take her home, to give her all she wanted, all she needed.

"Yes. That would be nice." She said blandly. There was a long stretch of silence, cutting the two apart from each other. Trent wanted to get her back.

"What are you thinking?" He asked, knowing that it would be of the man she once knew.

"I don't know who I am." She said after a while. "What is my real name? Who were my real parents? Do I have brothers and sisters?" All very good questions. Trent was determined to know the answer to every last question she raised. Luzetta turned to look at Trent.

"I know who you are. You are Luzetta Longwood, wife to Trent Longwood." He said, kissing her softly. "And don't you ever forget that."

"Thank you." She said, having a sense of belonging that she needed right now. She needed to rely on the new family she recently gained and knew it would get her through this. Trent held Luzetta until they smelled the bacon frying. It was too tempting to pass up.

When Luzetta appeared in the kitchen, everyone was instantly tongue-tied. They didn't know whether to say something or just keep their mouths shut, so most of them just kept their mouths full as an excuse to keep quite.

"Did you sleep any?" April asked with concern, noticing the circles around Luzetta's eyes.

"As well as can be expected." She answered as she bit off a piece of bacon and held on to a warm cup of coffee. "Thank you for being there for me last night." She said, not mentioning how horrible she really felt.

"Don't mention it. That's what family is for." April said, not thinking about her former family member betraying her as he had.

"Trent told me you caught the whole gang last night." She said to Aaron as he shoveled in another bite. He bobbed his head up and down until he could clear his mouth.

"We did. It was pretty close, though. It looked like they had packed up everything to set out at first dawn." He commended. "Thanks for the heads up." He was looking at her as if she were suddenly someone he could talk to freely, not as before when he more or less talked through Trent."

"Tell me something, Aaron. I want an honest answer." She asked him directly. He looked at her, knowing what she was going to ask. "Do you think my father was this Beck guy you were talking about?" She asked.

"What makes you think that?" He knew she was as sharp as a tack and there wasn't a doubt in his mind she saw the light last night.

"Because of what he wrote about. I'm positive he wrote the book because it's in his handwriting. Sam said that Beck knew just where to cause the most pain and the slowest death. A doctor would know that type of thing. I'm also guessing that you hadn't seen much of Beck's work recently. That's probably because he died sixteen months ago." She concluded.

"It's my opinion that he was more than likely John Beck" He confirmed after much consideration of the impact his words might have "but it would be better if there were some picture of him you could show us. Just to confirm." He offered. Luzetta thought, searching in her mind the last time she'd seen the only picture she had of her father.

"I can even give you more than that." She said, racing off to her room, pulling out her bottom drawer and withdrawing a box. April, Ma, Aaron and Trent had followed. "I have a picture of him with every man you caught last night. He said he didn't like this picture because it was before he grew a beard and it made him look like a little boy." Luzetta flipped through letters and papers she kept, stopping two thirds the way through and drew out a picture. Momentarily looking at it before handing it over, Luzetta took one last glimpse of the men she once cherished.

Chapter Thirteen

All four people scrunched together, angling and squinting to see the picture Aaron held. Ma turned away as soon as she saw him. There were Six men in the formal picture. Linus Fort, Manny Wainright and George Carbaugh were standing behind Russ Turner, Luzetta's father and Mack Crinshaw sitting on a couch. It was the small man sitting dead center that captured their attention. His black eyes and haunted features stared back at them. Ma couldn't bare to look at him more than a second.

Trent looked up at Luzetta, who was standing before them as if to be handed a verdict. "I'm afraid you're right. It's him all right." She looked momentarily shaken. Trent took her hand and led her out of the room.

"I'm sorry." She apologized.

"What for?" Trent asked

"I was just thinking about myself and not you or your family. How is Ma taking this?" She asked with concern in her eyes.

"Oh, Luzetta." He said, pulling her into him. "You are always thinking of others. Ma knew who killed our Pa when it happened." He comforted. "We are just so worried about you finding all this about your father." Trent pushed a stray hair from Luzetta's eye. "Your eyes have lost a little bit of their sparkle." He gazed down at the woman he knew he was madly in love with.

"I know." Her mouth, still unsmiling, was still just as enticing. He kissed her gently. She laid her head on his chest, hearing his heartbeat in perfect rhythm. "I'm scared, Trent." She admitted.

"What are you scared of?" He asked, stroking her back.

"I've had a past full of lies and a future that I have no idea what to do with." Luzetta heard the growl that she became to understand.

"Don't worry. We have the rest of our lives to make your future the happiest time of your life." He smiled. She looked up to him with her heart in her eyes.

"I love you, Trent." She said, not knowing how he would react.

"I love you, too." There was no tearing them apart, no talk of divorce, no pushing away. They stood staring into each other's eyes, seeing their future together. It was the sniffling from the doorway that broke their concentration. Ma and April had been watching and listening as they declared their love to each other.

"And that is the way it should be." Ma pronounced.

"Amen." April seconded. Luzetta looked back at Trent.

"How soon can we leave?" She asked Trent.

"How soon do you want to go?" He countered.

"I want to get as far away from here as soon as possible." She urged. "I need to get away from here." She pleaded. He held her and knew why Luzetta needed to get away, even if she didn't. He could feel and see her newborn sense of fear.

"You start packing. Me and Aaron are going in to see the others and I'll tell them what's going on." He began withdrawing from her. "Don't leave without me."

"I wouldn't dream of it." She confessed.

Trent and Aaron passed Mrs. Johensen on her way out of the jail. Looking at Trent rather peculiarly, Mrs. Johensen began walking a little faster as she headed for the other side of the street.

"An admirer?" Aaron asked as he watched the plump woman hustle it across the street.

"I'm afraid so." Trent replied. Sam, Isaac, Clint and Tray were lounging around the sheriff's office like cats in their den. Tray had his feet up on the desk as Sheriff Johensen had done while warming the roost.

"Now, don't this look like a fun crowd." Aaron gazed over the bunch of tired men, ready for a warm bed.

"It'd be funner if I had me a woman like April or Luzetta to come home to." Tray said, sliding his feet off the desk. "Got a message from the Boss. He's sending one of his troops to take over for us. Should be here by morning."

"Good. Then you can give them this." Trent pulled out the book he had kept close in his possession at all times.

"What's that?" Sam asked, grabbing for it. Trent pulled it out of his reach just in time.

"This" he waved the book before everyone "is what is going to see every man in that room hang like a dog." He said. Taking a chair and turning it the wrong way and straddling it, Trent sat and opened the book. He looked at Sam, knowing this was going to effect him just as much as it effected his family. "Let me read a little excerpt from the book." Trent read the marked passage. As each sentence was read, the room grew silent, eyes began to enlarge. Trent finished reading and closed the book.

"That's impossible." Clint whispered.

"At least we know why the Carbaugh boys kept their hands to themselves." Isaac concluded.

"How's that?" Tray asked.

"They were too scared of Luzetta's father to do anything." He said. "I wouldn't want to piss off Butcher Beck because I know I'd end up dead." Everyone knew it had to be so.

"Does Luzetta know?" Sam asked. Trent nodded. "How is she?" Genuine concern filled Sam's voice.

"She took it pretty hard. She wants to leave." He said. "I'm taking her home as soon as these dirt bags are taken away."

"I don't blame her." Sam said. "Have you thought about trying to find out who her parents were?" He asked.

"Just came from the telegraph office and wired a friend of mine. He should be able to find out something." Trent flipped the book end over end, back over front, contemplating deep thoughts.

"What's on your mind?" Sam asked with his usually brotherly tone.

"I was just thinking" Trent replied "how someone like Butcher Beck could have raised a fine woman like Luzetta." He pondered. "I can't believe someone like that could raise a child with the love and compassion Luzetta said he gave her."

"Well, friend, I guess that will always mystify us." Sam shook his head and put a hand on Trent's shoulder. "Just be thankful everything turned out right."

"I guess you're right." Trent sighed.

It only took Luzetta a few hours to pack. She wasn't taking any of the furnishings or memoirs. All she cared to take was her clothes, her medical supplies and medicines and the medical books and journals she used for reference. Even though it didn't sound like much, Trent had the entire wagon filled with Luzetta's belongings.

Wind In Hair helped with the packing and prepared foodstuffs for the trip. Luzetta noticed that Wind In Hair had assumed her responsibility to stay with Luzetta. "Wind In Hair." Luzetta took the woman to the side for privacy. "I just want you to know that I value your help and friendship, but I must ask you something. Is it your choice to go away with us, or it is out of obligation?"

"Both." Wind in Hair replied.

"I just want to make sure that this is your choice. That no one is forcing you to do something you don't want to do." Luzetta didn't want to see the old woman unhappy.

"I want to go." Wind in Hair smiled. "You need me more than Piqui."

"What do you mean?" Luzetta's brows furrowed at her comment.

"You are young, my Golden Hair." She fell back into speaking her native tongue as she took Luzetta's face into her palms. "New bonds need help to thrive. Houses and babies are a lot of work, too." She added, making Luzetta smile and blush.

"Yes, I am looking forward to having a family of my own, now that my fears are put to rest." She thought of all the heartache she had when she thought her lot in life would be as a barren spinster, destined to live alone without the love of another.

"And I wish you good fortune in producing healthy children. But I don't want you to worry about me. I am content with my new family, too." The two women embraced and knew that they were truly where they belonged. Luzetta, who had grown up motherless, now had two mothers, Wind In Hair and Ma, to look after her and to teach her the things a mother teaches a daughter.

"Thank you, from the bottom of my heart." Luzetta said, tearfully.

Aaron and Clint took Luzetta to town where she needed to tie up some loose ends before leaving. The first stop was the post office. Junior, who was tagging along, begged to go in with her.

"I would be mighty obliged if you would. A lady needs to be escorted by a gentleman from time to time." She said with a smile that didn't quite reach her eyes. She was helped down out of the wagon by Aaron. Junior jumped down on his own, showing her what a big boy he was becoming.

"Luzetta?" Junior looked up, squinting his face against the sun.

"Yes, Junior?" She replied as if addressing a real gentleman.

"Do you think Trent would mind if I held your hand?" He asked earnestly. "Seeing as you can't hold my arm without walking on your knees." He explained.

"No, Junior." She said, returning the smile she saw from the corner of her eye that Aaron was giving. "I don't think Trent would mind at all. Actually, I think he just might thank you for doing so." She qualified.

Junior's large smile covered his face as he took Luzetta's hand almost matched his father's prideful one. He was quite the gentleman when he walked up to the door and opened it for her, allowing her to enter before he did. He resumed holding her hand after closing the door, joining her in line behind the other patrons, the smile still plastered on his face.

There were three people in the Postmaster's office when they arrived. Every single one of them turned to look at her. She felt the discontented air grow thick. What had she done now? Had they found out who her father was? The thought that Trent or any of his family disclosing that sort of personal information caused Luzetta a moment of pain before she rationalized that they would never do such a thing.

Two more people arrived after Luzetta and Junior. They, too, stared at her as if she were a traitor. Luzetta was now very uneasy, knowing how easily the townsfolk got stirred up over things. She thought back to the other day when she intervened on Dr. Schumaker's attempt to deliver Elise's baby. She was sure that was it. Dr. Schumaker was probably singing her damnation throughout town and the townsfolk were lapping it up without proof positive to his allegations.

It was now Luzetta's turn to be helped by the postmaster. Junior studied the portly man with gray hair, a long mustache that flared out and came to points, and small, round spectacles. The Postmaster was looking at Luzetta like his mother looked at him when he was in trouble.

"Next." He said in a blustery voice. When Luzetta stepped forward, the man looked around her to the next in line. "I said 'Next'." The person directly behind Luzetta stepped around her without hesitation. With eyebrows furrowed she looked at the two men conducting business and the one behind her.

Again, when it was her turn the Postmaster ignored her. "Luzetta" Junior began "what's wrong with that man?" He asked with a perplexed look on his face.

"Well" Luzetta tried to gather herself "I guess some people enjoy being rude." She said it loud enough for everyone to hear. They didn't look up or pay her any heed. After waiting outside for Luzetta and Junior for longer than it should have been, Aaron came for them. He noticed people coming and going long after Luzetta had gone in.

Aaron entered the office and surveyed the situation. Luzetta had an anxious, bewildered look on her face and Junior was clearly disappointed with something. His eyes were saddened, but he wouldn't leave Luzetta's side.

"Daddy. This man won't take care of Luzetta. He's ignoring her." He said, pointing at the Postmaster. Aaron, who was just as big and intimidating as Trent, walked up to the postmaster, looking down at the man.

"What's going on here?" Aaron said, adding enough menace to his voice to make the man visibly cower.

"Nothing." He said, watching Aaron from the corner of his eye as he waited on Luzetta.

"I just have two requests. I have this letter to mail." She said, hesitating long enough to indicate he was to do this task first. After he was finished, she went on. "Secondly, I have need to post a forwarding address for any mail that may come this way."

"You're leaving?" He said with a too bright smile.

"Yes, sir. I'm traveling with my husband and his family to their home." Luzetta handed the man a piece of paper with the address on it. "Thank you."

She added hesitantly before turning her back to him and heading out the door. No need to pay rudeness for rudeness. What kind of lesson would that be for little Aaron junior?

"Doesn't look like there would be any love lost by leaving here." Aaron said as they stepped out onto the weathered boardwalk. When Luzetta didn't answer he looked back at her. She was looking over toward the jail. Aaron saw the longing in Luzetta's eyes and knew she was experiencing some of the loss all over again and knowing that the culprits were just down the way.

"Aaron?" She began, not knowing how he would react to her request.

"I don't see any problem with that." He said, reading her thoughts.

Luzetta stepped into the jailhouse. She didn't look around. She didn't look at Sheriff Johensen. She stared at the door she knew hid the only family she'd known. After a short repartee between the men, Sheriff Johensen unlocked the door to reveal nine caged animals lounging as best they could in their tiny cubicles. Linus Fort was looking right at Luzetta as the door opened. Linus nudged Manny Wainwright, who then turned to see Luzetta standing just outside the door. Soon everyone was staring back at Luzetta, knowing she'd learned of their transgressions.

"Luzetta." George was the first to speak up. He came to the bars and held out his hand, beckoning for her to come. Begging for the chance to explain. Luzetta warred with herself for only a second before she was told George couldn't be trusted, so she was not allowed to go past the threshold. Tears strained to burst forth from Luzetta's eyes.

"I trusted you." She whispered, fighting her emotions.

"I know." George said in defeat.

"Why?" She asked as she scanned the faces she came to love and trust. No one gave her an answer. Maybe it was because saying something would be admitting guilt, which no one wanted to do with a US Marshall standing just feet away. "Well" she said after she realized she wasn't going to get an answer "I just came to say good-bye." She was losing her battle over her emotions. "And to say thank you for keeping me safe all these years." Nine pairs of eyes looked at her as if she had lost her mind. "Even after learning all that I have, part of you will still be in my heart."

Luzetta turned and practically ran out to the wagon with Aaron at her heels.

"What's wrong, Luzetta?" Junior asked as he saw the tears in her eyes. "Why are you crying?"

"It's just that... . I am no good at good-byes." Luzetta said after wiping her eyes and composing herself.

Chapter Fourteen

"Hey, Wait up!" Henry Stout was riding hard and fast toward Luzetta.

"Aaron, slow down. Something's wrong." Aaron and Junior both turned to see the rider with a cloud of dust kicked up behind him. It was mere seconds before Henry caught up with them.

"Evn'in" Henry tipped his hat to Luzetta "hate to be the bearer of bad tidings, but I thought you should be the first to know that Doc Schumaker is rilin' up some folks against you at the church." Henry took a much needed breather before continuing. "He came into town like the devil himself was eatin' at his heels. Seems he came from Victoria Hamlin's place. I don't know nothin' more. I 'spect you auta see what's goin' on."

"How long ago was this?" Aaron asked after seeing Luzetta's face turn red at the mention of Dr. Schumaker and her friend in the same breath.

"About half an hour I 'spose. I heard that snippity Mrs. Criswald say that an emergency town meeting had been called and it was about Mrs. Longwood."

"Thank you, Henry." Luzetta said as she grabbed the reins out of Aaron's hands and drove off in the direction of Victoria Hamlin's home.

Victoria Hamlin laid in her bed, white with shock. She said nothing. She laid on her back with a blank expression on her face. She blocked out the noises her mother was making while busying herself. Milicent Bradford didn't know how to make her daughter's pain go away. All she could do is to tell Victoria that time will tell. There will be other children. Milicent would never tell her that she would forget the precious life that was lost, but she knew that time was the only balm that could soothe away the sharp edges of pain.

Milicent was sweeping the porch that hadn't a speck of dirt on it when the carriage pulled into view. She was unsure how to react to seeing Luzetta. Dr. Schumaker was adamant about the child being Luzetta's fault, but Milicent knew stillbirths happened all the time. Still, not like this, not this child. The wound was raw and she couldn't help but sound caustic as she greeted the two adults and small child.

"Mrs. Bradford." Luzetta approached the woman strangling the broom handle. "What happened? Is Victoria all right?"

Pain shown in the woman's eyes. Bright and clear. Luzetta recognized the emotion and held her breath. "Yes, she's in bed now." Looking away from the woman accused of such a horrendous deed. "I'll take you to her. You will want to see her."

Luzetta left Aaron and Junior as she walked back with Victoria's mother. The flattened abdomen was the first thing Luzetta noticed, then the empty arms, then the blank stare of sorrow, pain and rage.

"Where is the child?" Luzetta whispered.

"Laid out in the next room." She said after turning away from the room. Luzetta followed Mrs. Bradford. The white sheet covering the form was larger than that of a child. Was it laid out with a memento? The rag doll Victoria painstakingly stitched for months, wiling away the last month of her miserable pregnancy?

Luzetta could not have been more shocked if someone had shot her. She stared at the form in front of her. She couldn't even register it at first. After the shock cleared she knew exactly what she was looking at. It was rare. Very rare. They were conjoined twins. They were facing each other, sharing every vital part but their brains. They were attached from their collar bone to their pelvis. Their angelic faces were pressed together at the cheeks. Each had their own set of arms and legs. It literally looked like they were hugging each other.

"I have never seen anything like this. I supposed you haven't either." Mrs. Bradford said from the doorway. Luzetta knew this would be hard for anyone to take.

"Where is Charles?" Luzetta said without looking up.

"Off with the Doctor. He has Charles believing that you did all this." There was an awkward silence that Luzetta figured Milicent was trying to make her mind if she believed it too. "I don't know how this came about, but I suppose there is an explanation for everything in the world." Milicent left the room, not being able to bear being in the same room as the unexplainable, the unbelievable, the unknown.

Aaron's footsteps came in shortly after Milicent left. "Stillborn?" He whispered. Luzetta remained silent for just a moment, deciding how to explain.

"The children are dead, yes." She covered the children and began removing her hat, placing it on a chair. "I need you to get my medical bag.

"Anything else?"

"Place a telegraph to the American Medical Board in New York and tell them that we have a case of conjoined twins. They will want to come out and examine the children." Luzetta had spoken in such a calm manner that Aaron had to digest the information for a moment.

"What are conjoined twins?"

"It's when twins are formed inside the mother, but don't completely separate. Like when two tomatoes grow in close quarters." Passing him, Aaron looked puzzled still, but kept his thoughts to himself.

Victoria lain silently through the physical exam. Luzetta explained that she wanted to make sure that she was recovering after such a difficult birthing. Victoria sustained substantial tearing, but the stitching was impeccable. She would be able to have more children. It was the emotional scarring Luzetta was worried about.

"Victoria" Luzetta sat beside her on the bed "I would like to talk about your children." Victoria looked at Luzetta with such a horrified look, it almost hurt.

"What do you mean children?" Her voice was weak and raspy, but Luzetta heard pain, confusion and, most of all, the disbelief.

"Your children, Victoria, are what is called conjoined twins. It's very rare. Only a handful of cases were documented throughout the entire world." Luzetta let the news sink in. "I know this is hard for you, but I took a look at them. I found ... "

"But Dr. Schumaker said that it was a freak of nature. He called it a two headed beast that could have only been created by one who practices witchcraft." It didn't surprise Luzetta that the doctor was still against her, but he was clearly not a man of science if he would reduce natural rarity with such superstition and contempt.

"I can safely say that it is definitely not witchcraft. What happened was when your children were formed they were stuck together and grew together, like two tomatoes that grow off the same vine close together. I assure you that there was no way of knowing something like this would happen, but it will not happen again." They talked for quite some time, letting Victoria cry and express her sorrow. Milicent joined them a bit later and discovered what seemed like the most logical explanation for the child-creature.

"I want to look at them." Milicent and Luzetta looked at her with surprise and hesitation. "I want to see this rare miracle." She implored. "Please."

"She's strong." Milicent said to Luzetta. "I think she will be more at peace if she said good-bye, and to let her know she is part of history as one of the women who birthed conjoined twins.

Luzetta gathered up the children and gently placed them in their mother's arms, letting their heads rest on her arm naturally. Their multiple arms and legs were small and easily fit against her breast and belly.

"I have to name them, mother." Victoria spoke with tears in her eyes and her heart in her throat. "I want to give them names to remember." She stroked them. Their faces she committed to memory. Milicent clipped a bit of their hair and tied it in ribbons for the remembrance book she made for the baby. "Luzetta, is it all right if I see what color of eyes they have?"

"Yes. Let me help you." The first baby had brown eyes, but the second had blue. After a while, when Victoria said her good-byes and had fallen asleep with the children in her arms, Milicent took the children and placed them back in the next room. "Mrs. Bradford, I need your help." After taking some instruments from her bag, Luzetta stood beside the children.

"My God, you aren't going to dissect them now are you?" Milicent gasped.

"No, nothing like that." Luzetta didn't have the heart to tell Victoria what would happen once the medical experts arrive. "I just noticed something. These are supposed to be identical twins, yet they have different eye color." They opened each eye and found the left eye was brown and the right was blue. But the thing that really upset her was the small spots on the whites of their eyes. Luzetta looked closely and made sure both sets of eyes were the same.

"What is it?" Milicent asked as Luzetta acted as if she were to behead someone. "There must be a reason you are looking so pale." Milicent stood in the doorway and blocked Luzetta's way. Luzetta wasn't even sure she could speak any time soon. She brushed passed Milicent and walked into the dining room. Trent was waiting with Aaron and April, who automatically stood at the sound of footsteps.

"What's going on?" Trent said as he neared Luzetta. She was furious.

"I can't talk here." She whispered to him as she tied on her hat.

After saying good-bye to the puzzled Milicent with a promise to send word soon of any news, Luzetta directed Trent to turn the carriage around and head to town.

As they neared town they could see the lights burning high at the church. The doctor was high in his oratory of evil and damnation, with Luzetta and her witchcraft as it's source. Luzetta stood outside just a moment to listen an compose herself before entering.

Gasps sounded all around. How bold she is, they said. Satan gives her courage, they said. Don't let her speak, she may set a spell on us for talking down on her, one man said.

All the while she walked through the crowd listening to all the whispers and ridicule her eyes were trained on Dr. Schumaker. She paid no attention to the townsfolk she had treated that were now taking the opposing side. She paid no attention to Sheriff Johensen and his deputy leaning on the side door. She didn't even know if Trent, Aaron and April came in with her.

"Dr. Schumaker" she addressed the receding form of a man "would you care to tell all of these people where you got your license to practice medicine?" She said loudly enough for everyone around her to hear and hush others.

"New York." He said, puffing his chest out in bravado that didn't meet his eyes.

"Where in New York?" She countered. "What School? Who were your professors?"

"Why are you asking him this?" The minister had the right mind to ask.

"Because, anyone who has graduated Medical school within the last century would have recognized the case at the Hamlin's." Luzetta's eyes never left Dr. Schumaker's.

"What really happened at the Hamlin's?" The question was posed to Luzetta by the minister. "All we've heard was that you have been giving Victoria a tea, a potion, throughout her entire pregnancy and that caused her to produce a spawn of Satan. A two headed beast."

Luzetta shook her head, still not losing eye contact with her target. "Tell us, Dr. Schumaker, what is raspberry leaf tea used for?"

The doctor paled and began to visibly sweat. "Dear Lord, have you been giving a pregnant woman that have you? No wonder she had that demon child!"

"He's a crock!" A woman shouted from the back of the room. "A crock that had us believing he was a doctor. Every woman that has difficulty holding a baby knows to drink raspberry leaf tea. It keeps her from having contractions. Half the children here are because of that tea."

"Tell us, good doctor" Luzetta said with much more venom than anyone had ever heard her speak

"How did you determine that this child was a demon?"

"Wa, well... It was apparent."

"What was apparent to me, *Dr.* Schumaker, was that the only case of conjoined twins we will ever see has slipped through our fingers." Luzetta was yelling by the time she reached Dr. Schumaker.

"What's that?" Someone asked.

"A rare set of twins that are born stuck together." Luzetta answered, finally being able to break eye contact. "Very few, by that meaning only one set know to man, has ever lived."

"And the Hamlin twins died, right?" Sheriff Johensen asked, being drawn into the drama.

Luzetta pierced Dr. Schumaker with a cursed look of knowledge. She knew what he did.

"But I had to." He began. "As soon as I saw those two heads, I knew what I had to do." People began talking among themselves.

"No, Dr. Schumaker, you didn't. I saw the evidence of suffocation. They had to be drawing breath to suffocate." She was upon him again, not letting him flinch without her seeing it. "Which means there could have been a second pair of living conjoined twins. You just murdered the chance of a lifetime, Dr. Schumaker."

A mob of angry citizens ascended on the doctor. Sheriff Johensen arrested the doctor, charging him with murder. He would have added stupidity to the charge if it were a punishable offence. They jailed him and the last thing Luzetta heard was how the doctor was trying to turn the town into a possy to do that very thing to Luzetta.

"I hope you will stay on and be our Doc, Mrs. Longwood." The minister said.

"I'm sorry, but I've already made plans to move west with my husband and his family. I hope your next doctor turns out to be a capable one."

"Me too, seeing as the next doctor isn't for another fifty miles or so."

Chapter Fifteen

"What are you going to do with the house?" April asked Luzetta as they gathered the last of the provisions they needed for the trip.

"I signed the deed to the house and property over to the Piqui." She said, still full of raw emotion. "The lawyer in town wouldn't have taken kindly to that, so Sam and Trent signed as witnesses and I sent the deeds on to the title company. Everything should be in fine order. Now they have all the land." She said. "They can burn the house for all I care." Luzetta's acid tone told everyone exactly how she felt. Her hurt ran deep and would likely never fully recover from such a blow.

Trent helped Luzetta into the wagon seat before climbing in beside her. Ma, April and the boys were all ready to go in the wagon in front of them. Wind In Hair rode in the back of Luzetta and Trent's wagon, making sure everything was traveling well. The five men on horseback mounted and settled in for the ride home. Aaron gave a big whoop and a whistle to signify the trip had begun.

Luzetta hadn't even looked back at the house she was raised in as she was leaving. The only thought that kept her from crumbling into tears was the hope that she received from Trent the night before. He didn't say anything to try and comfort her or give her reasons to change her feelings of the events that transpired in the past few days. He just held her. He didn't pressure her to fulfill her marital duties as she laid in his arms, spooned up against him. He just held her with quiet strength throughout the night. She drew from his strength and built hope on that strength, knowing she could rely on it's integrity, along with whatever she could muster, to make their future bright. Everything had changed. Everything was different. But she was forging along in her new life, with her new husband, with her new family.

The trip was off to a good start. The sky was blue and only intermittent fat, fluffy clouds stood in their way of sunshine warming their day. At the latter part of the first day, though, one of the wagon wheels came off and threatened to toss Wind In Hair and almost all of Luzetta's possessions out onto the road as it lurched under the weight. The men emptied the wagon and set the wheel, putting everything back in after the chore was finished. Luzetta thanked each one for their efforts in helping.

On the second day April began to feel sick, taking to laying down in the back of the wagon with the boys. She hardly ate anything. Aaron became worried.

"Luzetta, do you think she's okay?" He asked. Luzetta smiled at Aaron.

"Yes, she's fine." Luzetta consoled. "Just give her a little time and she will get over it." She said, knowing what was causing April's sickness, even though April was in denial.

On the third day, as they stopped for lunch, Luzetta offered to put Walter down for a nap while the others cleaned up and scouted the lay of the land.

Luzetta was on a mission to find out as much as she could about the unknown. She rummaged through her books as Walter settled in. When she found what she was looking for, she sat next to Walter, stroking the boy's back in a soothing motion. Luzetta read a book between glances over her shoulder. It intrigued her, and fascinated her, to learn about the male body.

"That is a horrible picture." April said from behind Luzetta, laughing as Luzetta slammed the book shut in her embarrassment. Luzetta turned a bright shade of red and stuffed the book under some covers.

"I'm sorry." She apologized. "I didn't know you were there."

"I came to check on Walter." She admitted. "Listen, I wouldn't lean too much on books when it comes to you and Trent." She said straightforwardly, ignoring Luzetta's blushes. "When you and Trent get together it will all come naturally." She said. "Besides, if a man wrote that book and still drew man parts like that, he doesn't know what he's talking about."

Luzetta couldn't help but remember seeing Trent walk about naked in her house, delirious with fever. She also couldn't keep her blushing under control with the second memory of waking on top of him. "Just rely on the God given drive He gave you and let your heart guide you along." She said, leaving Luzetta with that advice. She didn't open the book back up.

On the third day, Trent noticed Luzetta hadn't been as uptight or wringing her hands as much as she had at the beginning of the trip. He knew from her facial expression that she was thinking of her father and was still in her grieving process. He just hoped she didn't turn bitter, but remember the good things that came from their relationship. Even though her father was a criminal, he was someone she had loved and respected, almost idolizing him.

Later that night Trent and Luzetta laid beneath the wagon, effectively separating themselves for some privacy that they both sorely needed. She'd taken her hair down from under her bonnet after supper. He watched her brush out the tangles as she stared into the fire, but not really seeing it. Luzetta braided it up for the night. Trent wished he could run his fingers through the golden curly locks again. The memory of finding her sleeping on top of him that first day came in full force, but he held it in check.

"So what is in that thousand yard stare? What are you seeing?" He whispered, trailing a finger along her cheek.

"I was imagining our life together, what our home looks like." She answered. "Describe it to me."

"It's not much. I bought it from an old lady that moved to Texas some years ago. It's a two story house with lots of windows and large rooms." He explained. It sounded spectacular to Luzetta.

"I don't have much by way of furnishings, but that will change." Luzetta laid down beside Trent, reveling in the feel of his embrace as he talked. "It isn't far from Ma's either. You'd like it." He smiled. "April called it a woman's house. I don't exactly know what that means, but it works for me."

"And ... what about the townsfolk?" She asked timidly.

"They're nice folk. I think you'll like them. And I know for a fact that they are going to love you." Trent turned Luzetta so she was facing him. He stroked her hair, placing soft kisses along her face. "We have a town doctor, but he's older than dirt. His spectacles are as thick as my hand. He's still sharp as a tack."

"He sounds nice." Luzetta reveled in Trent's loving attentions. "This is nice." Trent loved kissing Luzetta, teaching her how to kiss him back. Soon their kisses became heated, exciting, fierce in it's sensual grip.

Trent pulled away, breathing hard with excitement. He had to sit up, pull himself together. "I didn't mean to start something I didn't intend to finish tonight. I didn't want it to work out this way."

"I don't understand." Luzetta said, slightly shaken by his rejection.

"I don't doubt it." After getting a grip on his self-control once more, he laid down beside Luzetta. "I don't want your first time, our first time together, to be on hard ground under a wagon with our family only feet away." Trent cupped Luzetta's cheek in his palm. She pressed her cheek into his hand, feeling the love he felt for her. "I want to be in the comfort of our home, in a nice soft bed, tucked away where I can have you to myself."

"That sounds perfect. It will be worth the wait." They laid spooned together, talking about their future, their plans, their hopes, and their desires until they fell asleep.

Trent was right when he said she would like the house. The two story house was white with green shutters and flower boxes around the house. The wrap around porch was perfect for sitting around, visiting with friends and family. Inside, the rooms were large, although vacant as they were, with wood floors and large bay windows with seats. The large kitchen boasted an equally large cook stove and built-in washbasin.

"What is this?" She asked as she approached the sink.

"It is an indoor water pump." He explained, pumping the lever and watching the water flow out of the mouth.

"This is so great." Luzetta went from room to room. "A living room, dinning room and a kitchen, all huge." Trent furnished the house with pieces he picked up here and there. "Are the bedrooms just as large?" She asked.

"Just about. There are four upstairs." Trent took Luzetta's hand and led her up the staircase with a grand banister. The first three rooms were completely bare, but grand all the same. Each one had their own fireplace. "This is our room." Trent said, opening the door. Luzetta paused before entering the room. The largest room of all. The bed was larger than her bed by twice as much. Luzetta was sure the head and footboard were just as old and sturdy as the house, but not the least unattractive. Trent had a chest of drawers and a large, full-length mirror that sat at the side.

"This is very nice." She said, swallowing hard. Trent didn't seem to notice her nervousness.

"There's something else I like about this house. It has it's own bathing room." He ushered her to the hallway and proudly opened the door. "Isn't it grand?" He asked her as she stared at the largest tub she had ever seen. It would accommodate most of Trent's length with no problem. The cast iron mammoth had four claw-shaped legs to support it.

"It must have taken ten men to get it up here." She guessed. She was looking forward to using it tonight.

After going through the house, Trent and Luzetta helped unload everything out of the wagon. "I guess everything but my clothes will have to go into the living room." She said, not knowing quite what to do with all of her things.

"Maybe after you settle in you'll think about setting out your shingle." Trent suggested. Luzetta smiled, although it didn't quite meet her eyes.

"Maybe after settling in." She agreed.

Ma made a light supper and sent it over to Trent and Luzetta, knowing they were hard at work placing Luzetta's things in her new home. During the meal Trent talked about plans he had for the place.

"There are definite plans in the making for indoor plumbing. I would like to get one of those commodes that flushed like I saw back east. I also want to see about getting some running water to the bathtub. I heard that there is a way of getting hot water pumped right up to the tub without having to run it up there." Luzetta was in complete agreement. There would be no reason not to indulge in a bath every night if she had such a luxury. "I also want to do a bit more to make it more homey, but I never had the time or incentive." He said, casting a glance over to Luzetta, making her blush.

"You've done all right ... for a man." She smiled at her jibe. "It will come about before you know it." She confirmed confidently. "Us women will have this place shaped up in a jiffy."

"I'm terribly sorry that Wind In Hair has nowhere to sleep tonight." He said hanging his head low over the thought of her spending the night in the barn, albeit on her own suggestion.

"She knows that there isn't any bed in here." She consoled. "And, besides, I would rather sleep on barn hey than a cold, hard wood floor any day."

"I guess you're right." He said as he pushed his empty plate away from him. "Listen, I still have to tend to the horses. Is there anything you need? Any heavy boxes moved? I may be a while."

Luzetta looked at him knowing exactly what she wanted. "Yes. I planned on bathing tonight." Luzetta cleared her throat to dislodge the knot in her throat. "I was wondering if you wouldn't mind hefting a few buckets of water for me?"

"Certainly." Trent noticed how difficult it was for Luzetta to keep eye contact without giving herself away. It made him as skittish as a school boy.

After Trent filled the tub, he went to tend the horses. He couldn't stop thinking about Luzetta up in his bathing room, stark naked, enjoying a nice bath right now. He wondered if she was thinking of him. He could barely keep his mind on his chores, finishing in record time so he could go down to the creek and take a bath himself.

As Trent made his way up to the house he noticed all of the lamps but the one in the upstairs bedroom was blown out. He could imagine Luzetta's silhouette standing in the vast room they were to share tonight.

Trent suddenly became very nervous. He felt the butterflies in his stomach and the thud of an anxious heart. How ironic. He'd wanted her from the moment he laid eyes on her and actively pursued her up to this day. Why was he now starting to get cold feet? As Trent slowly climbed the stairs he knew why.

He wondered how much Luzetta knew about the act of mating. She had no mother or womanly influence, except Wind in Hair who may or may not have clued her in.

Approaching the open door of the bedroom, Trent stopped to look at Luzetta. She was sitting before the fire he prepared before he left her to bathe. She was using the fire's heat to dry her hair as she brushed it. She was wearing a white cotton night gown. Even though it covered her from neck to ankle, Trent could envision the body underneath, remembering seeing her in her father's snug-fitting long johns. Her long, curly blonde hair flowed down to her waist. Her profile was to him, allowing him to examine her face as she stared blankly into the fire. She was smiling an odd smile, as if she were remembering a special moment.

"A dollar for your thoughts." Trent said from the doorway, startling Luzetta. She made a small sound of surprise, then blushed.

"I thought it was 'a penny for your thoughts'." She corrected.

"I'm putting a higher bidding price for whatever was running through that beautiful mind of yours." Trent came closer. Luzetta noticed Trent's hair was wet. Apparently he washed up before coming back to the house. Trent held out his hands to her, pulling her up off the floor.

Trent was smiling a smile that Luzetta had never seen on him before. She wondered what he was thinking. "I'll tell you my thoughts if you tell me yours." She bargained.

"Okay." Trent's smile deepened as he took her into his arms. He was sure she could feel his heartbeat as she placed her hands on his chest. "You first."

"Actually, it's more of a confession." Luzetta cleared her throat. Trent kept quiet. "My curiosity got the best of me the other day." She began, staring into his chest at the third button from the top. "I . . um . . I decided to learn more about . . um . . male anatomy." She took a breath, careful not to look up at Trent's face. "I found a book that talked a little about the subject."

"And what did you find?" Luzetta could hear the smile in his voice.

"Not much." She began toying with his button. "April caught me."

Trent couldn't hold the startling whoop of laughter from coming out. "I can just imagine what she told you."

"She wasn't much help, either." Finally looking up at Trent with a frustrated look on her face. "There was a ... picture. April said that the artist didn't know how to draw."

"What else did she say?"

"She just said that when we ... get together" she blushed and went back to playing with his buttons "to not worry, that it will all come naturally and to show you what is in my heart."

"Smart woman." Trent interjected.

"So I've decided to do the only think I know how to do." Slowly, she looked up at Trent. "I'm going to examine you." Held within her eyes was a woman who knew what she wanted and was not going to give up until she got it. Determination was a trait Trent learned to recognize and respect at an early age.

Luzetta traced the outline of his muscles as they flexed. The restraint he displayed was physically apparent. Luzetta appreciated the tautness against her touch. The hard muscle bunching beneath her hand was something she remembered from when she woke up on top of him that first morning.

The glow of the fire played upon their skin as they took in the newness of their physical love. Trent was just as curious about Luzetta and she was about him. They went on exploring each other, reveling in the simplicity of their five senses.

Luzetta's stomach began uncoiling little by little. Trent showed her such tenderness and patience it almost made her cry. It must have been divine intervention that they met and married. Emotion swept over Luzetta as the man she loved, the one who saved her from herself, tortured her in so many magnificent ways.

Finally she was ready. The culmination of her love and the ebbing of her fears allowed her to release her deep seated tension, relax and concede to the desires Trent was stirring up within her.

It was beautiful. Each pinnacle and capitulation better than the one before. Each crescendoing to peaks never before reached. Reverence, awe and pure amazement flew about the room as they gave to each other, took from each other, worked vigorously toward the same goal.

Hours had passed before they tired and fell exhausted, spent in each other's loving embrace. They slept soundly until the fire died down and the chill stirred Trent.

As he woke with Luzetta's arm draped across his chest, her legs intertwined with his, snuggled up tightly against his side, he thought of the pure miracle that brought them together. The memory still fresh in his mind of when he woke to find this tiny morsel sleeping atop him. He lay staring at her for an exorbitant amount of time. Just watching her sleep.

"I promise, with all that I have to give, that I will always protect you. I will always keep you safe." He whispered with a lump in his throat and a tear in his eye. Never had he felt love this strongly. He knew she couldn't hear him, but that didn't matter. He had too much honor to let a little thing like that stand in his way. He would keep his promise to her if it were the last thing he ever did. He would gladly give his life for this amazing creature given to him.

Luzetta woke to Trent pressing a warm cloth to the tender insides of her legs. He smiled at her as he coaxed her legs apart to administer to her more intimate parts. "Are you sore?" He asked as he toweled her off.

"A bit." She didn't want to concentrate on the slight pressure of his strong hand or the crimson heat creeping up into her neck and face. Trent took her in his arms and held her close.

"It will be different the next time. You won't have any pain." He spoke softly into her ear, noticing it's rosy color.

"What about everything else?" She asked hurriedly, not realizing how eager her question sounded.

"The pleasure will be there. Better, even." Trent was intensely happy that Luzetta was able to enjoy making love with him. He could just imagine how interesting the future nights would be.

Luzetta came out of sleep still dreaming of last night's activities. She remembered examining Trent. Every single inch. It didn't stop her from wanting to learn more of her new husband. Of course it didn't come without a price. Trent made love to Luzetta two more times as a reprisal of her inquisitive nature.

"You are absolutely incorrigible!" He exclaimed with delight as the night grew on.

"I am not" she countered, letting her hands roam about where they pleased "I'm just persistent. And curious. And in love." She propped her chin on the back of her folded hands, gazing at Trent's ruggedly handsome face. His soft brown eyes speaking back to hers, telling her how he felt before the words spilled across his lips.

Chapter Sixteen

The next morning Trent and Luzetta slept in to midmorning. It was luxurious to wake up in Trent's arms. The warm sun streamed into the bedroom and across the bed.

"Ummm. Sunshine in the morning. I could get used to this." Luzetta purred as she stretched across Trent's naked form.

"I could definitely get used to this." Trent kissed Luzetta firmly, pulling her onto his chest. "Good morning, Mrs. Longwood. Did you sleep well?"

"Yes I did, Mr. Longwood." She smiled as she kissed his chest. The memories from last night's love making made her blush as she thought on how brazen she was with Trent, how brazen he was with her. It was so perfectly natural. She was glad they waited until coming home to share this experience. Somehow, she doubted that their love making would have been as carefree and natural anywhere else. "I want to wake up like this every single morning for the rest of my life." She said dreamily.

"I think I could accommodate that request." Trent pushed the blanket down to Luzetta's waist and began caressing her soft skin. "You are so soft. Just like a baby's skin."

Luzetta looked up sharply at Trent. Their eyes met. "Babies." She said, whisper soft.

"Babies." He echoed. They both began to smile at the prospect.

"I never thought it was possible. Any of this. Thank you." Luzetta's baby blues were turning misty with emotion.

Trent could only nod in acceptance. The lump forming in his throat forbade him to speak. Just thinking of Luzetta neck deep in the danger in made his stomach tighten and his heart race.

Trent watched as Luzetta moved away from him across the room, unashamed at her nakedness, reveling in her momentary lapse of self-consciousness. Her firm, naked bottom sauntered just as he imagined it would. She gathered some clothes and carried them to the wash basin. Her pert, young breasts were perfect. High, firm, perfectly rounded breasts topped with rosy nipples. Trent was blatantly staring at his wife's naked form as she performed her toilet in front of him without bashfulness.

Luzetta turned to see the hungry look in her husband's eyes as she was bathing. "I'm sorry, love. I don't think I can do any more love making. I'm sore as it is."

"Sore? How sore?" Trent's expression went from sultry to concerned before her eyes.

"Just enough to let me know I've had enough for now." Luzetta turned back to the task at hand. Luzetta dressed as fast as possible, not wanting to get caught up into lovemaking again. She left Trent as he reached for his pants. She headed downstairs with an appetite she never possessed before in her life.

"Good morning, Wind In Hair." Luzetta greeted her friend with a smile on her face.

"Good morning, Luzetta." Beaming back a smile so big it nearly took up her whole face. "I am glad to see you so late this morning." Wind In Hair took the blushing Luzetta by both hands, raising her arms in order to inspect her. Wind In Hair nodded her head. "Yes, I think we will have a baby by next summer." Luzetta grew even redder. "There is no shame in the wedding bed, Luzetta. Have no shame in it."

"I'm not ashamed, Wind In Hair. It's just that I am not used to people discussing ... baby making." She whispered.

"It is an age old practice. As old as time. Many women have done it before, many will do it in the future." Wind In Hair embraced Luzetta with joy. "Are you sore?"

Luzetta closed her eyes for the moment, hoping the embarrassment she felt didn't show in her eyes. "Yes, a little." "I have a balm you must use. The sooner the better." She pulled a small jar from her pocket of her dress. "Use this balm and your pain will disappear." Wind In Hair pressed the small jar in Luzetta's hand and left her standing in the hallway.

Luzetta was staring at the jar in her palm and was instantly transported back to the night before. She recalled Trent's tenderness and attentiveness. She had known no love as tangible as she experienced last night. Had she really done those things last night, had she acted as wanton as she remembered?

"Can I help you apply that balm?" Trent was standing at the top of the stairs leaning against the wall watching her with undisguised desire.

"No." She said, stuffing the jar into her dress pocket. She could feel her face burning bright and Trent's intent stare didn't help matters. She had to get out of his cross hairs before she burst into flames. She turned into the first room she crossed.

Luzetta stopped mid-stride when she caught sight of all the food laid out on the table, hutch and cook stove. There were two hams, one cooked chicken with all the dressings, three pecan pies, one sweet potato pie, pastries Luzetta didn't even know existed, and a bottle of whiskey. Luzetta was awe struck.

"Where did all this come from, Wind In Hair?" Luzetta said as she gravitated toward the delicious looking pastries.

"Strangers." She retorted. "The pies and pastries were on the back porch when I woke up. Other strangers brought the other gifts a short time ago." She watched Luzetta's face turn to ecstasy as she bit into a raspberry tart. "You will like your neighbors."

Trent strolled in just as casual as could be and poured himself a cup of coffee, grabbing a cream filled pastry before sitting at the congested table. "I couldn't agree more. Anytime anything happens, good or bad, the town has a habit of throwing food at the family involved." Trent took in the booty in his kitchen. "The hams are probably from the Prichards. They are a nice family you'll get to know real well. I think his wife has been pregnant every year I've known her. The chicken is from Mrs. Lorimere for sure. The pies are Etta Loraine's handiwork." Trent locked eyes on the whiskey bottle and grinned.

"What about the whiskey?" Luzetta asked as she noted the smile on Trent's face.

"That" he swallowed "could only be from Harold and Gerald. The two oldest coots this side of China." Trent picked up the bottle and shook his head. "They sure are a pair."

"Brothers?" Luzetta asked between bites.

"No, not in the true sense. They met when they were in their primer days. They used to mine coal down in Kentucky. Gerald saved Harold's life one day and they've stuck together since." Trent had to condense the story in order not to bore the ladies to death. They will get an ear full if they get within ten yards of either of the two anyway. Their way of telling their story is more colorful, especially if the two are together.

Luzetta was searching in the box of pastries for her second choice when a knock on the back door pulled her attention away. Wind In Hair opened the door to a boy who stood at the door with a note in his hand. He was practically beaming as he entered the kitchen.

"Grandma told me to give this note to one of you. It's an invitation for supper tonight." The boy said.

"Funny how you should know that, Matthew." Trent said as he was presented with the boy's back. He had already taken off toward his own house and running as fast as his little legs could carry him across the pasture.

"That was a quick how-do-you-do." Luzetta stood beside Trent to see the little boy running so fiercely.

"Oh, never mind him. He's what you call an overly literal child. I bet that his mother told him to deliver the note and head back home straight away." Trent lightly dismissed the child's behavior. "You will get to meet him and the rest of the family tonight." Trent looked back at the booty littering his - no, their - kitchen. "And a good portion of the neighbors if I had to venture a guess."

Chapter Seventeen

The gathering that night was a gala event with most of the townsfolk in attendance. It was their wedding party poorly disguised as a welcoming back for the family that was only gone for a few weeks. There was music, dancing, and food everywhere. Luzetta was enjoying herself immensely as she looked over the crowd of partygoers. People all around her were laughing and enjoying each other's company. Couples wondered off to distant corners, old friends drank together, children were skipping about.

"This is how it should be." Luzetta said out loud before she realized she was speaking aloud.

"Yes, I think so too." Luzetta hadn't heard Trent walk up to her, but she was glad to have him near.

"And to think that I never thought this was possible." She said with a hint of sadness in her voice. "I feel like the luckiest girl in the world."

"Before you get all teary-eyed on me." Trent bent Luzetta back deeply, supporting her back and head.

"I think I have something to say." Luzetta's heart pounded as Trent held her in his arms and descended upon her for a kiss.

It was a full minute before Luzetta noticed the clanking and clamoring accompanied by shouts and whistles bursting out at the newlywed kiss Trent was giving her. Trent was equally entranced, for as they realized they'd been spied, Trent brought Luzetta to a standing position and a twirl that took them to the other side of the trellis, effectively hiding them from the majority of the voyeurs present.

"Sorry about that." Both Trent and Luzetta were out of breath and entangled in each other's arms. "I didn't mean it to happen that way, kitten."

"No harm done." Luzetta had a hard time letting go of her new husband. Secretly she was hoping he would kiss her again. "They expect it, even hope for it. Did you think you could get away with not showing affection to your new wife with this crowd? They would pounded you soundly if you hadn't"

"You know them so well already." Trent pressed her firmly to his chest, smiling into her neck where he loved pressing his lips. Luzetta and Trent presented themselves back to the crowd holding hands and smiling as they made their way back through the crowd, accepting congratulations and well wishes from their fellow townspeople.

"Hey, did you hear?" Boyd Brewer said to his comrade, Luther Maxwell.

"Hear what?" Luther drank in any gossip Boyd would bring him.

"About Trent's new wife?" He asked, pushing his bowler's hat up with a filthy index finger.

"No, what?" By now Luther was foaming at the mouth awaiting the juicy morsel of information about the pristine beauty the marshal was parading around, gloating to everyone about his catch. She was a sight to see, all clean and fresh, and untouchable next to her husband.

"I heard she has a famous father." Boyd drew out the anticipation, loving every moment Luther was hungry for what he knew. "A *real* famous father." Luther was rubbing his grubby hands together hanging over every word. He could barely contain himself as Boyd paused for his dramatic unveiling. "Butcher Beck." He finally blurted, not able to hold out any longer.

Luther's face went slack in disbelief. "Not!" He barked. "There's no way *she* could be even slightly related to *Butcher Beck*." Luther shook his head in disbelief in the lie. "Butcher Beck was the most dangerous man in all these United States." Throwing his arms up in the air, Luther stalked away in effrontery.

"She is so!" Boyd called out. "I overheard Trent and Mr. Millson talking in his telegraph office just yesterday. Trent was saying the men they caught - the Carbaughs, Manny the Mangler, the whole gang - was keeping Luzetta tucked away safe because she was Beck's daughter and he wanted close tabs on all information about their transports and trials."

Luther stopped to listen to his friend, rubbing his stubble-covered chin pondering the words coming from his friend's mouth. "I still don't believe you." Luther eyed Boyd wearily. "I just don't. It's too wild of a yarn, Boyd."

"Well," Boyd thought "the only way we can be sure is if we ask her. We can slip over to her when Trent isn't around and ask her politely-like." It had never occurred to Boyd that there was no polite way to ask someone if their father was a murderer.

The boys set out to approach Luzetta when she was unattended. It almost didn't happen, with all the well-wishers and townsfolk wanting to find out all about their new neighbor, not to mention family that kept her within arms length. But the opportunity arose as she was saying her farewells and making her way to the carriage. Trent was making a second trip to into the house where wedding gifts materialized from smiling friends and family.

"Go, now!" Luther pushed Boyd toward Luzetta who stood by the carriage, waiting for her husband. The grubby boys didn't know how to act around such a woman, the daughter of a famous criminal. Awe struck them as she turned her eyes on the two teens who hem-hawed their way to her side.

"Ev'nin." The first one said. He was shorter than the second, but only by an inch or so. Luzetta noticed they had the same thickness of dirt covering them, though.

"Good evening." She replied with a smile on her lips and curiosity in her eyes. "Did you enjoy yourselves tonight?" She said when they didn't speak up.

"Yes, ma'am. The cake was 'spcially nice." Boyd rubbed his hands on his pants with nervous anxiety. "We was wantin', I mean we was wonderin'. Um." Boyd stammered.

"Yes?" Luzetta hoped to help the boy spit out what they wanted.

"We was hopin' you'd tell us somethin'." Boyd looked back nervously at his cohort.

"I would be glad to tell you anything. I would first need to know what it is you would like to know." Luzetta effectively shut Boyd's brain down by speaking directly to him, holding eye contact with him. She was the most beautiful woman he'd ever seen. He couldn't possibly ask her what he wanted to know.

Luther wasn't so inclined. With much impatience and a fare amount of less tact than Boyd would have asked, Luther blurted out the question. "Are you Butcher Beck's daughter?" He showed no signs of remorse at asking the heinous question. Luzetta only had time to raise her eyebrows and produce a small gasp of surprise before her husband took matters into his own hands. Trent grasped the back of the boys' shirts and escorted them away from his wife.

Trent took them far enough away from Luzetta that he could give the known troublemakers a earful. "You ain't got a lick of sense!" He accused. "I don't know if I should take you over my knee or call you out for disrespecting my wife." He said to the boys he had known all their lives. "You two misfits are going to grow up and quick. If I catch you ever talking to *anyone* - especially Mrs. Longwood - about this I will personally see to it that you do your growing up the hard way." He leaned over the boys to assert his power to carry through with his promise. "Do you understand?" He enunciated.

"Yes, sir." They said meekly.

"I can't hear you!" He shouted.

"Yes, Sir!" They shouted back with trepidation in their voices.

"Now," Trent continued, satisfied with the amount a fear they displayed "I want you to apologize to Mrs. Longwood. You will both be present at church this Sunday, clean and dressed in your Sunday best." Trent held up a silencing hand when the boys moaned in protest. "You will apologize after services in front of God and everyone. I mean it, Luther." Trent glared at the boy giving a hard look of rebelliousness. "You don't, and you know what is coming to you." Trent didn't have to tell the boys that he meant what he said. Trent was a man of his word and a U.S. Marshall to back it up. It was not good to cross him or any of his kin.

"Yes, Sir." They both said with as much enthusiasm as they could muster under the circumstances. They would have their tails tucked between their legs like whipped pups this Sunday or pay the price.

As Trent drove his silent wife back home, he wondered how many other encounters she would have to suffer under the same pretense of finding out if the truth be know of her past.

"How old were those boys?" She said breaking the silence that sat comfortable between them. "They seemed awfully young."

"Thirteen." Trent acknowledged their youth as a possible culprit in their actions tonight.

"I suppose they would be curious about someone like John Beck. He is famous all over, I suspect." She sat mulling over that fact.

"Don't worry about them. They are just ill mannered boys who ought to know better." Trent had known the boys were well on their way to a life of crime if their paths weren't straightened out. Their parents, poor and increasing their numbers without the ability to support them all, would rather see them take care of themselves as much as possible. One less mouth to feed. They had been on their own, so to speak, for well over four years now.

"I couldn't help but notice the layers of dirt on them. Do they have a home?" Trent was not surprised by the question. He was well aware that she thought of others before she thought of herself, and in doing so was setting herself up for a mighty task. Especially if she took those two boys on as subjects of charity.

"Yes, they have homes and families. They may need a little nudge in the right direction from time to time, but it is not for you to give Luzetta." The scornful tone in Trent's voice was well heeded. She would not concern herself with the boys and their thoughtless ways.

But she couldn't let it go.

Are you Butcher Beck's daughter?

It echoed in her head all night. She fell asleep hearing it. It haunted her dreams. It would not let her in peace. She looked thoughtfully into her plate of eggs, bacon and biscuits placed before her by Wind In Hair and wondered how it could be true.

After reading the passage in his handwriting, after seeing his picture with the others, after hearing the stories of Trent's family, Luzetta wondered how it all could have happened. How could she have been so blind?

She thought of Harriett Longwood, widowed with nine children to raise because of the greed and callous heartlessness of men. Men she'd known and cared for like family. How many other families had they destroyed? Her stomach rolled at the prospect of the far-reaching loss they caused.

Trent could not stand looking at his despondent wife any longer. Even Wind In Hair could not distract Luzetta from her transparent train of thought.

He took Luzetta's hand and pulled her outside into the sunshine and fresh air.

"If you need to talk it out I am all ears." Trent offered after the silent mile they traveled. She still didn't speak. "Listen, I can't have you like this. It just won't do. You are supposed to go see Grace today and she'll take your frown as a sign that something is wrong with her pregnancy. She is expecting twins and is scared to death. You show up with that frown and furrowed brow and she'll turn to mush."

"I'm sorry. I guess I let those boys get to me last night. The wound is still too fresh for things like that not to hurt." She confessed. "I just need a little time to let it pass." She walked a little further, realizing they were at a small lake just inside the trees. They walked quite a distance, she supposed.

Trent looked down at her, trying to put himself into her place. He guessed he would be out of sorts in the same instance. Unfortunately he couldn't think of a single thing to help her. He watched as she walked up to and leaned against an ancient Box Elder tree.

Trent towered over her with a serious look on his face, his hands on either side of her head and a twinkle in his eye. "Well, Mrs. Longwood. It seems to me that there is only one thing to do then."

"What would that be, Mr. Longwood?" She replied, missing the marked mischievous look he was giving her.

"You need to be distracted." Trent suggested, raising an eyebrow at her. The tell-tale growl she had grown to love brought her to wonder.

"But we are several miles from home." She stated matter-of-factly as he closed the space between their lips, capturing her neatly between himself and the tree.

"Um-humm." He agreed, pulling her away from the tree in order to reach the buttons on the back of her dress. Trent was half-way through his task before she realized his intent. She pulled away from his lips to gasp in mortification.

"Not out here in broad daylight!" She shrieked.

"Why not? There isn't anyone about for miles and, after all, we are married. Why not have a little bit of fun." Her face showed her emotion of the predicament he was putting her in. All the buttons were free and he began to pull the dress off her shoulders.

"I don't know about this." She said shakily. Trent continued to coax her out of her clothes, kissing her skin along the way.

"What happened to the woman that was so bold as to examine me the other night?" He cooed, getting a blushing bride in answer.

"That was in the safety of our bedroom, behind walls and curtains." She was losing the battle, she realized, as her breath became labored and she stopped looking around for spies.

Trent managed to get her undressed down to her thin cotton shift. He stood back to look at her in the light of day. She was utterly glorious nearly naked and looking thoroughly kissed. He couldn't wait to get her into the water. He stripped as fast as he could and took her hand, leading her to the water where he brought the hem of her shift up over her head without protest took his time distracting her in the most torturous of ways.

Trent pulled her into the water and his arms. After they reached the point where she could not touch bottom Trent brought her legs up to encircle his waist, letting the water carry her weightlessly. He kissed her and teased her with his tongue. The battle of torments had begun. His drugging kisses warred against her sense of propriety.

The bolts of pleasure shooting through her every nerve barely drowned out the sound of her thundering heart, thrumming blood past her ears.

Violent inhalations seized her lungs just to have them pushed out just as rapidly as they came.

Water swirled around them without notice. Trees clapped their leaves in exaltation of the love displayed. Sunshine rained upon the lovers in love. Warm summer breezes caressed them gently, lovingly as they displayed their ardent affection.

It was quite a while before Luzetta came aware again of where they were, but by then she really didn't care. She decided this distraction was quite effective and quite pleasant. She didn't have the heart to feign morose for long, although the thought had occurred to her.

Chapter Eighteen

"Here we are." Trent said as he pressed the brake on the carriage. Luzetta carried her black bag on her lap, wringing the handle the entire way. A thought had occurred to her as they made the trip to Isaac and Grace's homestead. It occurred to her that multiple births ran in the Longwood family tree. If she were pregnant as Wind In Hair insisted she was, what were the chances that she could bare twins? The thought was very sobering.

Trent helped her down gently and took her by the hand until they reached Isaac's front door. There was no need to knock, for Isaac had it opened to them before they alighted from their carriage.

"Come on in. Grace has been expecting you." Isaac beamed at Luzetta. "Ma and April have been singing your praises and she declares that the won't let anyone but you come near her when the baby comes." Trent led her inside the spacious ranch house. It took a moment to adjust to the light inside the house, but she immediately spied Faith and

Hope sitting on either side of their very pregnant sister-in-law, Grace. April was standing behind the chair with Walter perched on her hip.

In all her experience, Luzetta had never seen any woman as large or as uncomfortable as Grace Longwood. She was in a wooden rocking chair sitting on a pillow, a pillow at her back, a pillow under her feet atop a stool and a glass of lemonade in her hand. She was pushing against one of the arms of the chair either to relieve pressure or to stretch muscles, Luzetta supposed. The gown she wore was as thin as modesty would permit, short sleeved and large enough to be called a tent. Grace attempted to smile at Luzetta, but was only able to pull off sort of a smirk.

"Nice to meet you, Luzetta." She said, offering the hand that once had been pushing her oversized body to one side.

Luzetta nodded to her and took in the sight of her, unable to say a word. The smile she offered slid off her face. Tears formed in her eyes but they didn't dare show themselves. The men left the room as Luzetta put her bag on the floor beside the chair. Luzetta effectively ignored April as she rattled off question after question.

Luzetta approached Grace, taking in what she saw. Graces entire body was bloated with water and her face was more than flushed. Luzetta gently pushed on Grace's foot with one finger and watched as the deep indentation stayed.

"How long have you been like this?" Luzetta asked.

"About two weeks." She answered solemnly.

"Does it hurt when you use the chamber pot?"

"Yes, but how did you know?" Grace's brow furrowed.

"She knows everything about mamas and babies." April qualified, not liking the set of Luzetta's face.

"How long?"

"Just this morning."

"And the muscle spasms?"

"About the same time. I have also felt feverish and hot, not to mention emotional." She qualified. "Lately, though, my muscle cramps have been in my legs. Right here." Grace indicated her inner thighs.

"Can I examine you?" Luzetta asked meekly.

"Yes, please do." She said with more cheer than she intended. "I must admit that as soon as April and Ma told me about you I knew you were the one to deliver my babies." Grace said as she watched Luzetta pull out a long earhorn to listen to the lives within her.

Luzetta knelt beside Grace and placed her hands on her swollen abdomen. Grace immediately stirred, taking in a hissing breath, pushing against both arms of the chair, eyes large as saucers.

"What's wrong?" Faith asked.

"Nothing." Grace said as soon as she regained her breath. "Nothing. I think the brats just did a somersault inside me."

"It's a sign." Hope said reverently.

"Don't listen to her, Luzetta." April rolled her eyes at her sister-in-law. "She's rather romantical about things."

"It is a sign." Luzetta said, very seriously. Luzetta placed her hands in every position possible on Graces belly, then listened quite intently. No one had the nerve to ask her what she meant by the statement. All were in wonder of her findings, not wanting to interrupt her.

Finally Luzetta sat back on her heels and looked at the bloated Grace. "They need to come out." She stated bluntly. Grace stared at her, dumbfounded. Faith and Hope, though, began chatting almost hysterically at the proclamation. Isaac entered the room at the noise his sisters were making.

"What's going on?" He asked.

"We need hot water and lots of it. Blankets, towels, a bathing tub and ice." Luzetta issued.

"Ice?" Isaac said. "Why? She isn't due for another month."

"Those babies need to come out now, Isaac." She stated, the other women set out to complete the tasks needed.

"Why now?" Isaac, she assumed, was quite overwhelmed with the fact that his children were coming earlier than he imagined, much earlier than he was able to handle emotionally. She supposed he was like most fathers, scared out of their gourd of the responsibility that new life brings.

"Trust me, Isaac. It's for the best." Luzetta was rolling up her sleeves, washing her hands and arms up to her elbows with the lye soap Faith placed on the sideboard. "Now we need ice. Go get as much of it as you can. Trent, go get Ma and any other womenfolk you can."

When everything was gathered, Luzetta directed their placement. "Grace, I am going to have you stay in the chair." Grace made a grateful look to Luzetta for not making her raise from her spot.

"But I don't think it's time. I haven't had any contractions." She questioned.

"Yes you have, you just didn't know it. Those leg cramps you've been feeling are really contractions. I am guessing that when I check you, you will already be partly dilated." Grace's face went slack from the jolt of reality.

"Do you mean they will really be here. In my arms." Tears sprouted in Grace's eyes quickly. The joy and unpreparedness of it all overwhelmed her.

"Yes, but I have to warn you of a couple of things." Luzetta looked at her with dread. "There are some complications you may not be aware of. I need you to concentrate. This water weight is not good. I'm not delivering these babies because it is hard on them. It's because it is going to be hard on you. Hopefully it won't be fatal."

A pin drop would have been deafening at that moment. Harriet stood in the doorway as Luzetta began to explain to Grace the predicament she was in. She could have sworn her hair would have turned grey if it hadn't been already at that moment.

"You have to fight, Grace. Fight with all your might and will to see these babies." Luzetta set to work on Grace and getting the babies to come out of their safe, warm cocoon.

Isaac couldn't stand it. The screams coming from the other room were ripping him apart. If it hadn't been for his younger brother he would have barged in there and ... what... what would he have done? He realized there was absolutely nothing he could have done. It was the worst feeling ever. It would have been worse had he actually seen his beloved in pain, going through childbirth and not be able to do anything except pull his hair out.

Even after hours and hours of the bone chilling screams he would not abandon his post. It seemed disloyal of him to even think of leaving. Soon, there was a lull. A peaceful, anxious spot of quiet when he wondered what was happening. He wanted to go in there. He wanted to see for himself that Grace was alright and their babies were healthy. But he couldn't bring himself to stand, let alone walk across the room, turn the handle to the door and open it.

It was almost a relief when he heard the cries of mother and child. So many things went wrong with childbirth. He would think long and hard before he would agree to put Grace through this again. He felt like a heel for putting her through the pain and misery she was experiencing at this very moment.

Another wail of a baby. Okay. He can handle this. It was almost over now. His nerve was gathering it's muster. He couldn't sit still. Energy coursed through his body. After a few minutes of convincing himself that he was needed, he reached for the nob, turned and pushed.

The sight that greeted him was his wife's limp, exhausted body sprawled out on the rocking chair he built her with her feet propped up on stools. Her breathing was labored as her glossy eyes pointed in his general direction, even though he knew she didn't see him. The babies were being tended by two women each. Luzetta and April attended to Grace's limp body. No one seemed to notice him standing in the doorway gawking at the unfamiliar scene.

Grace began another horrible moan, one Isaac knew was a prelude to another blood-curdling scream. "What's wrong? Why is she still screaming?" Isaac's panicked eyes fell on Luzetta for answers.

"It's nothing to be alarmed about." She said calmly. "It's all about to be over." She didn't even look up at Isaac as she spoke. Instead, she palpated Grace's still swollen abdomen.

"Grace." Luzetta spoke forcefully. Grace looked at her with effort to concentrate on the face before her. "Grace. You're doing it! You're doing magnificently. I have good news." Luzetta waited until

Grace's next contraction passed. "Grace! Push. Push this last one out."

"Three?" Isaac shouted. "Three?" He said again, not believing the words coming out of his own mouth. He had the doorknob in a death grip and it was the only thing keeping him aground. Everyone turned to look at Luzetta in astonishment.

"There has never been three before." Ma said with disbelief.

The third and smallest babe produced itself at last. It's limp body laid in Luzetta's hand unbreathing, unmoving. She cut the cord and tried her hardest to make the babe breath it's first breath of life.

Then the worst happened. Grace's worn, exhausted body began to convulse. April took the baby and began working on it as she watched Luzetta work with Grace.

"Isaac help me get her to the floor." Isaac moved as if someone shot him in the rear. Trent came in and helped Grace to the floor, which was no easy feat considering she was convulsing like a fish out of water. Luzetta had prepared for this. How else would the palate beside the chair and premixed medicine be explained. After the men got Grace to the floor, Luzetta came with the medicine.

"What is that?" Isaac asked.

"Something that will help stop the seizures." Luzetta poured it down Grace's gullet and oddly enough left her with Isaac.

April had not been able to revive the child. It's lifeless form still in the tiny blanket being rubbed into life. April's eyes were spilling intense tears as she willed the child to live, thinking of the child that grow within her.

April fairly jumped out of the way as Luzetta approached. After seeing the situation it was time for some fast thinking. She took the child and unwrapped it. Holding it gently in her arms, she dunked the child in the ice water and cover it as quickly as possible with a quilt, holding it closely to her body.

The shocking cold water stirred the baby to take in a deep breath and scream it's angst. Everyone, excluding the barely conscious Grace, cried tears of joy and astonishment as each wail came forth. All three babies were wailing their hardest. It was a moment everyone would remember.

Grace lost and regained consciousness a few more times. Later she became aware of all three new voices. She smiled and cried and declared her love to her husband all at the same time. Isaac never seemed so relieved. For safety sake Grace remained on the floor as the last ministrations were attended.

Isaac helped Grace into a comfortable position while Luzetta perched herself between Grace's legs once more.

"So how did you know to use ice water on a baby?" Isaac asked.

"It was a last minutes decision." She said frankly.

"Last minute? But you had me get it hours ago." He complained.

"It wasn't intended for the baby." She qualified.

"Then what was it's intended use?" Luzetta didn't have to tell him the answer. She showed him. Since he was adamant about staying in the room while Luzetta finished, he was present for the display of the afterbirth, at which he promptly fainted.

Isaac came out of the ice water by his brother's hands. Luzetta's laughing eyes and smiling face didn't have to say a word.

"It's always nice when the men get the things they need instead of belaboring us women." She said jokingly.

Three days later Luzetta left Grace in the care of her husband, Ma, Faith and Hope. She was well cared for, as well as the three children. Everyone worried about the youngest and smallest, but he proved to be the loudest of all three. "It was probably the ice bath at birth" Isaac exclaimed, saying nothing of his own ice bath.

The walk back home wasn't but a mile or two and Luzetta was glad for the exercise. Every day Wind In Hair foretold her pregnancy, even though there were no signs seen by Luzetta herself, but just in case she wanted to keep active and healthy. Secretly she was hoping Wind In Hair was right. A baby. How wonderful it would be.

She was contemplating exactly which attributes would come from which parent when Luther Maxwell came riding up to her. The unusual set of his face set her to wondering what he was up to. And why he was out this way when he lived on the opposite side of the county. Where was his faithful sidekick?

"Hello, Luther." She called out. After all, he seemed to be riding straight to her.

"Mrs. Longwood I need you to come with me." He stated simply.

"Where's Boyd?" She asked the boy, still mounted upon his aged palfrey.

"He's with someone that needs you." He said, some emotion was pulling at his face Luzetta could not discern. "I don't know his name, but he said he needed the doc." It was a lie. Luther knew the man's name. They had gone searching for them when the news hit town.

"I'm just a mid-wife now. Where is Dr. Smith?" The boy seemed anxious about her question.

"He's up in the hills. I doubt if the old doctor could get up there." He watched pensively as emotions ran over Luzetta's face.

"Well, alright." Luzetta placed her foot in the stirrup after he took her hand. She had barely been seated on the back of the tired horse when it took off on the boy's instance.

The ride was quiet as the boy concentrated on directing the horse. Or maybe they were lost. Did he remember where the man in need was left behind with a boy that would not be of much aid? She was beginning to wonder as they entered into the thickest part of wood. Several caves loomed ahead of them. Luzetta got a very bad feeling that she had been lured into a trap.

Chapter Nineteen

Trent was extremely pleased with himself. After searching high and low, Trent had the perfect present for Luzetta tucked away. He patted the breast pocket of his shirt that held what was left of Luzetta's family. He was debating when to tell her when he heard his name called.

"Trent." Harvey Millson waved Trent down in the middle of the street, making his way across and almost getting trampled in the process. Trent stepped off the boardwalk to meet him partway. "This just came in. A couple days ago the Carbaugh gang escaped while they were being transported to their trial."

Trent's blood ran cold. "A couple of days ago?"

"Yeah. It took them that long to find the drivers. They said it looked like an ambush of sorts." Harvey was talking to himself. Trent was on his horse and riding home before he finished the sentence.

Trent's chest pulled tight as he rode hard toward home. He wondered, even hoped, that if George Carbaugh did get Luzetta if his affection toward her would stay his hand against her. Somehow he doubted he would bring her harm. It seemed at the jail in Montana that there was a kinship between them. He looked upon her with warmth and hurt when she confronted him with the truth. He hurt because she was hurt.

But now there was more on the line. The law had concrete evidence against them and were more hunted now than they ever were. They would feel the pressure creeping down their necks. Trent just hoped Luzetta was safe, tucked away safely at home.

When Trent arrived, Wind In Hair was sweeping the porch. She shook her head "No she hasn't returned home. She went to see Grace and babies." Trent rode the short distance between, scanning every inch for signs of Luzetta.

Trent burst in the door like the Devil himself, ready for murder if George Carbaugh even ruffled the hair on Luzetta's head. Isaac was stirring a pot over the fire, Kyle was sitting next to their four children making them behave while Martha, his wife, held one of Grace's babies. Elizabeth, who was standing by her husband Clint, also had a baby.

"Has anyone seen Luzetta?" Trent barked.

"She left over an hour ago. She said she was going home to work on some curtains." Isaac said. "Why?"

"She's gone." He said breathlessly, admitting it to himself at last. He felt like weeping. He had to take a deep breath before admitting he knew at who's hand her kidnaping had been. "The Carbaugh gang escaped."

A collective gasp resounded through the house. All the men jumped to attention and mounted their horses without blinking.

Luzetta stared up at the bewhiskered George and wondered what would become of her. She was bound and gagged, albeit loosely. She could probably push the bandanna out of her mouth with her tongue if she had time to maneuver her lips just right, but George sat with her. She suspected he didn't trust any of his boys with her. And, she realized, he had something to say. He tried most of the evening to convince her that he really wasn't all that bad of a man and that men were molded from birth as to their fate. He could see in her eyes that she was not accepting his explanation of matters.

"I don't expect you to understand right away." He stressed. "It may be a few years before you realize that even a criminal like myself is a fine man. I could make you a good husband, Luzetta."

Husband? Where had that come from? She had only thought of George as an Uncle of sorts. She couldn't think of him in a romantic sense if her life depended on it, which is exactly where she sat.

"What do you say, Luzetta?" George came to her, clearly with his heart in his eyes and removed the gag. "Will you marry me?"

"George." She said, keeping her voice calm and warm. "Dear George. I've loved you all my life. You have no idea how dear you were to me. I've always thought of you as an uncle, a father figure." Memories trampled over the new knowledge of George's past activities, but it was still there, present in her mind. He was a killer. A killer of her real parents. She tried to keep her disgust out of her voice. "I don't think I could think of you that way. Besides, I am already married."

"But that can change." He interrupted, placing an emotional hand beside her head and leaning into her but not touching her. He watched her face as she tried to dissect the meaning of that statement. "I can be so much more. Don't you see?" At first Luzetta thought George was going to kiss her but he pushed away, thankfully, turning his back on her as he made his plea. "All those times I visited you after your father …John… died. Those times you confided in me, trusted me. Couldn't you tell that I was pining after you, could you not tell I was courting you?"

Luzetta's shock turned into anger. Her temper was beginning to slip. She had to think of something. "All those times you looked at me after knowing you killed my real father, robbing me of my real parents, did you ever think your actions would come back to haunt you?" George sighed and looked to the ceiling as if to explain that away as well. "As far as being the wife of a criminal, now that the law has John Beck's diary with all the facts they need, you'll be a man on the run for the rest of your life. What kind of life could you give me, George? A life of looking over my shoulder, living in fear, wondering if you go into a town you won't get recognized and shot down leaving me to the mercy of strangers? Is that a life you want for me?" She asked the questions that stumped his brain.

"All I know is that it breaks my heart not having you with me. I promised John that I would protect you, and protect you I will. There are plenty of ships that make their way to Europe, the far East, even farther if you wish." Luzetta recognized the look in George's eye as the look of someone who was losing control of himself, of the situation, and becoming desperate. "We don't have to keep looking over our shoulder if we leave the States. We will be home free out at sea. I have plenty of money. You won't want for a thing." He pleaded.

"Is that your plan, to steel me away on some ship?" She asked.

"Yes. I knew even before we were captured that I wanted to take you and escape. Just to take you and run. I knew it was next to impossible, but we made it and now you're here." His pleading came more intense as the hours wore on. Luzetta was tired and hungry. He offered her the only food they had, bacon and coffee. Both were next to unpalatable, but she ate anyway.

The next morning George escorted her out to a tree where he instructed her to conduct her business as he turned his back. He wouldn't even give her the privacy she needed to complete the task - or room for escape.

As they came back to the caves she noticed the Carbaugh boys were in one cave together, Russ and Linus were in another, Manny and Mack were in the one below. They were dousing fires and packing up. They would be leaving soon.

Luzetta looked around for the boys, Boyd and Luther. There were so many other caves they could be anywhere. They were also dark inside. They could be hiding in any one of them. Or they could be dead. Luzetta didn't let the thought linger in her head too long.

It wasn't until just before they were leaving that she learned Boyd and Luther had been bound, gagged and held prisoner as she had been. Unfortunately they showed signs of ill treatment. Would they be let go when George and the others boarded the ship he spoke of? She doubted they would. They were liabilities and would be treated as such. What a fool she had been. If she didn't agree to going with him would she be a liability too? The least she could do would be to stall their departure and give Trent time to find her.

Luzetta was hauled up on George's horse. Her hands were bound and she was forced to sit in front of him, feeling his body pressed against hers. He positioned her so she would know how he felt about her. Luzetta felt like crying but she prayed instead. She prayed with fervor that Trent would find her and get her out of this mess.

Luzetta's mind traveled back to when they were both in jail. Trent had warned her that bad men were about and she stubbornly refused to believe it. Now she was neck deep in something she couldn't fix. Not without help.

Boyd and Luther were trying their hardest to keep up with the horse they were tethered to. Their hands were bound by a long rope tied to the horn of two separate horses. The boys were kept in separate caves last night and while they were traveling to keep them from talking.

Luther doubted Boyd would talk to him anyway. After all, he was the one who talked Boyd into searching out the Carbaugh Gang naively thinking they would be accepted with open arms.

Now they found themselves on the wrong side of the famed outlaws. Luther felt even worse that he dragged Mrs. Longwood into this mess. When George Carbaugh threatened Boyd's life if he didn't go fetch her, he wasn't thinking much of her fate. It was safe to say he hadn't done much thinking at all lately.

Now Mrs. Longwood was with George, forced to be at his side, ride with him, what else he'd made her do was even worse to think about. The look on her face this morning when she found them bound and gagged made him want the earth to open and swallow him. But not as much as he wanted it to open and swallow George Carbaugh right this instant, seeing him rub himself up against Mrs. Longwood. Luther didn't think George would physically hurt her but he knew George would keep her against her will regardless of the fight she would put up.

Luther began to think of ways he could rectify the situation and save the people he so carelessly put in harms way. He wouldn't be able to let Boyd in on his plans but he hoped Boyd would pick up any clues Luther would give him.

Chapter Twenty

It was pure divine intervention that the seven lawmen met up with the 134th battalion. The army of two hundred fifty men were sent out by the president himself to capture the Carbaugh gang. After laying out the situation to the captain, they made a plan of action. Hopefully Luzetta was still alive. Either way, George Carbaugh and his gang were going to die. They were now the judge and jury going to deal out the death sentence to each and every one of them.

It wasn't until almost noon the day after Trent learned of Luzetta's kidnaping that they caught onto the fresh trail. "I know this area like the back of my hand" Sargent McCullough, the second in command, stated with a mouth full of chaw and squinted eyes. "They're headed toward a clearing. Isn't a tree for five miles. If we cross before they do, we can hide in the trees on the other side and have the element of surprise."

Trent was in agreement with the Sargent. They needed to get close enough to the gang to get in the first shot, before they have a chance to take out Luzetta. The Carbaugh gang would do that. Trent had no doubt, no matter how close Luzetta was to George, he would take her down with him just to spite the law.

Especially because *he* was the law. And that scared Trent to death.

"I like it. Let's ride." Sargent McCullough lead the way around the clearing in breakneck speed. Urgency pushed them faster and faster until they reached the other side. The 134th battalion laid in wait for the most ruthless, gutless, depraved humans to walk the earth.

Luther and Boyd tried their hardest to maintain their hellish pace. If they fell, they were dragged. When they got up again, their captures went faster. They were tired, hungry and thirsty. They dared not raise voice of their discomforts.

They were half-way through a clearing when they spotted the tree line up ahead. Finally, the thick wood would slow the horses down enough to make it easier on the boys. It was high noon and the sun was beating down on their sweaty bodies. The shade would be comforting.

Luther looked over at Boyd. He didn't look so well. His face was flush and Luther could tell his strength was failing him. Luther knew Boyd wouldn't last much longer without water. He had to do something.

"Whoa" George called out for the others to stop. He was scanning the tree line with suspicion. He turned to the others. "I think we should stay away from the tree line for a while." He decreed.

"You gettin' that feelin' we're bein' watched?" Linus inquired. George only gave an almost indiscernible nod while peering into the trees. It was dark and plenty of places to hide. "Me too."

The men continued on cautiously, constantly gazing into the forest.

The pace was slower now, but they were still in the sun. Boyd was looking worse and worse. Luther couldn't see any sweat on his friend's face. He had to do something.

"What was that?" Luther said, trying to sound curious but ignorant of the weary men he traveled with.

"What?" Linus, his handler, piqued.

"Oh, it was probably nothing." He shrugged. The men looked from one to the other. Boyd dropped down to his knees and then lay on the ground in exhaustion.

"Boyd." Luther called out to his friend in concern.

"Leave him." Linus demanded, giving the tether a good yank, pulling Luther down to his knees.

Luther watched as the others ignored his friend, probably dying, and discussed the fear of the wood. He could feel the blood rush to his head, his breathing came deeper, heavier. His vision blurred at the injustice of their treatment, and the treatment of Mrs. Longwood.

The rage that built up in Luther was so strong, so fast, he had no time to think rationally. He acted purely out of emotion. Luther gritted his teeth and began to let his rage take over.

The six Longwoods, and Sam, were concealed along with the army in the woods up ahead. Just few hundred more yards and the gang would be right where they wanted them. Why were they stopped? Several of the men moved further down, closer to the fugitives, awaiting the signal to go. Trent was one of them.

If Trent could have talked he would have spewed a string of obscenities. They hadn't seen Luther and Boyd behind the caravan from the other angle. Trent remembered the awe-struck look on the boys' face the night when they confronted Luzetta about John Beck. Stupid, stupid boys. If they live through this Trent was going to paint them a new back side.

Suddenly Boyd fell to the ground. Then Luther was pulled down to his knees after expressing concern for his friend. And then the inconceivable happened. Trent could not believe his eyes.

Luther took a running start right toward the horse of his captor. He rammed his shoulder into the horse's hind leg, effectively causing it to drop his hind quarters and unseat the rider.

In an amazing display of skill nobody, even Luther, knew he had, Luther jumped over the fallen horse, stretched out his foot as he flew through the air and placed a neck-snapping kick to Linus's face. Luther grabbed Linus's gun and aimed it straight at his tormenter's head.

"Let us go or I'll shoot him." Luther ground out with a voice that sounded strangely possessed. Everyone sat stunned for just a moment of time. George was the first one to dismount. He didn't take the boy seriously, which was a deadly mistake.

As soon as George had turned his back on her Luzetta tried to make her getaway. She tried to dig her heals into the horse to illicit a response - but he didn't move.

George waltzed over to where his comrade lay, placed a finger on his neck and waited. Luther stood stock still, not knowing what to do. "Go ahead, boy. Show me what you got." George taunted. Luther knew then that he killed the man. And he was in neck deep in the smelly stuff.

Luther saw out of the corner of his eye Boyd stand on feeble legs. He had to keep their attention for his friend to make a get away.

Boyd pointed the gun straight at George's chest.

"Whoa, now." George raised up both hands in mock surrender. "You ain't never shot a man have you?" Luther was too afraid to answer. "Look, why don't we make a deal. You got guts, Kid. Why don't you put away that gun. It looks like I am in need of a new partner." George regarded the fallen man without remorse. "Why don't we talk about it?"

Luther was about to tell George where to go and then send him there when, almost simultaneously Boyd smacked the back of George's horse with what was left of his strength, sending Luzetta careening over the landscape and a war cry burst out behind him.

Luther watched George's face morph into something unrecognizable at whatever was behind him. Shots rang out, Luther and Boyd hit the ground.

Trent didn't give it a second thought. He would have loved to hand out justice to George and his gang, but he went after Luzetta instead. Her hands were bound, unable to steer herself to safety. She was at the mercy of a large, scared animal.

Luzetta thought she was seeing things when Trent pulled up beside her speeding horse, commanding the loose reins. She was never so glad to see him. After the horses were stopped, Trent lifted her onto his horse. She placed her bound hands around his neck and kissed him as fiercely as she could, tears still streaming down her face.

"It looks like you've saved me again." She sniffled.

"You'll get used to it." He said, wiping the tears from her face. "I did."

"You were very brave. Very, very, very stupid, but very brave." Trent lectured Luther and Boyd through jailhouse bars. He was going to give them a lesson they were not soon to forget. He didn't know how long he was going to keep them there, but he wasn't going to let them leave without undoubtably, unequivocally, undeniably spouting their intentions of becoming law abiding citizens for the rest of their natural lives. Then, and only then, can their parents have them to teach them their own lesson.

"I know. I figured I got us into it, I needed to find a way out. I was just glad you and the army were right behind us. I've never been so scared in my life." Luther confessed that he hadn't intended to kill Linus, just knock him out. He'd spent the last three nights laying on this stinking, hard as a rock cot thinking about it. He killed a man. It grated on him to know he was capable of such a thing. It didn't matter that the army shot and killed the others. That was them. Luther was Luther. He knew he was changed for the rest of his life knowing he killed a man at thirteen.

Chapter Twenty-one

Trent sat beside Luzetta, he contending with his excitement, her sitting in retrospect. Even though she pretended not to be affected by the events two weeks ago, she couldn't hide the truth from him. That haunted look crossed over her face every once in a while, and he knew.

Having her preoccupied with her thoughts allowed Trent to carry out his plan without any questions from his wife. When he hitched up the team in the middle of the day and told her to save picking berries for another day she didn't ask why. He supposed it was because she didn't want to be alone.

Now she sat beside him holding her hat on her head while she tilted her head back, allowing the sun to fall on her face and neck. She soaked in the rays with her eyes closed taking in deep cleansing breaths.

"God, it's good to be alive." She said without preamble.

"Yes it is." A smile grew on his lips, watching his wife's lovely neck thinking of how good it would taste warmed by the sun. "We're almost there."

The town came into view. There weren't any more people in town than usual, but all eyes seemed to be on Luzetta, making her feel self-conscious. When Trent lifted her down out of the wagon she straightened her dress and made sure her hat was on straight. Still people stared. She wished they didn't. A closed in feeling began grabbing her from nowhere.

"How long will you be. I want to leave as soon as possible." She stated under her breath.

"Not long. Pretend not to see them. Ignore them and they will go away." Trent lead her across the street on his arm. Luzetta had been so preoccupied with ignoring everyone that she hadn't realized they were at the hotel where the best restaurant in town resided.

"What is this?" She asked as he pulled her through the door.

"We are eating lunch at the restaurant with family." Well, this was unusual. Her eyes adjusted as she tried to focus on the well appointed lobby.

Trent left Luzetta to sit on the plush sofa beside a huge unlit fireplace while he spoke with the clerk at the counter. The clerk quickly disappeared into the hallway and Trent sat beside Luzetta.

"What is going on?" She asked, laughing at her husband's cat-like grin.

"Nothing." He stated, barely able to contain his emotion. Luzetta peered at him through suspicious eyes. Trent just chuckled and kissed her hand.

So she was going to be surprised. It wasn't her birthday. It wasn't their anniversary. What other occasion would call for a surprise. They haven't been married long enough for her to know if this type of 'thing' is something he would normally do.

They didn't have to wait long for the clerk to surface again. Trent took her by the hand and pulled her along the hallway, seeming to be in more of a rush to show her his surprise than she was to see it.

Trent and Luzetta entered the room after the clerk announced them. There were five people in the room. Three men of middle age, one of which pulled a spectacle glass to his eye to examine her, and two women.

The older of the two women stood regally at the window. She was dressed in black from head to toe with a grim look on her face. She was staring right at Luzetta.

Luzetta looked up at Trent, who was still smiling like a well-fed cat. Her brows furrowed together in misunderstanding.

"What is going on?" She asked her husband for the second time.

"Come here, child." The lady in black spoke, her voice broken with emotion. "Stand here in the light. My eyes aren't as good as they used to be."

Luzetta found herself inexplicably floating toward the woman, standing before her. They stared at each other in silence for a span of eternity. Gloved hands ran themselves over Luzetta's arms, holding them out in order to inspect her. The lady's eyes filled with tears. A huge sob broke from her lips.

"It will be all right." Luzetta placated when the lady threw her arms around Luzetta, sobbing her heart out. "Why don't you tell me what is upsetting you and I will try to help."

The lady in black straightened and pulled herself out of Luzetta's embrace. Not bothering to dry the tears streaming down her face, she took Luzetta's hands in hers and smiled a bitter sweet smile.

"Dear I am crying because I am happy. I found something that I thought was lost forever."

Luzetta went instantly stiff. There was too much to lose if she wished to hope. Her palms began to sweat. The blood rushed past her ears. Could it be? She looked over at Trent. He was smiling even bigger now.

"Please tell me. Tell me who you are." She said breathlessly.

"I am Morgana Westmorland . I am your grandmother." Before the words were out of her mouth Luzetta had her in a hug so tight it almost took the breath out of the old woman. The two women embraced and cried together.

"How did you find me?" Luzetta asked her grandmother.

"Your husband contacted my man of law through a private detective." She said after blowing her nose noisily. "I had to see for myself if it truly was you."

The two women drifted over to the couch, too loaded down with emotion to stand any longer. Morgana Westmorland sat Luzetta down beside her, looking at every feature of her face.

"When you weren't found with your parents, a widespread search went out to find you. Many claimed they were you in order to claim the reward. Many imposters tried to pass off their own children as you in order to secure a better place for their daughters." Luzetta's brows furrowed in misunderstanding. Morgana used her thumb to run over the area. "You look so much like your father. I knew as soon as you walked through the door that you were the one."

"Tell me about them." For hours Luzetta and her grandmother talked about the family Luzetta never knew. Her father was a railroad man and had been celebrating his success with a family train ride across the country.

"I was too old for such excursions and begged off. I had no idea ..." The old woman pressed her well soaked handkerchief to her eyes once more. "But now I have you I will never let you go."

Luzetta was given a picture of her parents. It had been taken just after they were married. Luzetta's mother stood behind the man she was told she favored. Luzetta inspected the picture until her eyes ached.

"What was my name?" She asked. "What was my birth name."

"Louise. After your mother's mother."

"And when was I born?"

"November 5, 1863 in New York."

"I'm twenty-five, then." She laughed.

Luzetta asked many more questions, practically letting her food go untouched until she exhausted her well of curiosity.

"Do I have any brothers or sisters?"

"No, you were their only. But you have uncles, aunts, and cousins. I didn't tell them the nature of my trip out here in fear of getting their hopes up if it were another ploy." She shook her head. "You see, Luzetta, your father was not only a railroad man but also a man of wealth. Both from family and from good investing. There are a lot of people that would love to be the one to inherit the money left to you."

"Money?" She thought about it. She shook her head. "No. I'm afraid I cannot accept."

"But dear, you can't refuse." She said disbelieving the words she was hearing, but Luzetta would hear nothing of it. They set aside the matter for a later date and continued in their quest of learning more about each other.

Epilogue

Early spring was the best time to have a baby. Love was in the air as the ground sprouted green and new life began. Luzetta sat up in the bed with several pillows propping her up as she nursed her new son. She stroked his head lovingly, marveling at the fact she had a beautiful baby boy. She named him Adam, after her real father. Trent lay beside her, staring down at the woman and child that made his life complete.

"He's gorgeous." Morgana sat across the room in the rocking chair Trent built for the nursery. She couldn't bare going back to New York without her granddaughter, and Luzetta's heart broke at the thought of having just met blood family and sending her away. Morgana had been living with Trent and Luzetta since the day after they met. The only reason they hadn't moved Morgana in that night was because she wouldn't have had a bed to lay her head on.

"Yes he is." Happiness flowed through Luzetta like electricity. She was unaware of the tears flowing down her cheeks.

"I felt the same way when your father was born." Morgana admitted. Much healing came from Luzetta and her new great grandson. She knew it would take a long time for the complete healing, but that would happen long after she went to her grave. For now she would stay by her granddaughter's side and look after her as her parents would have.

"Who would have known. The treasures we seek aren't the ones we need." Morgana's eyes swam with emotion. "It's the treasure of the heart. Love. The hidden treasure."

2547782

Made in the USA